1919

1919

The Search for Mankind's Greatest Killer

Ken Rosen

To order additional copies of this book, contact:
Xlibris
1-888-795-4274
www.Xlibris.com
Orders@Xlibris.com
765430

CONTENTS

Prelude

The news on Wednesday, September 29, 2004, did not appear to contain anything extraordinary. In his bid for reelection, Pres. George W. Bush was campaigning in Miami while the Democratic nominee, John Kerry, was trekking cross-country from Spring Green, Wisconsin, to Fort Lauderdale, Florida, trying to close the gap.

Simona Pari and Simona Torretta were finally freed by their captives in Baghdad. The Italian aid workers had been kidnapped three weeks earlier by insurgents. Gun battles on Haifa Street in Downtown Baghdad between US forces and insurgents were reported the day before. The troop surge was a long way off, and Iraq teetered on civil war.

Hurricane Jeanne had finally run out of steam in Pennsylvania but not before blasting her way up the East Coast, leaving a trail of death and destruction in her path.

The *USA Today* covered these stories in the front-news section of the paper. The paper's most popular section featured stories about the Red Sox history-making run to their first World Series Championship in eighty-six years. The Patriots were starting their defense of a Super Bowl Championship, and in hockey, the Tampa Bay Lightning were in danger of losing the right to defend their first championship because of an owner's lockout of the players. If no deal was reached, the entire season could be wiped out, and for the first time since 1919, Lord Stanley's Cup would not be raised.

On the second to the last page of the news section was a headline that read, "Thailand on the Alert for Bird-Flu Cases." Most Americans paid little attention to it. The war in Iraq, a killer hurricane, and a presidential election were far more compelling and closer to home.

Thailand was on the other side of the world, and how dangerous can bird flu be anyway?

Pranee Sodchuen was twenty-six years old and lived in Bangkok, but her eleven-year-old daughter, Sakuntala, was being raised in a small village in the northern province of Kamphaeng Phet with other relatives. Sakuntala contracted the virus known as H5N1, most likely from an infected chicken in her village, and was immediately hospitalized.

Within hours, Pranee was at the side of her sick child, whose temperature was spiking at 104. Her ears, hands, and feet had turned an ominous dark purple, and dark blotches were appearing all over her frail body. There, Pranee remained, never leaving her daughter. Three days later, she was physically removed from the dead child's bedside. But Pranee never left the hospital.

Half the world away, Dr. Jeffrey Taubenberger was following this case closely. As the head of the US Army's Institute of Pathology in Washington, DC, Taubenberger knew full well what these events could mean. A deadly form of the flu virus passing from one human to another was alarming, to say the least. Up until this point, fifteen people had contracted the bird flu in Thailand and ten had died. In neighboring Vietnam, twenty-seven cases were reported with twenty deaths—a shockingly high mortality rate, considering the ages of the deceased, not the customary very young or very old who succumb to the flu more easily.

The avian flu is highly contagious among birds but rarely spreads to humans. Millions of chickens and other poultry in the Far East have been purposefully destroyed in the past decade when other outbreaks occurred in an attempt to stop the virus before it spread. Since Pranee never visited the village where her daughter first got sick, it was logical to assume she contracted the disease from Sakuntala. Twelve days later, Pranee was dead. Pieces of her lungs were cut out from her disfigured body and carefully packed and shipped to the Centers for Disease Control and Prevention in Atlanta.

Taubenberger would have to wait for his turn to view the samples and compare them to the obese woman from Brevig, Alaska. Like most scientists, patience was a quality he had in abundance.

However, a biological bomb was ticking, and Taubenberger, the leading authority on the global pandemic eighty-five years earlier, feared a dangerous form of the flu virus was mutating and had been passed between humans. Could he be witnessing firsthand the history he had spent years researching?

This piece of history commemorates infamous shipwrecks and a world war but featured a far more powerful and effective killer than both. Estimates vary, but it is believed that influenza killed between fifty million and two hundred million people worldwide from 1918 to 1919, and then just as quickly and mysteriously, it disappeared.

1

Unforeseen Companions

Jubilee Arena, Montreal, Quebec

November 1918

The bloody puddle had finally stopped growing. Measuring about three feet in diameter meant that Montreal Canadiens star Edourd "Newsy" Lalonde had lost a fair amount of blood, but that wasn't anything new. Players and officials were working their skates, carving up the ice, and mixing the chips with the quickly freezing hemoglobin Newsy had left behind. Buckets of water were being carried from the benches on to the ice to help with the area being patched. The fresh water was mixed with the frozen blood and snow to create a new pink ice surface that the referee packed down with the pucks.

"Jesus Christ, I need to be paid more when you boys get together," one ref said to nobody in particular.

Joe Malone, a towering forward for the Canadiens helping with the repair, overheard the remark and smiled, turning to see Newsy being helped off the ice. A long red trail on the playing surface marked his exit. "Perhaps you should ask for ice-repair money as well."

The referee's hands had turned red from a combination of the cold and the bloody mixture. Clearly not in the mood, he looked up from his work to see Malone smirking and tilting his head in the direction Newsy just left. Looking down the ice, the ref became even more annoyed and disgusted with his predicament; trying to keep order in the young NHL has become almost impossible.

"Go to your benches, all of you! Get the ice crew out here. Let them fix this for fuck's sake," he sneered.

At the other end of the ice, Newsy had an arm around each of the men shuffling down the ice in street shoes. He slid on his left skate, and his right leg hung as though it were lifeless, with blood pouring off the right skate, marking his trail. At the door to leave the ice stood the toughest, most talented, and feared defenseman in the game, waiting for his nemesis.

"Not going to finish this one, Newsy?" Joe Hall asked with his Cheshire smile. "We'll miss ya!" Groggy from his loss of blood, Newsy was only able to lift his head and sneer at the man who just skated across his thigh.

Sensing his star player was heading into unconsciousness, general manager and part owner of the Canadiens George Kennedy was struggling to help the great Newsy Lalonde off the ice. Well into his late fifties, Kennedy carried an extra fifty pounds around his midsection caused by too many fine steaks, aged bourbon, and expensive cigars. Joe Hall was clearly out of Kennedy's league, but George can't let the Bad Man get away with literally adding insult to his star player's injury.

"Fuck off, you cheap bastard. You got some set of balls—"

"Got your stick boys doing your talking for you now, losey?" Hall interrupted. "What's next? They gonna fight for ya too?"

Suddenly becoming very lucid, Newsy regained his focus. *This jackass can't disrespect my boss like that. Only I can do that,* he thought. Reaching down to the wound, he cupped his hand, pulling it through the bloody mess. Wincing from the self-inflicted pain, he flipped a handful of fresh fluid in Hall's face.

"There now. Maybe you won't miss me quite so much."

Three thousand-plus Canadien fans turned from anger and concern into a unified eruption of laughter and celebration at their hero's defiance.

"Get me inside, Georgie," he said.

Claude, the equipment manager, couldn't hide his grin but managed to look away when Hall glared in his direction, wiping blood from his face. He was under Newsy's left arm and was first to leave the ice. He turned and helped Newsy navigate the narrow doorway while Kennedy tried to keep Newsy and himself upright as they exited next.

"Way to go Newsy! Don't let Bad Man get the best of you!" a man in the crowd yelled in support.

Everyone was standing, clapping, and reaching to pat the great Newsy Lalonde as the hockey god was carried down the tunnel to the dressing room.

The cheers faded as the dressing room door slammed behind the three men. Wooden benches lined three of the walls in the room. Most stood at crooked angles or leaned against the wall—well past their prime. Five feet above the benches, iron hooks protruded from the grey cinder block wall. Spaced three feet apart, they circled the room, and hanging from each of them were the street clothes of the players on the ice. In one corner, void of the player's benches was the skate sharpener and, next to that, what could be a carpenter's workshop. Wood planes, saws, and a hammer lay on the table next to rolls of black tape.

"Get him on the table, Claude. Let's get a look at it."

The carpentry tools were pushed aside, and Newsy was lifted onto the six-foot-long wooden table. Extra sturdy, it resembled something out of King Arthur's castle. Four thick wooden legs supported the three twelve-inch-wide and three-inch-thick planks of lumber that make up the top of the table. Newsy lay back as George gingerly slid down his hockey pants, revealing the sliced piece of meat that was, until moments before, Newsy's thigh. He reacted with revulsion.

"Jesus Christ. Where the hell is the doc? Newsy is going to bleed to death before he gets down here," Kennedy said.

"He's probably stopping to chat with the ladies on his way, the horny bastard," replied Newsy. "Claude, be a good lad and get me a brandy, would ya?"

"Sure thing, Newsy. Didn't ya see Bad Man coming?" the young man asked his idol.

"Nah, never saw him. Got spun around at center ice and lost an edge. Next thing I know, that bastard's jumping over me. He could've cleared me too. I saw him smile as he went over and dropped his skate just low enough." Newsy leaned forward and looked at the damage for the first time, reacting with disgust and anger. "Claude! Hurry with that brandy!"

"That son of a bitch needs to be taught a lesson. Cheap-shot son of a bitch. Here ya go, Newsy." Claude delivered his drink.

The dressing room door swung open and banged loudly against the wall inside the room. Doctor Jean-Michel Martineau jumped out of the way as the heavy door swung back, just missing him. Martineau was a short man with very sharp features on a weathered French-Canadian face. High cheekbones and a pronounced sloping nose made those features memorable but not attractive. Throwing his hat on the bench along the wall revealed a hairline in retreat. What's left on his balding head was long and not well groomed.

"Hello, boys!" Martineau shouted in his usual over-the-top booming delivery. "Jesus, it stinks in here! How's it feel, Newsy?"

"Smell the hockey, Doc. Kid, another brandy!"

"Make that two!" yelled Martineau while inspecting the wound. "Very nice, clean cut, good skin on the edges. Doesn't look that deep either. At least, not deep enough for any muscle damage. When are you going to learn to stay away from that baboon? He could have killed you last week."

Martineau had walked up the length of the table and was inspecting the stitches in Lalonde's head, the result of his last encounter with Joe Hall. The wound just above his forehead's hairline was healing nicely. *In another couple of days, those stitches will need to be taken out,* the doctor thought.

"Checking you from behind and into the fence! The man is Neanderthal. Boss, you still thinking about pressing charges?" Martineau asked Kennedy, who had been trying to thread a needle for the doctor with no success.

"I'm . . . considering . . . it. Shit! Fuck! Piss!" He missed the needle's eye again.

Claude had returned with two more brandies and handed them to Martineau and Newsy.

"Thanks, kid," Martineau said.

He took one sip and poured most of the brandy on the open wound. Newsy, in the midst of gulping down his glass of liquor, moaned, then spit a mouthful of brandy on George Kennedy.

"What the fuck?" yelled Kennedy.

His face and suit covered with the sticky liqueur, Kennedy fought to regain his composure and calmly lay the needle and thread on the table before turning toward the bathroom.

Newsy and Claude were giggling like schoolchildren as Martineau shook his head and thread the eye of the needle smoothly and confidently on his first attempt. "What's the bet?" he asked.

"Haven't made one yet. I'll say 20," Kennedy muffled, returning with his face buried in a towel.

"Looks like 25 to me, Doc," followed Claude.

"I'll go 28," added Martineau.

"Can we hurry this along? How 'bout more stitchin' and less bettin'? I'll say 22, and get me up and back out there," urged Newsy.

Martineau had toweled off the wound and started stitching it closed. He shook his head and chuckled at Newsy. "Forget it, Newsy. You're done. You can watch the rest of the game with me. The crowd's full of dolls tonight. I always seem to do better when you get hurt. 'Doc saves hockey superstar yet again! How does he do it? What magical skills does he possess?'" Martineau said, doing his best newsreel announcer impersonation while stitching the wound.

"Why can't he get laid on his own?" followed Newsy in his version of the newsreel announcer. "And I'm *not* done. Hall ain't gettin' rid of me. You're right, kid, Mr. Hall is about to get an education. One he's desperately in need of. Hand me that piece of cardboard and that newspaper."

Newsy wrapped the eight-inch square rigid piece of cardboard with several pieces of newspaper he'd crinkled. He then wrapped black electric tape around the makeshift pad and nodded at Martineau. Doc poured alcohol on the stitches that shot a mind-numbing pain through Newsy's body. He muffled a groan as Martineau bandaged the area. Newsy placed his new "pad" over the injury and taped it down with black hockey tape, right to the skin surrounding the wound. He slid his hockey pants back up and attached them to his suspenders. The entire sequence was done quickly and seamlessly, almost as if it had been performed numerous times before. Which it had.

Still not thrilled with Newsy's decision to return, Martineau shook his head and asked, "Who guessed twenty-five stitches?"

"I did," Claude responded with excitement.

"You win, kid," Newsy said, brushing by the young man. He grabbed his stick, opened the door, and was gone.

The Jubilee Rink's scoreboard showed Toronto leading 4–2 when Newsy arrived at the door to the ice surface. The game was on, so he'd have to wait for a stop in the action. His blood trail was lighter but still visible in the ice. The crowd, intent on following the action, hadn't noticed an overanxious Newsy, who had one hand on his stick and the other on the lever to pop open the door to the ice. A few fans sitting nearest the door briefly took their eyes off the game and spotted their injured hero waiting to return! They stood and cheered. Others sitting near them turned to see what's going on. The cheering spread through the crowd until the entire Jubilee Arena was filled with thunderous applause.

The puck left the ice and flew into the crowd, momentarily stopping the game. Newsy popped the gate and exploded on to the ice, doing his best not to favor the injured leg. The roar of the crowd grew with every stride. The face-off would be at center ice, and Newsy was going to take it. He glided over the frozen pond, glaring at Joe Hall who smiled and nodded his respect to Lalonde's surprising return. Newsy smiled and winked at his antagonist.

The linesman gave the customary instructions to the two opponents prior to the face-off and slammed the frozen puck to the ice. Newsy won the face-off, dropping the puck back into his own zone. The puck skipped deep to the corner and winded around the backboards behind the net where Montreal goaltender George Vezina stopped its momentum and waited for Newsy to retrieve it. Gaining speed, the great Newsy Lalonde circled back to his own goal line and, with a flick of his stick, started the puck up ice. Not having enough time to say anything to his captain, Vezina could only enjoy the breeze as Newsy passed him in a blur.

Breaking out of his defensive zone, Lalonde effortlessly danced around two Maple Leafs as he continued his charge up ice. His speed had eliminated the threat of all the other Leafs and only Joe Hall now had a chance to interrupt his sprint to the Toronto goal. Entering the Maple Leaf zone, Newsy did the unthinkable: he glanced down at the puck to make sure it's where he needed it in relationship to his stick in anticipation of his deadly wrist shot. Hall seized his moment and stopped his backward momentum by planting his left skate in the ice. In an instant, he was moving forward at the defenseless Lalonde.

Newsy knew Hall has taken the bait. He slid the puck slightly forward and to the right and tightened the grip on his stick. The moment before Hall delivered his crushing body check, Newsy lifted his stick to shoulder height. Hall's collarbone was the point of impact for Newsy's lumber. The snapping sound could be heard throughout the arena, but Newsy's stick was still intact. Bad Man Joe Hall crumbled to the ice, grabbing his shoulder, and the back of his head bounced off the unforgiving ice. In his last conscious moment, he saw Newsy regaining his balance on one leg while picking up the puck at the precise spot on the ice he slid it, prior to the collision. Hall's shoulder felt like it has been doused with gasoline and lit it on fire, but what hurt more was the sight of Newsy Lalonde cruising in and beating his goalie "top shelf" with his deadly wrist shot. The crowd's cheer quickly faded as Hall blacked out.

The Montreal dressing room was filled with incredulous reporters and celebrating hockey players in various stages of getting dressed.

"Hey, Newsy, this reporter here wants to know how it feels to play with the great Newsy Lalonde. What should I tell him?" asked George Vezina.

"Tell him Lalonde has the chance to win games because his peerless goaltender keeps the Canadiens close in every contest!" responded Newsy.

Vezina smiled at the compliment. "There's your answer."

Newsy crossed the dressing room to where Vezina was being interviewed. He put his hand on the back of Vezina's neck and leaned in. "Great job in overtime, George. You keep playing like that, and the Stanley Cup will once again be property of Les Habitant."

They shook hands.

"What did he just say to you?" the reporter asked.

"He said your suit is horrible. Perhaps the worst he's ever seen," Vezina responded with a smile.

"Hey, Newsy! You buying tonight?" asked Joe Malone.

Lalonde had grabbed his hat and top coat and headed to the door. "No, Joe, you boys are on your own tonight. Gotta head over to the hospital to see my girls."

He flashed a smile, heading to the door. Just before he left the dressing room, Newsy turned and shouted, "Les Canadiens!"

The players erupted in celebration, responding to their captain.

The tunnel beneath the Jubilee Arena was still busy. Arena workers mop and sweep the food that had fallen through the cracks of the bleacher seats. A crew of four young men struggled to roll the rubber matting that led from the two dressing rooms to the ice and provided a skate-friendly path on the cement floors for the players and referees to enter and exit the arena. Others were packing up the large containers of chips, dogs, and beer not sold this night, but the season was young.

Each time someone reached for Newsy's hand in congratulations, he stopped and graciously accepted it. He spent a few moments with each, patiently discussing the game and his goals numerous times while signing autographs. Newsy made every person feel like they're special and important and he'd been waiting to speak with them all night. This was the part of being a hockey superstar Newsy appreciated and still enjoyed. His role as the leader of Montreal's best professional hockey team was as important off the ice as it was on it, something never lost on Newsy.

Further along, the fans waited near the building exit for a glimpse of the great Newsy Lalonde.

Newsy gently rubbed the stitches on his thigh and took a deep breath before signing his final few autographs. He loved the smell of the old Jubilee down here. A combination of stale beer, musty cement, and the cool air coming off the ice combined to create the unique odor that was a hockey arena. Having just left the dressing room where the stale sweat of old hockey gloves, pads, and skates dominated the senses, this was an improvement. But Newsy relished the odors, this moment, and his blessed life.

He continued toward the building's exit, his shoes sticking to years of spills on the floor, shaking hands with as many fans as possible, even in his hurried state.

One father and son stopped Newsy in his tracks.

"Great game tonight, Mr. Lalonde. I'm glad I was able to witness that comeback and even more happy to be able to share it with my son. He probably wouldn't have believed me if he hadn't seen it with his own eyes," said the father.

"That's very kind of you. And this young man is a Canadiens fan?"

"You bet, sir," said the boy, staring at his idol who literally seemed larger than life. "I'm your *biggest* fan, Mr. Lalonde. I'm glad I was here tonight to see you put that bastard Hall in his place!" he continued.

"Michel!" His father was clearly upset with his son's language, even though he used that word and many other profanities dozens of times during the game.

"No, he's right. Joe Hall is indeed a bastard. Aren't you, Joe?" Newsy asked Hall, who had walked up behind the father and son.

The father cowered as Hall shot his infamous stare in his direction. They thanked Newsy again and quickly departed the company of the Bad Man of professional hockey.

"How's the leg?" Hall asked.

"Took twenty-five stitches. How's the arm?"

"Your fucked-up-looking doctor says it's a broken collarbone. I'll be out a couple of weeks. You're leaving quickly. No press tonight?" Joe asked.

"Gotta get to the hospital. Not for the leg, I'm going to visit my wife and new baby daughter."

Hall was surprised at the news and felt a little guilty for what he'd done. "I'm sorry."

"For what?"

"Didn't know about your baby girl. I wouldn't have, well, you know, if I had known."

"Yes, you would have. Cut the crap, Joe. Wanna come along and meet them?"

George Kennedy interrupted them, huffing and puffing from the short run down the hallway accompanied by two policemen.

"There he is. Arrest him! I want Joe Hall arrested!" he shouted.

"Are you going to arrest me too, George? Forget it, officers. It's part of the game. And besides, George, if I didn't have to play *against* the Bad Man, just think of the money you'd save on stitches," Newsy suggested, smiling and shoving Hall toward the exit.

"What the hell is all over your suit? Smells like brandy. You been drinking already, Georgie?" asked Hall. Lalonde burst out in laughter as they head out.

"Hey, Newsy, great game!" yelled one of the policemen.

"Thanks, Officer. You're doing fine work," Newsy responded over his shoulder, shoving Hall out the arena door.

Kennedy wasn't sure what just happened. The two stars left the arena after they nearly crippled each other, arm in arm and laughing together!

"Pain in the ass. Fuckin' guy gets everything he wants, when he wants it. It's like dealing with Rockefeller," Kennedy mumbled.

"Makes about the same money," said the policemen, still staring in the direction of the odd scene of the two combatants hurrying down the exit ramp together.

"Worth every penny. He's just . . . gifted."

George just picked up on Newsy's "stitches" comment. He excitedly waddled down the hall toward the Toronto dressing room.

Newsy hated hospitals; all athletes do. Yeah, they served a purpose and the people were nice enough, but this was the place you came when things went wrong. Injuries, illness, death. That's why hospitals were in business. But they did smell good. At least, a lot better than the Jubilee. *I bet one hockey bag filled with Vezina's goalie gear could infect the entire building,* he thought. *The entire city block.* He smiled.

He rushed down the hallway and around the last corner to Iona's room. His dress shoes, now wiped clean of the sticky substance from the Jubilee floors, caused him to slip and lose his balance. Instinct took over, and he grabbed the only thing nearby to keep from falling, his brother-in-law walking the other direction.

"Gotcha! Jeez, Newsy, slow down. They're not going anywhere, and besides, shouldn't you be resting that leg?"

"Oh hey, Gladdy. Thanks for the assist. How are my two lovely girls?" Newsy asked Gladstone.

"Doing fine, just resting. I gotta get home, but I've been meaning to talk to you about that radio company you wanted me to look in to."

"That's right. Radio Corporation of America. Got a pretty good tip from someone in the States. He says with the war ending, this RCA company will be the leader in this new radio thing," Newsy said excitedly.

"Who gave you the information?"

"Ah, Gladdy, I told you. Can't give you the fellow's name. But trust me, he's reliable."

"Well, my sources are telling me this radio thing is going to be a passing fad. Most people don't even believe it'll work. I would advise you not to invest your hard-earned loonies. Especially since you're so adamant about protecting your source. Sounds a little fishy to me. Stay away, and we'll find something more secure for you to invest in."

"Really? You sure? This guy seemed pretty confident in the technology."

"Technology? Sounds more like voodoo to me. Voices flying through the air with no wires. Trust me. It won't last, and you'll lose your money."

"All right, Gladdy. Oh, this is—"

Gladstone interrupted, "Joe Hall?" He nervously nodded but didn't reach for Hall's outstretched hand. "We'll talk tomorrow, Newsy," he said while backing away cautiously, then turning to walk briskly down the hallway and disappeared around a corner.

"You sure have a way with people, don't ya?" mocked Newsy.

"Yeah, I get that a lot in this town," replied Hall. "And other towns," he said under his breath.

Iona's hospital room was large and barren. A small table in one corner of the white cinder-block room supported a large bouquet of flowers with a card from the Montreal Canadiens Club de Hockey. The bed was made of iron and rested upon four wheels, which are locked into place. The rest of the room was empty and cold except for the six-foot lamp next to the bed, which didn't provide enough light for the sizeable room. Even in this light, Iona looked stunningly beautiful. Her waist-long brown hair was gracefully brushed to the side and hanging off the bed. The delicate features that first attracted Newsy were still full of youthful appeal. Just two days since giving birth, she exuded the class, confidence, and elegance that was Iona Letters Lalonde.

Newsy crossed the room quickly and silently as Iona took notice, smiling at the proud father. He bent over, kissed Iona lovingly on the forehead, and took the baby from her arms.

"Here are the two most beautiful women in all of Quebec. Joe, this is Iona, and this here is the newest Lalonde. Hello, sweetheart, how is my gorgeous little princess tonight? Daddy won again. You missed a very exciting game."

He turned toward the light and began counting tiny fingers and toes as he had done each time he saw his new baby.

Iona's expression had changed. She recognized the other visitor in the room.

"Congratulations, Mrs. Lalonde. She is indeed beautiful. It's a pleasure to meet you both," he said.

"I wish I could say the same, Mr. Hall. By your appearance, I can only hope that your arm is in a sling because of my husband," she said with as much disdain as she could muster.

"Then, you'll be very happy this night, Mrs. Lalonde," Joe replied through a smirk.

"Happier still had you not paid this visit. What you did last week was—"

Newsy interrupted, "Now, now, honey. What happens on the ice, stays on the ice, you know that. I think it was a nice gesture of Mr. Hall to come see our little princess. Want to hold her?"

"No!" Iona and Joe practically yelled in unison.

"How is our newest Canadiens fan this evening?" asked George Kennedy, whose timing, for once, was perfect. "Laurene, you would have been very proud of your pappa tonight," he leaned in and said to the baby girl.

"What happened?" asked Iona.

Kennedy looked at Hall and Newsy, surprised that no one had told her yet. He's going to enjoy getting this reaction from Iona.

"Well, after we put twenty-five more stitches into Newsy's leg, courtesy of Joe here, he scored two goals in the third to tie the game and then got the game winner just a couple of minutes into overtime," George explained while watching the blood boil to Iona's cheeks.

"Mr. Hall, I must ask you to leave my room immediately. I will not have my daughter in the presence of a . . . a barbarian!"

Now Newsy felt embarrassed as Joe raised his good hand to Newsy as if to say it's okay. Kennedy burst out in laughter. His face turned red this time from the scene that just unfolded. "And just what seems to be so humorous, Mr. Kennedy?" Iona asked, not understanding his amusement. Newsy and Hall were wondering the same thing.

"Well, Mrs. Lalonde, you better get used to his presence. I heard what you said after the game, Newsy, and decided you were right. I'm tired of paying Martineau more money each time you play against each other. I made a trade, had to throw in some cash, which I didn't want to do, but that son of a—" Kennedy caught himself, remembering there were women present. "Excuse me, Joe, you're a 'Hab.' Welcome to the Montreal Canadiens," he said with pride.

Newsy grinned and let out a "woo-hoo!" while rushing over to shake Joe's hand. Hall just stood still, amazed and a little shocked.

"The Bad Man a Canadien! I never thought I'd say this but, Joe, heal quickly and hurry back. We got us a Stanley Cup to win," Newsy excitedly proclaimed.

Hall can only manage a smile in response when an annoyed nurse entered the room.

"Excuse me. Excuse me! It's late, and your party has to end. Sorry, Mr. Lalonde, wonderful win tonight, by the way. But you're all going to have to leave. Especially you, Mr. Hall. There's a train leaving for Toronto in fifteen minutes. Please be under it," she whispered, taking a sleeping Laurene from Newsy's arm and returning her to Iona.

Newsy, Joe, and George suppressed a laugh at the nurse's insult. She'll read about the trade in the morning newspaper along with the rest of the Province of Quebec.

"Sleep well, sweetheart. I'll see you first thing tomorrow before practice," Newsy whispered to his wife and kissed her softly on the lips. He then kissed the tiny forehead next to Iona. "Good night little, Laurene. Come on, Joe, we gotta find you a place to stay."

"You can stay with me until you find a place," offered Kennedy.

"Love ya, sweetheart. See you tomorrow," Newsy said and rushed out of the room.

George and Joe were already well down the hospital hallway, ahead of Newsy. They eagerly discussed everything from Hall's new defensive partner to the best restaurants and bars in Montreal. Lalonde hurried to catch up. He turned one corner, then another, barely making up any ground on his boss and new teammate.

I've only seen Kennedy move this fast at closing time in Murphy's pub. Lalonde smiled to himself, also realizing he hadn't bought cigars for the boys yet. He reached into his pocket and pulled out a Cohiba.

Something suddenly stopped him in his tracks, a smell that was foreign in this place. The clean hospital aroma had been replaced with a foul stench. As he slowly moved down the hall, the odor increased and was joined by a chorus of coughing, wheezing, and moaning. The sound was muffled but clearly growing louder as he walked toward the nurses' station. Kennedy and Hall have disappeared around another bend, but Newsy was confounded and growing concerned. The two nurses behind the counter were occupied with returning files to their proper drawers and didn't notice his investigation.

Across from the nurses' station was another long hallway that connected with his, creating a T. He peered around the corner and realized the smell and sounds were coming from a door about twenty feet down this hallway. At the top of this hallway was a red sign with large white letters, warning in French and English, "Quarantine: No unauthorized admittance past this point."

"Mr. Lalonde? I'm sorry for my behavior in your room, but you were making a lot of noise and Joe Hall, well, I just don't like the man," said the nurse who just ended their visit.

She was walking with Newsy, slowly, along the hallway now, talking about the hockey game or the baby, but Newsy was not listening. He stopped at the door. The upper half was a window that was partially fogged. He thought he saw people in beds but couldn't quite make out what was behind the glass. The smell and the sounds emanating from behind the door were description enough.

He interrupted the nurse, "Madam, what's wrong with the people in this room?"

"Flu."

"Pardon?"

"Spanish influenza. Most are military, just returned from overseas. Some of them came back sick, others were healthy as oxen, then became ill at the military camp, outside the city. Last week, there were only two. As of this morning, the count stood at 163 patients. Twenty-five have already passed since they arrived," she explained.

He reached for the doorknob to enter the room but only had the door open an inch when the nurse grabbed his hand and shoved the door closed, surprising Lalonde. He turned to her. "I'd like to visit with them."

"Mr. Lalonde, that's very nice of you, but this flu is extremely contagious and just as dangerous. There's a very good chance that most of the men behind that door will be dead within a week."

"Then I insist. Perhaps I can offer them . . . a distraction. Ease their minds." He gently took her hand off his and turned the doorknob again. Stepping inside, he said, "My god. They're so young."

She handed him a mask. "Here, put this on, and please don't get too close."

Each bed was separated by a white sheet from floor to ceiling. Some patients were visible as Newsy walked down the center of the room, but most beds were completely shielded on all sides by the sheets. He held the mask to his face, then started tying the strings behind his head. The nurse grabbed the strings and tied it for him. He turned, not realizing she had come into the room behind him. Only their eyes were visible. Hers were professional and focused. His had become glassy, filling with tears on top of shock.

"This side of the room are the advanced cases. All we can do is try to make them comfortable," she explained in a tone, trying to calm him.

He stopped at one of the beds where a young man lay in a fetal position, rigid and shaking. He struggled to breathe, almost gurgled with every gulp of air. The only parts of his body not covered were his feet that have turned black and his face, which appeared to be a dark gray/purple. Newsy took a couple of steps closer and saw a frothy red liquid dripping from his lips each time he exhaled. The nurse grabbed his arm and stopped Newsy's advance. She gently pulled him by the arm, leading him away from the man who within the hour will take his last labored breath.

2

Outbreak

Camp Jackson, South Carolina

September 1918

Six miles east of Columbia, South Carolina, lay a vast area of wilderness known as the Congaree Sand Hills. Nearly two years before Joe Hall became a Montreal Canadien, a small contingent of military and civilian planners had surveyed the area. Its rolling terrain included lakes and swamps and was overgrown with blackjack oak and loblolly pine, thriving in the sandy but firm soil, which was what attracted the planners to this sight. After intense storms, the porous soil did not turn to mud but rather absorbed the moisture and remained solid. The combination of this unusual draining phenomenon, the terrain, and the climate was what made the sand hills ideal for year-round training.

The United States had successfully isolated itself from the war in Europe, but that was about to change, and the military needed new modern training bases for their doughboys. On May 19, 1917, Maj. Douglas MacArthur announced that the army had decided this location would become one of sixteen National Cantonments constructed to support the impending war effort. Two months later, pursuant to General Orders No. 95, it was established and named Camp Jackson, in honor of Andrew Jackson. Major general of the army and a hero in the Battle for New Orleans, Jackson also served the United States as its seventh president (1829–1837).

The contract to transform this backcountry into an operating military base was awarded to the Hardaway Contracting Company of Columbus, Georgia. Hardaway's general superintendent, Henry B. Crawford, oversaw the massive construction project that would need to house the more than forty thousand men in an infantry division, their thirteen thousand horses and mules, as well as the eight thousand additional officers, hospital force, quartermaster or supply force, utilities force, depot brigade, security force, and the continuing construction crews needed for repairs and new construction.

In six months, Crawford's crew built a city containing 1,519 buildings that featured everything needed to house the arriving army, including an airfield, roads, bridges, sewers, a heating plant, laundry, and even a 3,000-seat theater. The base covered 2,727 acres, and Camp Jackson featured another 12,804 acres for training, establishing it as the largest and most active Initial Training Center (ITC) in the US Army.

Pvt. Roscoe Vaughn arrived at Camp Jackson in early September 1918. The twenty-one-year-old joined thousands of other inductees to begin what they believed to be the adventure of their lives.

Private Vaughn was smart, tough, and in tremendous physical condition—the perfect infantryman candidate. He took pride in being part of 1st Company, 321st Infantry Regiment, 81st "Wildcat" Division. The eighteen-hour days of long marches through the sandy marshes and bushy thickets took their toll, but he knew that he was being prepared for combat with the Kaiser's war machine. The training bordered on torture, and the officers showed little mercy for their men. His morning drills completed, Vaughn felt more stiff and sore than usual. He had a terrible headache and decided to lie down in his bunk before reporting to the mess tent. *Just a couple of minutes and I'll be good as new*, he thought. *I always recover quickly.*

Capt. K. P. Hegeforth, one of fifty doctors and dentists currently stationed at Camp Jackson, was part of the group of original doctors assigned to the training facility. Earlier that summer, Hegeforth had dealt with the measles epidemic, which was quickly followed by a meningitis outbreak. Nearly 1,500 soldiers-turned-patients entered the base hospital, taxing the staff. Since August, however, things had calmed down, and the majority of his time was spent diagnosing and treating minor injuries and the occasional accidental gunshot wound.

It was nearly noon on this typically warm and humid September day. Hegeforth stepped out of his sweltering office in to the blinding South Carolina sun. The medical complex covered fifteen acres at the highest point of the camp. From this vantage point, he could survey nearly all of Camp Jackson. Companies marching in unison, new trainees unloading at the train depot, and still others heading to the mess tent. It never failed to amaze him how this was all coordinated. To Hegeforth, it was organized confusion being played out on a massive scale.

"Another day of worm-baking out here, Ms. McKenna," he said to the chief nurse in the office behind him. "Probably going to turn into a frog strangler this afternoon. So much moisture in the air and all," he continued.

Hegeforth loved using the metaphors he learned from his father, growing up in a small town in Central Alabama. Nurse McKenna smiled to herself; she loved hearing them too and kept working on the medical chart in front of her. Hegeforth was about to return to his desk when he noticed something peculiar, even for the typical anarchy below him. From practically every direction, soldiers were struggling to walk, even stumbling toward him. At first, he thought it may be some new training formation or battle exercise, but that couldn't be. Not the way they labored up the incline to the hospital.

"Nurse McKenna, we're going to need some help out here," he instructed. Hegeforth hurried down the hill to help the man he thought was having the most difficulty. "Here, let me help you, son. What's your name?"

"Pvt. Roscoe Vaughn, sir," he said, holding his head and shielding his eyes.

"Can you tell me what the problem is, Private?" Hegeforth asked, cupping his palm to Vaughn's forehead. *Damn, must be over 102 degrees,* Hegeforth thought, supporting him with both hands under the private's left arm.

"Thought I was just tired from morning drills but got this headache a while ago, and now I feel like I'm freezing," he said as they stepped into the hospital. "Something ain't right."

"Here ya go. You just lay still, and we'll figure out what's what, quicker than you can whistle Dixie," Hegeforth said reassuringly.

"I'm from Jersey, Captain."

"Nobody's perfect, son," he said, trying to calm the private's fears. He laid a thick wool blanket across Vaughn, who rolled on to his side, crawled into a fetal position, and continued shivering, despite the intense heat inside the building.

As Hegeforth turned to leave Vaughn's bedside, he became aware of what was happening behind him. A dozen soldiers suffering the same symptoms as Vaughn were filing into the base hospital and dropping into cots.

"Nurse McKenna," he shouted across the room.

The chief nurse looked up from helping one of the men and rushed to meet him, helping two more young men into bed along the way. "Yes, Doctor?"

"Get the word out. All medical staff on base are to report to duty immediately."

"What's going on?"

"I'm not sure, but we gotta get on top of this thing right quick."

The next morning, over eight hundred of the hospital's one thousand beds were filled with ailing soldiers. All night long, they came. Hegeforth and his medical staff piled blankets on top of the men as nurses pleaded with them to drink water for hydration. But their conditions continued to deteriorate. At first, purple blotches appeared on their skin as they drifted into unconsciousness. However, sleep provided no reprieve from the agony.

Hundreds of men moaning and coughing was cause for great concern as more and more reported to the hospital complaining of headaches and fever. Hegeforth was taking the pulse of Private Vaughn, concentrating on the number of heartbeats while eyeing his watch. When he had nearly completed the task, Vaughn moaned and rolled over in his direction. Hegeforth reacted in a way he had never done before. He jumped back a few inches and dropped Vaughn's arm. The private's face had turned color from a healthy pink a few hours earlier to a nightmarish dark purple. His breathing was becoming more labored, and around his mouth was a frothy pinkish liquid.

"Nurse."

"Yes, Doctor?"

"Hand me that VC10 and a towel, please." He carefully wiped a few ounces of the liquid from Vaughn's mouth into the small glass container and then placed the cork in the top. He wiped the exterior down with the towel, then wiped Vaughn's mouth clean. When Vaughn exhaled again, new liquid appeared. "Take this to Dr. Park in the lab and have him take a look, will ya, dear? Thank you much." He attempted to appear relaxed.

Next, Hegeforth placed his stethoscope on Vaughn's chest. *Sounds like a bathtub half-filled with water in the middle of a twister,* he thought. *A sure sign of influenza, but these patients are the wrong age. These are some of the healthiest young men in America. Why are they succumbing to something that they're typically capable of fighting off?*

Hegeforth visited a dozen of other patients in just under an hour. Vaughn's condition had progressed the furthest, and others were still reporting with early symptoms, but some had shown improvement. They were, however, a very small minority of the nearly one thousand cases the base hospital was now caring for. Returning to Vaughn's bed one more time before consulting with Dr. Park, Hegeforth was staggered by his breathing, if it could be called that.

The hospital's lab featured the newest most powerful microscopes. Hegeforth startled Dr. James Howard Park Jr. who was concentrating on the sample Hegeforth sent over an hour earlier. "Well? What are we dealing with?"

"It's definitely influenza. But a strain I'm afraid I'm not familiar with. I've never seen it progress this fast and kill this quickly," responded Park.

"Kill? I just left my most advanced patient, a Private Vaughn. His condition is serious, but he's very much alive."

"Captain Hegeforth, on my way here this morning, I witnessed a private drop to the ground about fifty yards ahead of me. By the time I reached him, he was dead. Pvt. James Downs is the first mortality," Park explained.

"Dr. Hegeforth! It's Private Vaughn, come quick!" Nurse McKenna interrupted.

The three rushed through the lab door, running through the hospital to Vaughn's bed. Blood was everywhere. Vaughn's body lifted off the bed at his waist with every breath he attempted to take. A bloody froth spewed from his lips with each exhale. His eyes were wide with terror as his hands clutched the bedding.

"Clear this area!" Hegeforth ordered, but before anyone can move, Vaughn's body twisted to the side and he dropped back to the cot. His lifeless eyes were fixed on Hegeforth as the bloody mixture bubbled out of his open mouth.

Five days later, a special military courier arrived at the Old Red Brick Building in Washington, DC, original home of the US Armed Forces Institute of Pathology. Established in 1862 by an executive order of Pres. Abraham Lincoln to house specimens, the institute is home to millions samples.

The pathologist carefully opened the package revealing two thumbnail-size pieces of lung tissue belonging to Privates Vaughn and Downs. The samples had been injected with formaldehyde and wrapped in paraffin wax. They were categorized and placed in boxes, then shelved in the massive warehouse where they would be left undisturbed for almost eighty years.

3

Pandemic

November 1918

Seward Peninsula, Alaska

On July 26, 1771, members of the Second Continental Congress meeting in Philadelphia agreed "that a postmaster general be appointed for the United Colonies, who shall hold his office at Philadelphia and shall be allowed a salary of $1,000 per annum for himself and $340 per annum for a secretary and comptroller, with power to appoint such, and so many deputies as to him may seem proper and necessary. That a line of posts be appointed under the direction of the postmaster general, from Falmouth in New England to Savannah in Georgia, with as many cross points as he shall think fit."

In 1902, 127 years after Benjamin Franklin was appointed the original postmaster general, a cross point was established in Wales, Alaska, the westernmost point on the Continental United States. Nearly four thousand miles away from Philadelphia and located at the tip of the Seward Peninsula, Wales became a hugely successful whaling village because of its proximity to migratory routes of the planet's largest mammals.

For these reasons, Andrew "Shorty" Edgar made his home here. Once a month, he performed his mailman duties, traveling the 117 miles south to Nome and back, stopping at smaller villages to deliver and pick up parcels along the way. The rest of the time, he worked as a whaler. What many believed was a difficult life was, in fact, fun and adventurous to Edgar. But the lure of the post office and whaling ships was not what originally brought Shorty to Alaska.

Well over six feet tall, Shorty was always the largest man in the room. His broad shoulders, full beard, and long brown hair provided him with a stunning, some would say intimidating, appearance. A natural outdoors man, Shorty was a deadly shot with his rifle or pistol and could handle a knife as well as anyone in the territory. His size and skills made him a foreboding opponent for any man or beast. It also accorded him respect and admiration. Everyone loved Shorty, most out of fear, but they just didn't know the man. His smile, manners, and sense of humor were as much a part of his legend as was his mental and physical toughness.

Born in Seattle in 1870, Andrew Edgar often heard the tales of the California gold rush growing up. It sounded like a wonderfully magical time when ordinary people struck it rich. So when Jafet Lindeberg, Erik Lindblom, and John Brynteson discovered gold in tiny Anvil Creek in 1898, Andrew joined the tens of thousands of other prospectors boarding ships and sailing 2,500 miles north to Nome, Alaska.

Overnight, claims were staked and villages sprung up throughout the territory. Edgar lived out of his tent, panning for gold in places named Willow Creek, Elephant Creek, First Chance Creek, Surprise Creek, and Disappointment Creek. For three years, he made large sums of money from the nuggets he found and then spent it drinking and fighting in the bars, gambling halls, and bordellos that followed the prospectors. It was during this time he received his nickname and his well-earned reputation.

By 1902, the more easily reached claims were exhausted and so was Shorty. Large mining companies with bigger and better equipment took over, and at thirty-two years of age, Edgar needed a new profession. He was hired on the spot at the Wales post office mainly because the head postman, like everyone else in the territory, knew his legend.

Shorty made the Wales to Nome run starting on the fifth of each month. The timing had less to do with the post office's schedule and more with the payment schedules of the whalers who were paid on or about the first of every month. With cash in his pocket, Shorty spent the next few days resting from the arduous work on the seas, enjoying the camaraderie of other whalers and the native Inupiat Eskimos at the pub as well as preparing his dogsled.

November meant all the streams and rivers would be frozen solid, making the trip much easier and quicker than the summer months.

His dog team had been together for several years now and worked like a well-oiled machine. The lead dog, Fifi, steered the other seven and could probably navigate the trip by herself, if need be. The dogs provided a means of transportation in this unforgiving frozen environment, but they were also family. Every musher had a special relationship with his dogs, especially the lead dog. Fifi was one hundred pounds of muscle, discipline, and personality, which Shorty relished on the lonely trail.

The three-day trek was the same as it had been for the past sixteen years. Forty-five miles to Brevig Mission, another seven miles south to Teller, and then the seventy-mile run down to Nome. Shorty arrived at the Nome post office in the early afternoon of November 8, 1918.

"Welcome back," greeted H. Roy Hunter. The postmaster in Nome for three years now, Hunter was younger and much smaller than his mail carrier and always looked forward to Shorty's arrival. "What's new up north?"

"Hey, Roy. Same ole, same ole," he replied while unstrapping the mail bundles from his sled. "Am I in time for lunch?"

"Just ate but come in and make yourself something. The missus has got some Arctic char on the fire."

"Be there in ten minutes," Shorty replied, throwing Roy a large bundle of mail and nearly knocking him off the steps of the small wood building. "Let me get my girls situated first."

Roy smiled while Shorty unstrapped the dogs and led them to the pen on the side of the post office.

"Hey, Anna. How ya been?" asked Shorty, entering the back room of the building the Hunters called home and office. Shorty towered over Roy's petite wife who wore wire-framed glasses and her hair pulled back in a bun. "You look great."

She didn't, but Shorty loved her cooking and her company.

"Hello, Andrew," she said, rushing to the doorway to meet him.

Anna was the only person who called him by his given name. Although Shorty was several years her senior, she treated him like a younger brother, perhaps even a son. Shorty held a special place in Anna's heart, most likely because of the reputation she deemed inaccurate for the man she had come to know. Or maybe she felt sad for him because of the loneliness he must experience on the trail. Regardless, it was heartfelt, and Shorty enjoyed her caring, loving attention.

"How was the trip down?" Anna asked.

"Easy. This time of year is my favorite. Everything is frozen, the snow ain't that deep, and the weather is just so comfortable. Gotta enjoy it while it lasts. And of course, I get to see my favorite Nome-ites. Is that what you call yourselves down here?"

"I hope not, sounds like a bug," replied Anna.

"Nome-ites? How the hell'd you come up with that?" asked Roy.

Anna placed a plate in front of Shorty that contained a large piece of Arctic char and boiled potatoes.

"Thanks much, Anna. I didn't come up with it. Fifi did. I think it's good. Nome-ites, a people who live in Nome, connect the Seward Peninsula with the rest of the world, and never grow taller than a pickax," Shorty said, smirking.

"Fifi came up with it, huh? You having lots of conversations with your dog?" inquired Roy nervously.

"Nah. Don't want to distract her when we're moving, and she's been drinking a lot at night. Gets real surly when she's had a few. Can't stand her when she's like that. I think something's bothering her, but she won't tell me what's on her mind."

Anna looked at Roy, who was staring at Shorty with the same look of concern Anna had. His postman must be losing his mind. *Too many miles and too much time alone on that cold desolate trail,* he thought.

Shorty looked up from his fish dinner and smiled.

"I thought you'd have a problem with the pickax comment!"

Anna let out a relieved giggle at her guest's creativity. Roy just shook his head. "I got the only grizzly-sized postman who wants to be a comedian. Jeez, Shorty, you scared me!"

"Comedian? Nah. You know me. Gotta keep it loose and fun. I'll run your mail forever. At least, that's what Fifi wants me to do."

"Shut that fuzzy trap of yours and finish lunch. We got some sorting to do," cracked Roy.

"Yes, boss," smirked Shorty.

After lunch, Anna cleaned the dishes and started preparing dinner while Roy and Shorty worked in the front room, sorting mail and servicing the Nome-ites, who had business with the post office or just stopped by for their monthly visit with Shorty. Every so often, Anna would hear a burst of laughter, which meant her two boys were going at it. A tremendous thud shook the building and was followed by a terrible moan and then a scream. She went rushing into the post office to find Roy on top of Shorty, his arms locked around Shorty's huge neck, applying a headlock and a pile of mail knocked to the floor next to them.

"I give, I give!" shouted Shorty, laughing at his much smaller antagonist.

"Boys! Dinner is almost ready. Cut the crap and finish your work."

Roy and Shorty looked at each other and burst out in laughter again. Roy rolled off Shorty and landed with another thud on the floor.

"Yes, Mother," replied Shorty.

"Sorry, hon," added Roy, tears rolling down his cheeks.

The November mail load was heavy, so it took most of the afternoon to separate and sort for Brevig, Teller, and Wales. Anna was convinced that it would have taken much less time if the two men would quit acting so juvenile, but what the hell, she thought. Roy loved the bizarre camaraderie he shared with this huge outdoorsman. She never would have thought her refined, educated, and quiet husband would get along so well with a man who couldn't be further opposite in size, manner, and social graces. Roy and Andrew could be poster boys for the expression "opposites attract," she told her husband constantly. What they did share and perhaps was the cornerstone of their relationship was a warped sense of humor. Once a month, they laughed with each other and at each other for hours. Either way, it didn't matter. They were always laughing and never stopped enjoying each other's company.

The post office was located just a few hundred feet from the Bering Sea. More of a large village than a traditional city, Nome did not feature streets and blocks. Rather, the white buildings with reddish-brown roofs were scattered haphazardly around the brown sandy beach. Shorty often wondered if people went to the wrong house on a load because they all looked alike. Lucky for him, Roy and Anna were always there to help him find his way back after their monthly night out. After dinner, Shorty was the first to step out into the cool salty night. Anna and Roy followed. All three breathed in the fresh crisp air.

"Lord have mercy. Look at that sky. Seems like you could just reach up and pluck one of those stars outta the sky," observed Anna.

The eternal optimist, she would regularly begin one of her "the glass is always half full" sermons when properly inspired. Shorty and Roy shot each other a look as if to silently say, "Here it comes."

"It really is amazing. Makes you appreciate what we have and where we live. It also reminds us how little and insignificant we are in God's grand universe. It's quite humbling and, at the same time, inspiring."

"Amen," Roy and Shorty said in unison, trying to conceal their sarcasm. It worked.

"Another delivery from the lower 48 coming in, I see," said Shorty in an attempt to stem the monologue that was sure to continue. A ferry was making its way through the narrow inlet toward the bay. Since Nome had no deep-water port, passengers and material were ferried from the larger ocean-going vessels into the city.

"Yep, more prospectors looking to find their fortune. Someone should really let people know down there that the gold has all but run out," remarked Roy.

"They'll be disappointed and looking for real work soon enough," agreed Shorty.

"They'll be drunk and disorderly before that, my friend," added Roy.

The sky was cloudless, and the three continued to enjoy the star-filled sky as they made their way to the Crystal Palace, their favorite night spot, which they frequented every month when Shorty was in town. The name was utterly misleading since there was no crystal to be found, and the "palace" was simply another weathered white building with a dozen and a half tables that wobbled on the uneven floor, a large bar that dominated the room and an old piano. To the locals, its name was unimportant, just as long as it was open—that was critical.

Shorty held the door for Roy and his wife.

"Hey, PJ!" Roy shouted to the bartender.

"Hey, Roy, Anna. Shorty! Welcome back, buddy. Good trip?"

"Easy and fast," Shorty told his favorite barkeep as both men extended their right hands.

PJ was in his thirties, tall, and thin with a shaved head and a goatee mustache that could not conceal his twenty-four-hour-a-day scowl. He always seemed to be in a sour mood to visitors, but to the locals, they knew it was just his personality and actually enjoyed his sad-sap stories that were endlessly entertaining. Roy was Nome's postmaster delivering mail, and PJ was the town's distributor of the most current information, gossip, and news, most of which he picked up from newly arrived 48-ers, the moniker given to the hordes of people coming north from the lower forty-eight states, looking to strike it rich.

"What's the good word, PJ?" Shorty asked, pounding his huge hand on the aged bar and clasping PJ's hand in his.

PJ squeezed as hard as he could as always but still felt the blood being forced from his hand. "Latest is, the war in Europe may be coming to an end. Supposed to sign the treaty anytime. Don't know if it's going to happen, but hopefully . . . it's gone on long enough. Complete waste of time and lives if you ask me."

"That is good news."

"What can I get you?"

"The usual?" Shorty asked Roy and Anna who had just sat down at a table near the piano and away from a group of twenty or so 48-ers, who had pushed three tables together on the other side of the barroom and were clearly overserved already.

"Sure, Short-man," responded Roy.

"Three pints and a bottle, PJ. How long they been here?" Shorty asked, motioning with a head tilt toward the large boisterous group.

"Way too long, bunch of fuckin' assholes. Must've arrived this afternoon and been here ever since," replied PJ.

"They're always entertaining, that's for sure," Shorty said, grabbing the three pints of beer, three empty tumblers, and the bottle of whiskey.

"PJ happy tonight?" asked Roy.

"Pleasant as always. Those boys in the corner aren't helping his mood."

Roy leaned forward around Shorty to view the spectacle just as one young man looked in his direction with an expression of "what the fuck are you looking at?" Roy quickly leaned back, finding comfort in Shorty's large frame breaking the man's view. "Oh boy, another drunk group with an attitude. Just what we need."

"Relax, Roy. They're not bothering anybody. At least, not yet." Shorty turned in the direction of the group with a glare. "So what are we drinking to tonight?" he asked, turning back to his hosts.

"How 'bout another safe trip for our favorite mailman?" asked Anna.

"Hear, hear. Safe trip home, my friend," said Roy, lifting his mug of beer.

All three glasses met at mid-table with a *cling*.

"Thanks to you both for the hospitality, as always," Shorty responded and downed the entire mug in one gulp. Wiping away the froth from his mustache and beard, he was suddenly jolted from behind, causing his chest to pound into the table.

"Sorry, buddy." Shorty looked up to see two of the men from across the bar now standing beside their table. "We just got into this shit-hole of a town, and we're wondering where all the women are," said one of the young men.

Shorty figured him to be about twenty-two, young, foolish, and full of piss and vinegar, like most 48-ers. His smaller partner seemed to be smiling at something, though Shorty wasn't sure what was so amusing.

"It's still early, friend. Be patient, they'll be here," replied Roy, trying to diffuse the coming situation. "So why don't you return to your pals and enjoy your evening?"

"Nah, not those kinda women. You know. Where are the whores?" Smiley asked through slurred speech. "We've got our land legs back and now we want to use our land dicks on some fine local meat," he continued.

"Fuck me," PJ said to himself, overhearing the conversation and reaching under the bar.

"You see the lady sitting with us? You need to show some respect. Now you've been asked once to leave us. Don't make us ask again," Shorty said calmly.

"I'm s-sorry. But is she available to rent for a few hours?" Smiley mockingly asked, pointing his thumb at Anna. His taller friend burst out laughing, but his mood was about to change.

Shorty stood up, slowly and deliberately.

"Apologize" is all he said. The two men looked stunned at the size of the man for a brief moment, then regained their composure, realizing that they had numbers in abundance. Smiley looked over his shoulder to his friends at the table across the room as if to say "help."

"They'll never get here in time," threatened Shorty, staring down at his two antagonists, who refused to back down. "They'll arrive too late to save your sorry asses. So I say again. Apologize," he repeated, this time with a threatening firmness in his voice and a lean to his body.

Smiley and his beer-muscled buddy saw the group get up out of their chairs across the bar. They knew the cavalry was on its way, so why wait any longer? Smiley's friend dropped his right foot back, twisted his right side, and loaded up his fist in preparation of landing the first blow on his huge adversary. But the alcohol had slowed his reflexes more than he realized. Before his fist came forward to find its mark, Shorty quickly loaded up his own right hand and poked a short powerful jab into his face. The massive weathered fist collapsed the sinus cavities and drove his nose a full half inch to the left side of his face. Next, it impacted his right eye socket, fracturing that as well. Roy leapt out of his chair to grab Anna and usher her out of the way, but he was too late. He was showered with blood exploding from the maimed visitor but managed to shield his wife. The eight pints of beer no longer dulling his senses, an intense pain shot through his entire body, and then, Smiley's friend went limp. The knees buckled, and he started toward the bar floor. Smiley reached for him, but Shorty grabbed him by the collar first, spun him around, and slammed him on to the table that Shorty, Anna, and Roy had just toasted over.

The shock of being slammed to the table had snapped him back to consciousness, but that wasn't a good thing either. His hands were now cupping his face, but he couldn't remember why. They were covered with his blood. The pain was worse than anything he had ever experienced.

I feel something hovering above my face, but I can't touch it, he thought through the agony and the blood. Suddenly, he remembered what had happened just moments before. Above him a blurry huge bear of a man had his hand raised above his head. It seemed as if Shorty was moving in slow motion, and as the hand swung toward his head, it became apparent it held a large Bowie knife. *This guy was right,* he thought. *My friends didn't get here in time.*

Shorty slammed the knife into the table, taking a piece of the bloodied man's ear with it. Smiley and his friend screamed in unison. Shorty turned and grabbed Smiley as PJ hopped over the bar to intercept the crowd charging toward Shorty, Roy, and Anna. He fired one round from the double-barreled shotgun into the ceiling just above their heads. They all stopped instantly and were showered by wood chips and dust falling from the hole in the Crystal Palace ceiling. A few fell to the floor and covered their heads. The odor of human feces filled the room.

"Time for you, assholes, to move on," PJ warned the crowd, pointing the gun at the lead man's face.

Shorty's hands had a firm grasp of Smiley's overcoat, just below his neck. With seemingly little effort, he lifted Smiley nearly two feet off the floor until they were nose to nose. Shorty let out one long calm breath while staring straight into Smiley's eyes. Smiley realized there was nothing he could do but capitulate to this man's demands.

"Apologize?" Shorty asked softly in a mocking tone. He held him there for another instant, sealing his own fate before he slowly lowered the man to the floor.

"I surely do apologize, ma'am. Didn't mean no disrespect. We'll be leaving you all now. Won't be any more trouble from us, I promise you that."

Smiley helped his bloodied friend off the table and on to his feet. Cupping his ear which was missing a piece, he was happy that was all that was stuck to the table under Shorty's knife. The rest of the group had moved toward the door, so PJ lowered the gun to his side as the group exited into the cool Alaskan night. PJ turned to see Smiley helping his friend who struggled to stay upright.

"Wait a minute," PJ said forcefully. He picked up the bar rag and tossed it at Smiley. "Clean up that blood, shit-head."

The sun had just peeked over the horizon, and Shorty had already strapped Fifi and the rest of the team to his sled. Two of the three bags of mail were tied to the sled next to his provisions for the trail. Shorty was making his way up the back steps of the post office when the door swung open. Anna walked through the doorway, dragging the third bag of mail behind her.

"Good mornin'," Shorty said with a smile. "Sorry if I woke you up."

"You plannin' on leavin' without sayin' goodbye?" Anna asked.

"Don't much like goodbyes. You know that."

Anna smiled and handed him the bag of mail, which Shorty took and returned to his sled, strapping it next to the other two.

"Besides, I'll be back before you know it for more fun and games at the Crystal Palace," Shorty said after the bag was secured to the sled. He turned and looked at Anna who extended both arms toward him. *Ah shit,* Shorty thought and walked up the steps. Anna wrapped her arms around her huge friend.

"Please be careful. I worry about you so," she said caringly. "And last night, I was so frightened for you—"

"Don't worry," Shorty interrupted. "You know me, I'm always fine, and I'll be back here picking on your husband in a month."

Anna smiled at that. She lifted the wool cap on Shorty's head and kissed him lightly, as a mother would kiss her son. "For good luck. Oh, wait a minute," she said, rushing back inside. A moment later, she reemerged with a sack.

"Take this. It's the rest of the char and potatoes," she said.

"Thanks, Anna. See you in one month. Oh, and when Roy finally wakes up, punch him in the arm for me. I was just about to do that when you scolded us yesterday. I still owe him." Shorty smiled, grabbed the reins, and yelled, "Hike!"

Fifi took the command, bolted into a gallop, and the rest of the team followed her. Shorty gave the sled a powerful push, took a couple of steps, then jumped on the runners of the sled.

"Safe travels!" Anna called out.

Shorty just waved, never turning around. "Haw, haw, Fifi!" he called, and the powerful lead dog leaned to the left, pushing with all her strength as the rest of the team followed. The sled turned left and raced out of Nome.

The first leg of the trip was approximately seventy miles to Teller, Alaska. If Shorty wanted to, he could cover the distance in one day, pushing Fifi and the team hard. But why make his girls work like that, he thought. The weather was clear and mild, the terrain frozen and beautiful, so he set Fifi into a comfortable trot to the northwest and enjoyed the ride. The rolling hills of Seward Peninsula were dotted with the towering white spruce which still had snow on one side of each tree. The November sun melted the snow on the other sides, but the north side remained out of the sun's warming rays, providing a constant compass for Shorty and Fifi. Shorty thought back to what Anna had said and smiled at the previous night's shenanigans. *Good, clean fun,* he thought.

The following day, November 10, Shorty broke camp early again. They were just fifteen miles outside of Teller, and the weather was starting to turn. The clear sky he and the girls enjoyed the day before was now overcast with low-hanging gray clouds. Shorty knew a storm was blowing in off the Bering Sea, and he hoped to get as much of the trip behind him before it hit.

"Easy, girls, easy, Fifi," he called to his lead dog as they entered Teller, located on a spit of land between Port Clarence and Grantley Harbor on the peninsula. The wind had picked up, and the small wood buildings of Teller appeared to be swaying with the gusts. Fifi led the team to the proper building as always and stopped without a command from Shorty who hopped off the sled, untied the bundle of mail for Teller, and tossed it on the porch.

He checked to make sure everything else was securely tied to the sled, walked to the back, yelled, "Hike!" and again, the sled was underway. It was a short five-mile run to Brevig Mission where he would stop in to eat with Lucy before the final leg of the trip.

Fifi led the team down the embankment and on to the frozen Port Charles inlet. The storm was now racing his team, and snow flurries gathered on the sled as the wind whipped the cold arctic air into his face. His head began to ache, but that was probably just the weather, he thought. Shorty pulled the wool cap down lower on his head, turned up his collar, and pulled the hood of his jacket up, tying it in place. With just his eyes and nose facing the elements, the pain from the cold should go away, he thought. But it didn't. He yelled again, "Hike, Hike!" and Fifi led the others into a full sprint across the smooth ice of Port Charles toward Brevig.

The sled bounced up the opposite bank and back on to land. Shorty held tight nearly being tossed from the sled. His head was pounding as he entered Brevig, and the snow was coming down at a severe angle being blown in off the Bering.

"Easy, Fifi," he called again, and the dogsled slowed to a stop in front of Lucy's home. He stepped down off the runners and knocked on the door. Shorty could hear her approaching from inside the building even over the howling storm.

"Hey, Shorty! Another month's gone by already? Wow!" Lucy's frame easily filled the entire doorway. A little over five feet tall, she appeared to be five feet wide as well. She wore the same bright red dress she had on every time Shorty saw her. Grossly overweight, she rarely left her house, which was one of the reasons her home served as the local post office; she was always here, and the people of Brevig could pick up their mail at their convenience.

"Hey, Luce," Shorty said, placing the bundle of mail inside the door for her.

"You're not thinking of going right out, are you? This storm is getting worse," Lucy advised.

"No. If it's okay with you, I'll hunker down for the night and finish tomorrow," Shorty asked.

"Of course." Lucy noticed Shorty wasn't his usual self. "You okay?" she asked.

"Got a headache is all."

"Get the dogs in the house. They can't stay outside in this storm, and I'll fix you something to eat," she said.

"Be right back" was all Shorty could muster.

Lucy's house was typical of most in Brevig. Just two rooms with one serving as kitchen, dining, and living area and the other as a bedroom. The larger room always seemed to be filthy and contained large mailbags filled with God knows what, Shorty thought. She must save everything that enters this shack, but she never changes out of that horrible red dress. The floors were filthy with years of dirt now covering the wooded planks, having never been washed, he assumed. On top of all this filth, Lucy had two cats that were also overweight and exuded a privileged attitude. Cat hair littered the shack and angered Shorty's allergies. However, on this night, the cats were nowhere to be found, obviously finding shelter from Fifi and her team.

After eating, Shorty lay down on the floor next to the fire. The warmth felt good as Shorty's headache was now accompanied by chills and body aches that he just couldn't shake. He pulled his blanket up to his neck as Lucy struggled to bend over and place a pillow beneath his head. "You ain't look'n' too good, Shorty."

"I ain't feelin' too good, Luce. Nothing a good sleep won't take care of. Thanks for everything. I'm going to get some rest, if you don't mind," he mumbled.

Lucy shook her head with concern, but there was nothing she could do. The closest doctor was in Teller, and there's no way he's going out in this storm, she thought. She carefully placed two more logs on the fire and turned down the oil lamps in the room. As she made her way to her bedroom, she noticed Fifi pick her head up and look over at the now shivering Shorty. Fifi stood, looked at the other dogs as if to say "Stay here" and crossed the room. She sniffed around Shorty's head for a moment and then lay down beside him, placing her head on his chest. Shorty coughed a couple of times, and Fifi whined softly, staring in Lucy's direction.

"Nothing I can do, girl. He'll be fine, just needs a good night's sleep," she said and turned to enter her bedroom, the floorboards moaning under every step she took.

Shorty shook awake, not knowing if he'd actually slept. His dreams were frightful, and his restless sleep had not eased his condition. He realized a hand was resting on his forehead. Shaking the cobwebs, he realized who this pudgy hand belonged to.

"You're burning up, Shorty. You got some kind of fever or something I think," said Lucy, stating what was now obvious to even Fifi.

Shorty managed to sit up on the floor.

"Oh boy. Yeah, this ain't good," Shorty realized. He looked out the window and noticed the sun was already up. "What time is it?"

"Almost noon."

"Ah shit. Gotta get going."

"Well, I've fed the dogs so they're ready, but I don't think you are. Maybe you should wait another day. I'll see if I can get Doc to ride up from Teller," Lucy offered.

"That's kind of you, Luce, but no thanks. Don't care much for doctors, and I need to finish the run today. My ship leaves dock the thirteenth, day after tomorrow. I'll be fine." Shorty struggled to his feet, rolled up his wool blanket, put on his jacket, and called for the dogs to follow him outside. They obeyed immediately.

Tasks that were normally simple and routine were difficult and time-consuming. Shorty had trouble strapping in the dogs and tying down the sled through the pounding headache. His shaking hands were not cooperating. At least, the weather had cleared, he thought as he finished strapping Fifi to the front of the team. He grabbed his lead dog's face in his hands and asked, "Ready, girl?" She whined in response as if sharing his torment.

"Shorty, I got a bad feeling about this. You sure you should be going?" asked Lucy from the porch.

"Jesus, I got a bunch of mothers all over the goddamn state!" he said to himself, then turned toward Lucy. She stepped back into the doorway and raised her hand to cover her open mouth at Shorty's appearance.

"What's wrong?" he asked, then coughed.

"Come up here," she ordered. Shorty climbed the porch slowly, his muscles seemed to ache more with every step. He stopped on the second step from the top so as not to tower over her. Lucy cupped his face in her hands and turned his head to the side. Only a piece of his ear was visible beneath his wool hat, but what she could see had turned color. She lifted up the hat, and what she now saw took her breath away again. The ear was ashen and purple. Shorty had only been outside for about a half-hour and was wearing his wool hat, so it couldn't be the cold.

"Your ear. It's, it's purple," she struggled to say.

Shorty lifted his hand to touch it, but that didn't confirm or negate what Lucy had just said. He coughed again several times but wasn't able to turn his head quick enough to avoid coughing on Lucy.

"Thanks. Now I'll probably catch this death of a cold." She smiled.

Shorty managed a return smile. "Sorry. I'm sure it's nothin'. I'll be seein' ya."

"Hike," he said meekly, struggled to push the sled, then hopped on to the runners clumsily. His right foot slipped off, and Shorty lunged forward and to the right onto the sled and handrails. Finally righting himself, he pushed the team down the lane and out of Brevig for the forty-five-mile trip to Wales.

It was well past noon and only a couple of hours of light remained. Shorty looked forward to dropping off the mail at the Wales post office, settling the dogs, and crawling in to his bed. *That would certainly make me feel better.*

"Hike, hike, Fifi! Let's get home!" he yelled.

The dogs sped up into a comfortable gallop, slicing through the new blanket of snow. It was another beautiful clear Alaskan day, but Shorty wasn't enjoying the scenery as he had two days ago. The sun's warmth was unable to penetrate his layers of clothing and heavy coat. His hood tied tight around his head and his collar up, he was confused and growing concerned over this chill that was persistent and getting worse. As was his cough. Each time he coughed, his chest burned and felt as if something was pressing against it.

A little over half the way home, the sun had started to set, and his health continued to fail. He was coughing constantly and spitting up a milky phlegm. Orange and red hues from the west turned the entire landscape another color. When he noticed the phlegm had turned red, he first thought, or maybe hoped, it was caused by the sunset. *But that's not it,* he thought. *It's blood. I'm coughing up blood. And I can't breathe!*

He ripped the hood off his head and peeled down his collar as he felt panic attack him from a lack of oxygen entering his body. But it didn't help.

He let go of the handrail and tugged at his jacket near his throat, pulling it away from his chest. He leaned back, trying to expand his chest, raising his open mouth skyward, but that just intensified his coughing. There just wasn't enough air entering his body. He held his hand to his chest to make sure it was expanding and tugged forcefully at his layers, hoping that would offer some relief. It didn't, and for the first time in his life, Andrew "Shorty" Edgar felt true fear. *What the fuck is wrong with me?*

He coughed more violently, and a reddish froth sprayed from his mouth, landing on the sled in front of him. He leaned forward from the pain inside his chest and to get a closer look at what he just coughed up. *Why is this happening to me?* His vision narrowed and blurred; he coughed up more mucus and fell forward onto the sled. Barely conscious, his thoughts turned to the sea. *All those times I've set to sea, like every whaler, wondering, Would this trip be my last? Would we lose the battle with earth's largest creature or simply with the sea itself? Drowning. Every sailor feared it. Feeling the ship sliding out from beneath us as we plunge into the frigid deep. My lungs filling with water as I gasp desperately for air I cannot reach. It's said to be the worst possible death imaginable. And it's happening to me on my dogsled twenty miles from the sea.*

He coughed and passed out.

The dogs barking outside of Shorty's house signaled he was back from his mail run to Nome. But this time, it was different. The dogs kept barking. Neighbors looked out windows and saw the familiar sled outside the home of their mailman. One by one, they came out of their homes to see why Shorty had not quieted his dogs. As they approached, the answer became obvious. Two men grabbed Shorty and pulled him upright. His beard and face were covered with a thick red ice. He was barely breathing and was shaking uncontrollably.

They got him inside his home and laid him down on his bed.

Shorty coughed up more of the liquid and rolled on to his side, curling into a ball. Two women wiped his face with damp towels as the men built a fire. A small group of concerned neighbors stood by watching the horrific scene. Questions filled the small room. "What should we do? Where's the doctor? Shorty, are you okay? Can you hear me, Shorty? What happened to you?"

On the eleventh hour of the eleventh day in the eleventh month of 1918, hostilities finally ceased in Europe. The First World War was over and in its wake, millions were dead, but not all from wounds inflicted in battle. Of the fifty-seven thousand US deaths during the war, forty-three thousand died of the improperly named Spanish influenza. Something unseen and untouchable was a far more effective and merciless killer than anything man had devised. At that same moment, on the other side of the world, this potent murderer accompanied Andrew "Shorty" Edgar to a territory that had been unscathed to this point by this war or this disease.

His eyes opened wide. A look of fear on a face unfamiliar with that emotion frightened everyone in the room. He coughed twice. Exhaled through the frothy blood and then went silent. His eyes wide and locked. Eyes that no longer held life behind them.

Within a week, one-third of the six hundred residents of Wales were dead with many more ill. Forty-five miles to the south, it was much worse. With a population of just eighty people, Brevig was a tiny isolated village. However, seventy-two of its inhabitants were dead. The eight who avoided the illness had not visited Lucy for their mail that week, and most were Inupiat Eskimos living on the edge of town.

Virtually, every family had a team of dogs for transportation in Brevig, Wales, and Teller. When the residents suddenly died, there was no one to care for the dogs. Wild with hunger, they ravaged food reserves, and when those were emptied, they turned to the human remains. Dogs ran wild through towns and fought over the arms and legs torn from the frozen bodies of the dead.

In Brevig, the Inupiat Eskimos piled the bodies onto sleds and made numerous trips dragging them to a small hill just outside of town. They dug a massive grave using picks, shovels, and dynamite, left over from the gold rush, to loosen the frozen ground. Next, they lay the bodies, first side by side then on top of one another in the grave. The permafrost-laden dirt was replaced, filling the common burial plot, and two large white crosses were placed at each end of the mound to mark the grave.

4

Friend / Adversary / Hero

January 18, 1919

Jubilee Rink, Montreal

The first half of the NHL season was coming to a close. Each of the three NHL clubs would play one another one more time, which meant two games for each club. Montreal, with a record of 6–2, could clinch the first half championship with a win tonight against the Ottawa Senators, who had a record of 4–4. The Toronto Maple Leafs, at 2–6, were out of contention and would have to look forward to improving in the second half of the season.

The morning skate just concluded; the Montreal Canadiens were back in their dressing room working on skates, sticks, and other equipment in preparation for the upcoming game that evening. The dressing room was busy, bustling and boisterous from the confident professional athletes. The door opened slowly, and in walked a man dressed in military fatigues. Preoccupied with their tasks and their jokes, no one noticed him for several moments, making him feel uncomfortable. Just as he was about to turn around and head out the same way, Joe Malone yelled, "Punch!"

Immediately, every player turned to Malone, then to the man in uniform at the door.

George Vezina looked over his shoulder, and standing just a few feet away stood Harry Lawton "Punch" Broadbent. Vezina dropped his gear, took two steps, and grabbed his right hand firmly. "Punch! Welcome home."

"Thanks, Georgie, it's good to be back," Broadbent replied sheepishly.

Within seconds, the entire team was heartily patting the hero on the back, pulling him in to the room and offering him a seat. Punch was a star player for the Senators before entering the war, and when news from the battlefields of Eastern Europe filtered back to the dominion that he was awarded the Canadian Military Medal, every NHL player, executive, and fan shared the glory and swelled with pride.

"When did you get back?" asked Malone.

Punch sat down on the bench with the rest of the team standing nearby or pulling up benches to join the impromptu party. He grabbed Malone's stick with both hands; it was like holding an old friend. It had been years since Punch Broadbent touched a hockey stick. He placed the blade of the stick on the floor in front of him and leaned into it with a portion of his weight, testing the stick's flexibility and give. He leaned back, tapped the stick on the floor a few times, and placed it back on the bench where he found it.

"A couple of weeks ago. Good to set foot on Canadian soil again. I can tell ya that, boys!" They all chuckled, a few clapped, and others patted him more. "I don't get officially discharged until March, but they let me join the team for this game. Got here a little while ago. My boys are about to go out for their skate, so I figured I'd come over here and say hello."

"Welcome home, Punch. Looking forward to seeing you on the ice soon," Joe Malone said from his heart.

"Not me. But good to see you safe and sound," said Montreal goaltender Vezina with a grin.

A number of other players shook his hand and welcomed him home one more time before getting back to their post-skate, pregame routines.

Newsy sat down next to Malone, placing his right arm around Punch's shoulders.

"It's good to see you, Newsy. I've read you boys are playing well."

"We've had a good first half," Newsy said.

"You know what hit me first when I came in here? The smell. God, I missed that. There's nothing like the smell of hockey," Punch remarked fondly.

"Stale sweat, burnt lumber, and foul-smelling men. Yeah, there's nothing like it, Punch," observed Newsy, looking around the room.

The players chuckled. Odie Cleghorn raised his arm and shoved his underarm into George Vezina's face, which didn't go over well.

"It beats gunpowder, sulfa, and rotting corpses," replied Punch. "You know what I mean. It smells familiar, like home."

Timing it perfectly, Malone got up, returned to his stall, and exploded his own noxious gas too close for Newsy's comfort.

"There ya go, boys, now it smells like *my* home!" he cracked.

The entire room burst out in laughter, and Newsy, smiling at Malone's all-too-familiar calling card, gave him a shove. "Jeez, Joe! Take that outside."

"I missed that too. Well, not *that* exactly, but the dressing room and the fun, the laughter," Punch said through a relaxed grin.

Joe Hall came out of the bathroom in street clothes, and even though he had heard of the trade, it took Punch by surprise.

"Holy cow, I had forgotten the Bad Man was a Canadien. You two getting along?" he asked Newsy and Hall.

"Like peas and carrots, Punch," said Hall, shaking Broadbent's hand.

"Like scotch and soda," followed Newsy.

"Like Romeo and Juliet," added Vezina from across the room. "Hey, Joe, read Punch the Valentine you had printed in the paper last year for Newsy. You still have it?"

"You sent Newsy a Valentine?" Broadbent asked incredulously.

"Yep, got it right here," Hall said, pulling his wallet out of his overcoat. He dug through it for a moment, then found the piece of folded-up newspaper.

"Ahem," he started, and the players chuckled.

"From Joe Hall to Newsy Lalonde.
I'm sorry if your face I've kicked
Or if your head with dents I've nicked
But dirty play I didn't mean,
I hate to crack you on the bean,
And thus, to show my love, you swine,
I send you this cute Valentine."

The room erupted with laughter and a standing ovation. Hall bowed at the waist for his audience, folded the newspaper back up, and returned it to its special place in his wallet.

"Put your wallet in your pants. Then that Valentine would be next to your heart," Newsy shot at Hall.

The laughter was mixed with oohs from their teammates.

"I gotta run, Punch. See ya tonight?" Hall asked, still smiling and proud.

"Sure thing, Joe. Good luck tonight," said Punch.

"Thanks, buddy. And again, welcome home." And Hall was on his way out.

"It's so good to see ya, Punch. You made us all so very proud. It is indeed an honor for me and everyone in this room to be able to call you friend," Newsy said, rubbing the back of Punch's neck firmly.

His head down, the smile gone, Punch seemed to be concentrating on his hands. He flashed a crooked smile, part pride and part embarrassment. Then he cocked his head and looked up at the hockey legend. "Thanks, Newsy. I was just doing my duty."

"Come on then. The returning war hero is too humble. Share some stories of battle and glory. What was it like over there?" Newsy requested, trying to raise his spirits again.

"It was, well, it was, it was war. It was just, I don't know, war."

He dropped his head, focusing on his hands again. Newsy felt a pain of sympathy. Newsy took his arm down and put both elbows on his thighs, leaning forward so his body was even with Punch's.

"You okay?" he asked softly.

"Yeah. Well, at least I will be," Broadbent said, taking a deep breath and tying to compose himself. "Not a lot of people have asked me that. Everyone is so wrapped up with the celebrating. They don't know what it was like. The trenches. The bombing. The sleepless, silent nights waiting to be attacked. But worse than all that, well, perhaps not worse but certainly adding to all that was this sickness. It just ravaged us. Friends of mine, boys who were like brothers to me, were fine one day, then sick and dying the next. It was as if God Himself was trying to stop the war. This thing, this influenza, pretty much ended the fighting. We didn't. Nobody won. It just stopped.

"There were times I thought if Gerry attacked right now, he could just march through us, killing everyone 'cause most of us were unable to fight. Then after it was all over, I learned that they were worse off than we were, which was hard to believe.

"People are so happy, celebrating the victory. There was no victory. Influenza was the only victor."

They sat there for a time. Newsy digesting what Punch had said. Then he broke the silence.

"I've seen it. Here in Montreal. When Laurene was born, I would go to the hospital to visit her and Iona. Each time I went, the ward with the sick and the dying became more crowded. The last time I was there, the room was so crowded, they had some of the boys in the hallway. They quarantined the entire area. And the doctors could do nothing but stand by and watch as these young men, in the prime of their lives, just slipped away."

Punch took his eyes off his hands and looked at Newsy. "I'm afraid it's followed us. He's followed us home. The wrath of the Lord. Maybe he's punishing all of us for what we did over there. I don't know.

"When it ended, that cool, cloudy day in November, the eleventh it was, I was in the hospital in Paris. The next day, celebrations just erupted in the streets. The sickness had run its course with me, and for some reason, I was spared. Don't know why.

"Well, when we heard the noise, a number of us who felt well enough went down to join it. People were hugging each other and kissing each other all over Paris. Total strangers. Just happy to be alive and to have lived through the worse of what man could muster." He smiled remembering the scene. "Servicemen from every country began marching down the main street in Paris, the Champs-Élysées. Nobody told us to do it. We just did it.

"First a few hundred, then what seemed like thousands. French, English, American, and Canadians. All in uniform. All marching. We marched with pride, our shoulders back and our heads held high. As if we had actually won the war. One woman ran out into the street and handed me flowers, kissed me on both cheeks, and thanked me. I think she believed I killed the Kaiser myself. Incredible," he continued, shaking his head, still in disbelief.

"So we marched and we waved and we shook hands and received kisses. All of Paris was celebrating. Probably all of Europe, I would imagine. As I walked with a few boys from my battalion, we came up on an American lad, struggling along to keep up with the crowd but not able to keep pace. He was coughing and wheezing like those who had very little time left." His smile had left his face and was replaced by a distant stare as if Punch was back on the Champs- Élysées. Reliving what he was describing for Newsy and the rest of the players who remained in the still dressing room.

"He stumbled and fell to his knees. I was right behind him, so I grabbed him. His face was familiar. Not that I knew who he was but the blotches. The purple ears and hands. I told him, 'You're not well. Let me take you back to the hospital.'

"He lifted his head, looked me in the eyes, and said, 'I fought. Now I will march.' So I lifted him back to his feet. Another soldier, again that I didn't know, grabbed him under his other arm and we marched on.

"The poor lad didn't make it a hundred yards. He died there in our arms. Marching through the streets of Paris. This poor American boy. Just passed away in our arms. I never got his name. I didn't know who he was, where he had fought, where he was from in the States, if he was a husband, a father. Didn't know anything about him other than he was a brother in arms and I knew that his last wish was to march. So he marched. We carried him for blocks to the Place de la Concorde where the marching ended. In the middle of thousands of celebrating soldiers and civilians, we lay this lad down on a ledge near a fountain. We summoned the police. And we left him."

Punch broke his stare and seemed to return to the dressing room. He looked at Newsy, then back down to his hands. He wiped a tear from his cheek. "I've never told anyone that story. I don't know why I just told you boys," he said.

"We're glad you did, Punch," Newsy said. "People need to know what you boys did and what you went through. We need to know."

The Jubilee Arena was typically full, standing room only. Tonight's game against Ottawa held a special importance in the standings, and the Montreal crowd was even louder and more intimidating than most nights. Both hockey clubs had concluded their pregame warm-ups and were standing by their benches, getting last-second instructions from coaches and captains. All the combatants wore their game faces now, ready for the coming battle.

Standing on the ice next to his bench, Newsy placed his stick over the board on to the bench side, then took his gloves off and placed them on the top of the boards. He skated over to the ref and said something in his ear. The ref reacted with a look of mild surprise, then gestured as if to say, "Sure, go ahead." Newsy skated to center ice.

The crowd rose to their feet in thunderous applause and hollered for their hockey hero. Newsy smiled, raised both arms, and flapped his hands downward to the ice. The fans had never seen him make this gesture before, but they knew what he wanted. The cheering faded, and the Jubilee Arena became silent.

Newsy cleared his throat and began speaking as loud as he could. "Ladies and gentlemen. On behalf of my teammates, I want to thank you for your unbridled support. Tonight, we have a special guest joining us."

Newsy turned toward the Ottawa players where Punch Broadbent sat at the end of the bench in full-dress military uniform. "His name is Harry Broadbent. He is a member of the Ottawa Senators."

A few jeers from the crowd were quickly stifled when Newsy raised his hands again.

"Harry returns to the rink tonight for the first time, in a long time. He is just back from Europe where he was part of the Canadian Expeditionary Force, 7th Artillery Brigade. He was awarded the Military Medal for bravery in the field."

He was interrupted by a respectful cheer, and this time, Newsy joined the crowd and clapped. The players from both teams banged their sticks on the ice, the bench, and the boards in admiration and respect. When the cheering died down, Newsy continued.

"We are honored to have him in attendance tonight. Harry Broadbent is a respected opponent, a trusted friend, and a Canadian hero. Harry, we look forward to your return in a Senators' sweater. Three cheers for Harry Broadbent! Hip, hip!"

"Hurrah!" the crowd shouted.

"Hip, hip!"

"Hurrah!" the players joined in.

"Hip, hip."

"Hurrah!" the Jubilee Arena erupted in unison for Punch. Newsy skated to the Senators' bench where Harry met him with an embrace. Both waved to the Canadiens' crowd. The rest of the Montreal team skated to the Senators' bench and, one by one, welcomed home Punch again. Newsy waited until the last Montreal Canadien, George Vezina, shook Punch's hand and then extended his hand once more. Punch pulled him in close and shouted into Newsy's ear above the roar of the crowd, "Thanks, Newsy. You're a class act. Now take it easy on my boys tonight."

Newsy smirked, still shaking Punch's hand and simply shook his head no. Punch knew he would get that reaction and rubbed the top of Newsy's head forcefully before he skated away. Broadbent turned to face the crowd behind him, waving to the adoring fans and relishing the moment.

Newsy kept his word to Punch, scoring two of Montreal's five goals and assisting on two more in a 5–3 victory over the Senators, clinching the NHL's first half championship.

5

Johan's Near Miss

Nome, Alaska

June 1951

"Don't worry. I've flown in much worse weather than this. This is nothin'!" the bush pilot yelled over his shoulder to his passenger.

The Piper J-3 Cub rolled to the end of the beach and turned back into the wind. In the back seat, Johan Hultin felt his heart rate pick up, not in fear but rather in excited anticipation.

"No worries. Let's get this thing in the air!" he yelled back.

Walter Jamouneau smiled. Perhaps his young Swedish passenger would keep his breakfast down. Jamouneau had become accustomed to cleaning his back seat of everything the human body can secrete from his paying passengers.

The pilot eased the throttle forward, and the Continental A-65-8 air-cooled engine roared to life, pulling the plane down the beach. The propeller became a blur, and as the speed of the wind rushing by the open window increased, so did the adrenaline coursing through Hultin's body. The olive green single-wing plane bounced down the beach, picking up speed. Jamouneau pulled back on the wheel, and they were off.

Hultin wanted to let out an exhilarating scream, but that would be unbecoming of a scientist. He was off on the adventure of his young life, which had begun just six weeks earlier at the University of Uppsala in Iowa City, Iowa.

Raised in Sweden, Johan Hultin was brilliant, handsome, and adventurous with shoulder-length blond hair and mesmerizing blue eyes, typical of his race. At twenty-three years old, he took advantage of an opportunity the Swedish university system offered. A student could apply to schools abroad and continue their education while not losing credits or time accumulated and graduate on schedule. The United States had always appealed to Hultin. Choosing Iowa City was an easy choice since it had a large Swedish population, and Uppsala had an outstanding microbiology department so Johan could continue his research and studies. In addition, it was located nearly dead-center of the country, he thought, allowing him and his wife Gunvor to travel the Land of the Free and the Home of the Brave, which they did on every break from school.

"I'm going to try and climb out of this muck. Can't see a damn thing in this crap!" yelled Jamouneau from the pilot's seat.

"Okay, whatever you think, I'm with ya," replied Hultin, as if he had a choice.

"We have to find our navigational marker so we're heading in the right direction," Walter continued.

"What's our navigational marker?" asked Hultin.

"A house on a bluff, about ten miles north of Nome. Once I find that, turn slight left, and it's a short two-hour flight to Wales. But we can't be sure we're going in the right direction without finding that marker. You know what? I'm *not* going to climb. We may miss it. Going to drop down and maybe we can fly beneath the weather. Okay?"

"Okay," said Hultin. "But not too low, right?"

Jamouneau smiled again. "No. Not too low."

Six weeks earlier, Hultin was working in his lab at Uppsala when he noticed Roger Porter, the head of the microbiology department, escorting William Hale, from the prestigious Brookhaven National Laboratory, who was perhaps the best known virologist in the world.

"Mr. Hale, this is one of our brightest postgrad students, Johan Hultin. Johan, meet—"

Hultin interrupted him.

"Dr. Hale, it is an honor," he said, shaking Hale's hand. Porter smirked with pleasure and pride at his student's reaction.

"Join us for lunch, Johan," Hale said.

"My pleasure," Hultin excitedly responded.

"I haven't gotten a visual on the marker. We're going to have to circle and come back around a little lower," the pilot advised.

"Okay," said Hultin, growing nervous now.

His plan was to go ahead of the rest of his team, find the permafrost, and dig into the grave site to make sure the bodies had not deteriorated. Once he had found the well-preserved bodies, he would call the other two team members who would meet him and perform the lung extraction. But he would have to be alive to accomplish all this. Flying low in this thick cloud cover, looking for a house on top of a rocky bluff overlooking the Bering Sea was not part of his itinerary. And dying in a plane crash was never contemplated. The Piper banked to the right, and Walter pushed the wheel forward, lowering their altitude. Johan felt his stomach turn over.

Hultin was one of seven select students who were invited to the lunch. The conversation around the table centered mostly on science, but topics varied and the discussions on each were kept short. Hale was the featured guest, and as such, he kept control of the topics for conversation. No one topic ever lasted for more than a few moments before he was on to another. It was lively, entertaining, and educational. The microbiology postgrad students were infatuated by this legend in their field of study.

Then Hale said something that stuck with Hultin. It was a statement in the middle of the conversation perhaps no longer than ten to fifteen seconds that came and went. It seemed no one at the table thought twice about it as the discussion raced off to a different topic from the 1918 influenza epidemic.

"Everything has been done to elucidate the cause of the epidemic," Hale said. "But we just don't know what caused that flu. The only thing that remains is for someone to go to the northern part of the world and find bodies in the permafrost that are well preserved and that just might contain the influenza virus," he theorized.

What was said after that was lost on Hultin. He fixated on what Hale had just thrown out to this group. The simple yet brilliant idea! Some of the people who lived in the northern part of the world and died from the most horrific killer man had ever known should be buried in permafrost. If someone could locate those bodies, the frozen lungs may still contain that virus.

I could do this, he thought. *I am uniquely qualified to do this, perhaps more than anyone else at this table. Hell, more than anyone else in the world. I know how to locate permafrost from my youth in Sweden. I know how to take tissue samples and how to preserve them. I know how to coax viruses to grow in the laboratory. And my department head, Roger Porter, is one of the renowned leaders in influenza research. He could help figure out the virus's secrets. This is for me.*

"Did you see it?" Hultin yelled above the engine from the rear seat.

"No. Did you?" asked Jamouneau.

"No. What's the plan?"

"Plan? This is the only plan. We're going to have to try again. I'm going to circle back and come in a little lower," replied the pilot.

"How much lower?" asked Hultin, more nervous now as the Piper banked to the right again.

"One hundred feet should do it." And the pilot pushed the wheel forward again.

Five minutes later, they were flying straight again! Hopefully, toward the location of the marker. The thick gray clouds would not relent. Hultin also couldn't see the instruments in the cockpit ahead of him in front of his pilot. *Good thing,* he thought. *Less information is better right now.*

But every so often, Hultin thought he could see the water below them through pockets in the clouds, just for a moment. Walter noticed it too and dropped down a couple more feet for better visibility. "Oh shit!"

The Piper's nose lurched up as Jamouneau went to full throttle and yanked the wheel back. Hultin had been looking out the right side window when his body slammed back into his seat. Straight ahead was the bluff, and it was coming closer at an alarming speed. Off to his left, Hultin saw the house on the bluff just a couple of hundred feet off the side of the aircraft. And most startling, it was above them.

The engine whined and moaned to climb above the oncoming cliff. Jamouneau pulled with all his might on the wheel, his teeth gritting and his mind running numbers. *This aircraft can climb at four hundred fifty feet per minute. We're about three hundred feet away, air speed is sixty-two knots, and we need another one hundred feet in elevation. Fuck it,* he thought. *Climb, you fucker!*

Behind him, Hultin's eyes were wide open. He shut them, no longer wanting to see that rock wall rushing at him. Suddenly, he saw Gunvor at his funeral. Crying. Alone.

The Piper was climbing at a near-vertical ascent, and at this angle, Jamouneau expected that they might just make it when the plane went into a stall. The pilot could hear the engine still hard at work and could feel the plane vibrating as it continued to drive at full throttle. They were nowhere near their altitude ceiling of 11,500 feet. He thought, *So why are we stalling?* The updraft!

Powerful winds were blowing in with the storm off the Bering Sea. The cliffs that were about to violently end their short flight blocked the wind's path and thrust them skyward, which countered the airflow over the Piper's wings, causing the stall. Jamouneau nosed the plane to the right at the exact moment before forward momentum was lost. The plane slowly nosed over and turned 180 degrees back toward the sea.

Hultin expected the impact, but instead, he heard, "Woohoo!" from his pilot. With the wind now in their face and the engine still at full throttle, the plane rocketed out toward the sea and to safety.

"All right! Well, that's enough fun for one day. Let's head back to Nome. Now that I have my bearings. We'll wait for this crap to clear and try again tomorrow," Jamouneau suggested.

Hultin's eyes were still shut. Not knowing how much they missed the cliff by was a good thing too, he thought. A short while later, he felt the Piper touch down on the beach at Nome. Walter taxied up to his usual spot and cut the engine. It was then he realized he hadn't heard anything from the young Swede behind him since their near miss. He turned around to find Hultin still holding on to both sides of the plane, his blond hair standing straight up and his eyes shut tight.

"Is it over? Are we dead?" Hultin asked.

"It's over, and no, we're not dead. Do I need to clean anything out of that seat back there, boy?" he asked.

Hultin checked himself. "Nope," he said, opening his eyes and smiling with pride for not soiling himself or Walter's plane.

The two broke into laughter. They grabbed each other's shoulders, pushing and pulling each other, celebrating their victory over death. Hultin had heard the stories of bush pilots and their brushes with death, but no story measured up to what old Walter Jamouneau had just dealt with—and survived!

"Walter, thank you!" Hultin said, calming down and realizing how his big adventure had nearly ended on a wall of stone outside of Nome. "I need a drink," he said.

"I'm buying," offered the pilot.

The Hotel Nome was located in the middle of town. The rooms were clean and reasonably priced, but most importantly right now, was the Hunter's Pub located on the first floor.

Thirty-five-year-old Roger Porter was in his room toweling off after a shower. Porter was not the typical microbiology professor. Tall and lean, he kept his body in as good a shape as his mind. An avid skier and runner, Porter believed that the mind and body were intertwined and worked better together when both were challenged and active. He had just completed a five-mile light jog and was planning on spending the day reviewing the research on the 1918 epidemic when there was a knock at his door.

"What the hell are you doing here? I thought you were on your way to Wales?" Porter asked, surprised to see his student and team leader.

"Well, come down to the bar and have a drink with me, and I'll tell you why we're back. Where's Gary?" asked Hultin.

"Haven't seen him in hours. Why did you ask him to come along anyway? He never stops complaining," said Porter, putting on his clothes and then closing the door to his room behind him.

"He asked. It wasn't like there was a great number of volunteers for this trip. He'll be fine," Hultin said.

Jamouneau waved to Hultin and Porter from across the bar. The two scientists sat down at his table. Hultin's hands were still shaking a little from their short trip.

"So let's have it. Why are you back in Nome?" asked Porter.

Walter and Johan shared a look and then started in. They took turns retelling the story to Porter, who sat in silent amazement.

"Couldn't see a thing."

"Suddenly, all we could see was the huge wall of rock."

"Pulled back with every muscle on the stick."

"The plane went into a stall."

"Shut my eyes and prayed."

When they were finished, Johan slumped in his chair and shook his head. "Jesus, that was close," he said.

Porter just stared.

"Okay, I know you boys are looking for permafrost and that you're both scientists but little else. What are we looking for exactly?" Jamouneau asked.

"Are you familiar with the influenza epidemic from earlier this century?" asked Hultin.

"A little," said Walter.

"Between 1916 and 1918, the influenza virus was mutating, and it became this very potent, very deadly strain of flu that was never seen before," explained Hultin.

"The alarming thing was how quickly it spread and how quickly it killed. Extremely lethal, extremely efficient," joined Porter.

"How many people died from this thing?" asked Walter.

"Conservative numbers are around one hundred million people," replied Hultin. "Some scientists think the number, worldwide, was double that. Six million people died in India alone," added Porter.

"But no one knows for sure as the census back then wasn't overly accurate," Hultin continued. "We're here to find people who died from the virus and are buried in permafrost. Hopefully, it preserved their bodies enough for us to extract lung tissue and analyze it."

Walter sat listening as the stories and the numbers continued to flow from the two scientists. Dead bodies piled in the streets of Philadelphia. Churches in Boston and New York filled with decaying corpses. The epidemic struck all over the world at the same time, something unprecedented in recorded history.

Walter sat for a moment, trying to digest what Porter and Hultin just described.

"Anna," he called to the woman behind the bar. A woman in her sixties looked up but not in the direction of Walter. She looked confused, feeble and weathered. "Anna. Over here." She looked at Walter. "When you have a moment, please?" he asked.

Hultin and Porter were confused. Could Walter have lost interest and thought of something he needed this old woman for? *Who could lose interest in this story?* thought Hultin. The woman behind the bar said something to the other bartender, lifted the bar door, and walked over to where the three men were sitting.

"Hi, Walter. I thought you were going on a trip?" she asked.

"Ran into a little weather (*And nearly a stone wall,* Hultin thought). I want you to meet these gentlemen."

Hultin and Porter stood before the frail old woman whose hunched posture made her appear as if she carried a heavy load for most of her life.

"This is Roger Porter and Johan Hultin," he introduced them. They shook her hand tenderly so as not to hurt her. "They're scientists working on something that may interest you," he said.

Hultin sat back down as Porter excused himself and went to the bar for another round. Johan briefly explained why they were in Nome and what they're looking for. Then Anna sat down.

"Terrible thing, that flu," she said softly. "Took my husband from me. And most of my friends. Hell, it practically killed everyone in Nome. And those of us lucky enough to have lived through it, well, we weren't too lucky either." She stopped briefly.

Porter returned with three pints of beer. Anna looked at the glasses and remembered a night a long time ago. A night that she didn't know at the time would be her last night of normalcy and happiness. The night before the influenza came to Nome. And killed it.

"I wish you good luck with your work, gentlemen. I hope you find what you're looking for," she somberly said. She pulled her wire-framed glasses from her face and wiped a tear. Then she got up and returned to the bar.

"What was that about?" asked Porter.

"That's Anna Hunter. This is her place. She lived through the time you boys are researching. She survived what you're looking for," said Walter.

"Who was her husband?" asked Johan.

"Never got the full story. People who lived through that time don't seem to want to talk much about it," Walter realized.

The three men drank their beers quietly for the next few moments when a short stocky man with three large brown bags rushed into the pub. Gary Collins was another student at Uppsala and the third member of the Hultin team. Only a couple of inches over five feet tall, his large shoulders and full body made him appear to be square. Combined with a scalp he kept shaved, if Porter and Hultin were the dashing young scientists, then Collins was their "Igor." He was obviously very excited and rushed over to their table.

"Johan! What the hell are you doing here?" he asked.

"Long story. I'll tell ya later. What's in the bags?"

"I solved our problem of getting the tissues back to Iowa," said Collins. He reached into the bag and pulled out an ordinary thermos. About ten inches tall and three inches wide with a twist-off top. "Ta-dah," he proudly said.

"A coffee thermos?" asked Porter. "That's just great. And how do we keep the tissues frozen?"

"Ah, but wait! There's more." The other two bags contained two small fire extinguishers each. Gary took one out and again said, "Ta-dah."

"Hey, that's pretty good. The dry ice in the fire extinguisher should work to keep them frozen. Nice work, Gary," Johan complimented.

"I bought four of these smaller ones for the trip home. I got a large one in the truck we'll take with us to the site. I've done the math, and this should be enough for us to get the job done," he concluded. "Buy me a beer?" he asked.

Porter shook his head in amazement. Hultin laughed.

"Sure. A job well done deserves a reward," said Johan.

"Then you can buy it," said Porter.

"So why are you here?" Collins asked Johan again.

"Well, we took off and we couldn't see a damn thing . . ."

The skies had cleared the next the morning, but the storm was still being an annoyance to Walter and Johan's travel. The beach was filled with debris washed ashore or blown onto the beach from Nome. It was early, and the cool air was just starting to be warmed by the rising sun. Seagulls and other water fowl hunted for their breakfast as Walter, Johan, Roger, and Gary walked the beach, clearing a runway of every piece of refuse left behind by the storm.

"This sucks. I'm a scientist, not a custodian for Christ's sake," Gary said, already in midday complaining form. "I'm out here like a common field hand. Look at the size of this log! Where the hell did this come from?" he asked the group.

At his feet was what appeared to be a piece of ship that washed ashore in the storm. The four by eight lumber was at least five feet long and had to weigh over one hundred pounds.

"I'll tell you where I'm going to shove it if he doesn't shut the fuck up," Roger whispered to Walter farther down the beach. Jamouneau smiled and shook his head.

"Looks like a ship's plank or piece of a mast maybe," speculated Johan. "Here, let me help you move it," he said, bending over and grabbing one end of the plank. Gary grabbed the opposite end. Not accustomed to the physical labor, they struggled with the load.

"This is bullshit," Gary moaned. "My hands are finely tuned instruments for delicate procedures, not carrying water-logged lumber off a beach," he continued. They moved the log far enough off the makeshift runway and let it drop into the firm sand. "It will be a miracle if I didn't get a splinter!" Collins continued.

Down the beach, Porter had heard enough. "Would you shut the fuck up?!" he shouted.

"Boy, who pissed in your oatmeal this morning?" mocked Collins.

"That's it, he's dead," Porter started down the beach toward Collins when Jamouneau grabbed him from behind. Fifty feet away, Johan had already stepped in front of Collins in case Porter made it that far.

"I think we've cleared enough of the beach. We're done here, so let's everyone calm down. Why don't you two go back to bed or something?" Jamouneau said, restraining Roger who was finally calming down. "I'll make final preparations on the plane, so go ahead and head back to the hotel," he said, momentarily defusing the situation.

Roger took a deep breath, composed himself and looked at Jamouneau as if to say, "Okay."

But Collins never knew when to let up. "Maybe you should go sit on the toilet, Porter. You're obviously constipated. You're lucky he stopped you or we'd be cleaning your ass off this beach too!" he said, smiling.

Roger looked at Jamouneau, who stared down the beach incredulously at Collins, then turned to Roger. "What an asshole. Go ahead, he needs a beating," he said.

Porter took two steps toward Collins, who bolted from the beach in the direction of the hotel, his squat legs working feverishly in the sand to escape. Porter sprinted after his antagonist and closed ground quickly with his longer more athletic strides.

"Roger, just ignore him. He's an idiot. Everyone knows it," Johan shouted as the two men disappeared into town.

"Should we be worried for the wee man's safety?" asked Jamouneau, walking back toward the Piper.

"Nah. This goes on all the time with them."

"That kid is going to get his ass handed to him someday with that attitude," Jamouneau observed. "That day just might be today if Roger catches him," replied Johan.

"What the hell smells?" Johan asked, buckling his seat belt in the rear seat of the Piper.

Jamouneau chuckled. "Oh, that would be this." In the front seat, he held up and away from him, a brown paper lunch bag that sagged at the bottom. Then quickly placed it back on the floor near his seat. "We're going to need it after takeoff," he continued.

Walter was finishing his preflight preparations, but that had become so routine for him it was easy to multitask.

"What the hell is it? It smells like shit."

"It's our ordnance. AKA, shit bomb!"

"There's actually shit in that bag?"

"Yep. Personally deposited it myself this morning."

"Why are you carrying your shit in a brown paper—"

Jamouneau maneuvered the Piper to the end of the cleared runway on the beach, facing into the wind. He throttled the engine to full before Johan finished his question. The thrust of the engine and the rush of the wind drowned out Hultin's words.

"Hey!" shouted Hultin above the noise immediately after takeoff.

"Yeah?"

"What's with the bag of shit?"

"My neighbor has been washing off his boat and throwing the dirty water on mine. I've caught him at least twice, and both times he acted like it was an accident. It's *no* accident!"

"You live on a boat?" Johan asked.

"Yeah, why?"

"I just never knew anyone who lived on a boat. You live on the water and work in the air. It's an interesting life you lead."

They had taken off and turned right toward the ocean to use the incoming breeze for added lift. Jamouneau then made a severe left turn, the Piper's wings almost becoming perpendicular to the ground. In a few moments, the marina was in sight.

"See that large cabin cruiser at the end of the dock? That's mine. Our target is the one next to it. Hold on!" Jamouneau said with an excitement to his words.

He pushed forward on the wheel and dropped down to just one hundred feet above the water. He came in low and throttled the engine just as they passed over the neighbor's boat, which caused all the docked vehicles to sway and shudder. Jamouneau pulled up and eased back on the throttle while looking back over his shoulder. Again, he banked to the left; this time, he made a wide looping turn, all the while looking down at his target. Then, just as he had hoped, the neighbor stepped out onto the deck of his boat. It was hard to see the man from this distance, but he was younger—probably in his thirties, with dark hair and slim. His body posture made him appear cocky and very upset.

"Ha! Okay, buddy. Get ready 'cause payback is coming," Walter said confidently.

He pulled back on the wheel and throttled up again, gaining altitude about a mile from the marina. Johan held on in the back seat as it looped to the left and started back toward the target at an alarming rate of speed and descent. Heading straight down for the man's pristine boat, Walter leaned forward over the wheel, adjusting his angle and trimming his course as if he had done this many times before. Just when it appeared to Hultin they would never be able to pull out of the dive, Walter hung the brown bag at the window and let go. He then pulled up and out of the dive and yelled out the window, "Enjoy, asshole!"

Johan thought the bag was released to early and would fall harmlessly into the water. But Jamouneau had calculated the speed of the plane and his angle of descent. The bag flew toward the boat, spinning and tumbling before it impacted on the white hull with a *splat*. Johan and Walter watched the bomb's impact as they climbed away from the target and broke into uncontrollable laughter.

"That is tremendous!" Johan shouted, tears running down his cheeks.

Walter banked to the right, another long looping turn. Below them, a large brown blotch with streaks running in all directions marked the neighbor's boat as he stared first in disbelief at what just happened to his pride and joy, then back into the air at his attackers. Jamouneau lowered the plane to a hundred feet again and slowly came around to admire his successful bombing run. The neighbor stood on the deck of his shit-soiled vessel, waving a fist and shouting in their direction. Walter rocked the wheel, causing the wings to wave up and down in response. Johan couldn't help himself; he stuck his head on the Piper's window and waved back.

"That's the funniest thing I've ever seen. But aren't you concerned he's going to do something to your boat while you're gone?"

"Not at all. Look," a very proud Jamouneau said. Below them, his boat was backing out of the dock. "I asked a friend of mine to wait until after our mission and then take my boat to another marina. I've had enough of that shit head of a neighbor. Okay, back to your mission. Let's find our nav marker, shall we?" Walter asked and turned north following the coastline. A couple of minutes later, they located the house on the bluff. "Got it," he said and turned slight left, gaining altitude for the short flight to Wales.

"Okay, I've got to ask. Where did you learn to do that?" inquired Johan.

"Do what?"

"The bombing run," said an impressed Hultin.

"Oh, Army Air Corp. I was a fighter-bomber pilot in the war. Over fifty missions. That was nothing, the target wasn't moving," Jamouneau casually responded when the engine sputtered and died.

"What's wrong?" Johan shouted, even though he didn't need to in the eerie silence.

"It's nothing. We're going to have to land and fix a wire that came loose from a magneto terminal," Jamouneau said.

Two thousand feet in the air and losing altitude in the silence didn't seem to cause concern with the pilot, Hultin realized. It must have happened numerous times before.

When Jamouneau banked the glider to the right, beginning their descent, the engine sputtered back to life. "There we go. The wire must have found the terminal again," he said. "We're fine."

He adjusted his course back toward Wales, but the engine cut out again after the turn to the left. So Walter banked right again and again, the Piper shook and the engine roared. This time, he continued a long 360-degree looping right turn, realizing the turn to the left caused the wire to fall off the magneto terminal. Ten minutes later, the engine sputtered and quit, and Walter repeated his loop to the right. During the hour-long trip, this routine was repeated six more times before they landed on the beach in Wales.

"Well, that was an interesting trip," said Jamouneau after he cut the engine.

"It never got boring, that's for sure," replied Hultin. "I saw the grave I'm looking for up on that bluff. It doesn't look promising, but I'm going to go have a look anyway."

"I'll fix the wire while you're up there. Good luck." Walter lifted the engine hood while Johan retrieved the pick and shovel from beneath his seat.

The large white cross marking the mass grave was originally reported to be inland, but the sea had caused erosion here in Wales and the years had moved the water closer to the grave. Hultin could tell the way the sun was shining on the bluff above him and with the ocean water so close that his chances of finding permafrost were not good.

Approaching the grave, Hultin's fears were becoming true. The victim's bodies had been buried at least six feet down in the permafrost, but the ground he stood on was soft. He had little difficulty digging with his shovel. After three feet and no sign of permafrost, he stopped digging. Wiping his brow and looking down to the village along the sea, he thought about the 178 bodies lying beneath him. His research had revealed that they all died within one week, nearly half the village. It had to be terrifying to have been in this isolated, desperate place, he thought. He replaced the dirt back into the hole he had dug and started back down toward town.

The weather was changing, very typical of this area in the northwest, Hultin thought. What had been a beautiful morning was now becoming overcast with threatening storm clouds as the wind whipped the Bering into a violent sea. He wondered if they would be able to take off in this. One last shot at finding permafrost here in Alaska, and that was in Brevig. Porter had believed they might find it in Nome, Wales, and Brevig, but his belief was now proven wrong. The great fire of 1934 in Nome had destroyed most of the town and its records. The location of the grave from 1918 was now lost to history. The encroaching ocean combined with the warmth of the sun had rendered the grave in Wales worthless to his project. *Yep, it was all down to Brevig. If there's no permafrost there, there's no reason to stay here in Alaska. Gunvor will be happy to have me come home early.* Hultin's feelings were mixed.

Jamouneau had completed repairs to the engine and was clearing debris from the beach when Hultin returned.

"It's no good. The permafrost has obviously melted at times in the recent years. One last place to look," he said, placing the pick and shovel back in the Piper.

"You wanna go now?" asked Walter. Hultin turned and looked out to sea. The Bering, which was glassy smooth this morning, now featured four- to eight-foot waves crashing against the beach. A slight but constant rain had been falling for an hour, causing puddles to form on the sand. "What do you think?"

"I think if we're going to try it, we gotta go now before the weather gets worse," the pilot said. "Okay. Let's go," Hultin agreed.

"Buckle in tight. I've got just enough runway to take off, but we're going to have to turn west immediately to gain lift from the wind blowing in off the water. It's going to be close," Walter said while performing a brief preflight check. In the back seat, Hultin was buckling his seat belt and regretting his decision.

"What do you mean, 'close'?" he asked.

"If we don't have enough speed, we're going to have to ditch in the water. But don't worry, the Inuits will pull us out," responded Walter, motioning with his head to a group of four Inuits up the beach, watching this lunacy with no intention of jumping in the dangerous sea to rescue these two morons.

The Piper taxied between puddles that were growing larger, making the runway shorter still. When he had reached the preplanned spot that was the start of the runway, Walter pointed the plane straight down the beach. Hultin peered over his pilot's shoulder, confident he was going for a swim.

Walter throttled the engine to nearly full, and they started down the beach, gradually gaining speed and bouncing over small dunes. *The runway is impossibly short,* thought Hultin. *This is crazy. Tell him to stop. Tell him to stop!* "Forget it. Let's stay here tonight!" he yelled.

"Too late!" was the response, and Jamouneau pushed the throttle to full.

The Piper bounced up slightly, landed with a thud as they ran out of runway, and then hopped a few feet in the air. Walter immediately banked the plane to the right just above the water. It started to climb into the wind as the rain pelted the windshield.

We're going to make it, thought Hultin. *This guy is nuts, but he's good.* But his confidence was premature as a wave caught the Piper's wheels and pulled the plane's nose down, dragging them toward the Bering. Walter pulled back on the throttle, and the Piper adjusted, regaining the lost altitude when another larger wave hit the belly of their aircraft, pulling it down farther.

"Fuck me!" Hultin yelled, or at least, he thought he did.

Walter again pulled back on the wheel, and the Piper hopped up a good twenty feet, well clear of the oncoming sea.

"I don't know if you have good luck or bad luck, son. But we just dodged another close call," Walter said as he banked the plane left and south for the short flight to Brevig.

Located forty-five miles south of Wales and about one-third the way back to Nome, Brevig was a small village decimated by influenza in November 1918. Of the eighty residents, seventy-two perished from the flu. Unlike Wales, Hultin had no way of communicating with anyone in the village ahead of time to gain permission to dig at the grave site. The village was originally named Brevig Mission after the missionary who established the village to bring God's word to the territory. Hultin had learned a man by the name of Otis Lee was the current head of the mission, but that was about all he knew of Brevig.

A half-hour south of Wales, the weather had cleared somewhat. The sky was still overcast, but the wind had died down and the rain had not yet arrived. Walter touched down on the beach and taxied up to the largest building in the small village. The old structure was weather-beaten and in need of repair. The steeple at the front of the building caused Hultin to believe that this was where he would find Otis Lee.

A man in his middle forties, Lee looked every bit the part of a missionary. Slightly overweight with thinning gray hair and glasses, Lee was accommodating and friendly to the two weary travelers. Hultin explained the purpose of their visit and asked Lee to call the village council together. That night, a dozen people attended the impromptu meeting in the church. Most were Inuit who spoke very little English, so Otis Lee translated Hultin's message.

As it turned out, three of the elders were part of the eight survivors of the flu epidemic. Hultin asked them to tell the story of what happened, and for the next half-hour, the story of the flu coming to Brevig, Alaska, unfolded in first person for the scientist and his pilot.

They explained how a woman by the name of Lucy was the first to get sick. None of the three knew how or why, but the illness raced through town, killing nearly the entire village in just five days and then it disappeared. The agony of remembering was clearly visible on their faces as they told their painful story, perhaps, for the first time.

"I am a scientist. I'm here to try and find out what happened and why," Hultin began as Otis Lee translated. "It is now possible to prevent this from happening again. But I need your help. If you allow me to dig in the grave, I will do my best to find specimens. And once we have the virus, we can produce a vaccine. And the next time the disease comes, you will be immunized and you will not die."

A short council discussion led by the survivors followed as Lee, Hultin, and Jamouneau stood off to the side. The terrible story of death as told by the survivors was so overwhelming for the council that they quickly and unanimously gave Hultin their permission, wishing to never have to live through that again. The villagers said their goodbyes politely to the two strangers, and Otis Lee offered them the shelter of his home. The next day, with his supplies packed, Hultin walked to the grave about a mile outside of town. Unlike Wales, the grave was located in a raised mound and a good distance from the sea. This location was promising.

He picked a spot in the exact center between two crosses that marked the grave and began to dig. Nearly three feet down, Hultin was becoming despondent when he finally hit permafrost. His mood and his energy drastically improved. Next, he widened the hole to about six square feet in diameter. But the digging was becoming arduous. The exposed permafrost layer was hard and rubbery, like trying to dig through a car tire. He would have to melt it before digging further.

Hultin built a fire from wood he found nearby and waited. The permafrost began to melt, and he was able to scrape a couple of inches off the frozen earth where the fire had been. He realized that by building a fire on one side of the pit, then moving it to the other side, his digging time would be cut in half. He could dig on the thawed side while the fire melted the opposite side. His theory worked, and Hultin took advantage of the long summer days where sunlight was present nearly around the clock, working sixteen hours, alternately moving the fire from side to side, digging his hole a few inches at a time.

When the hole was nearly five feet deep, another problem arose. The fire not only melted the ground beneath it, but the sides of the pit as well. Water would trickle down the walls and douse the fire. A few times, small sections of the wall collapsed, resulting in additional digging for Hultin.

The work was backbreaking. Hultin's hands were covered with mud and blisters that stung and oozed a milky substance. The smoke from the fires choked his lungs and burned his eyes, but he kept at it for four days until he saw a head appear at the bottom of the grave. It was a young girl, perhaps ten years old, and even though he was anxious to find a specimen, it took him by surprise.

Her black hair was braided, and she wore a red ribbon to hold it in place. He exhumed the young girl a little farther and realized the dove-gray dress she was buried in looked like new. This lifeless body, entombed more than three decades earlier, looked as if she was ready to attend her friend's birthday party that afternoon. Hultin stood and stared at her for a moment, waiting for his feelings to settle. He reminded himself why he was here and what this discovery could mean. He decided it was time. He would call the rest of the team.

The following day, Porter and Collins drove the seventy miles from Nome to Teller in just over four hours. The Alaskan roads were little more than leveled dirt, and in the summer months, melting snows and storms blowing in from the Bering Sea caused them to all but disappear. Teller was six miles southeast of Brevig, and it was decided that would have to be the location where Porter and Collins met Hultin. North of Teller, the land was a soggy bog that the truck would not be able to cross. The short trip to Teller was Jamouneau and Hultin's first event-free flight. Walter said his brief goodbyes and then continued to Nome to refuel and wait on the call to return and pick them up.

He heard the truck before he saw it. The GM pickup, carrying their supplies, was nearly covered with mud as it stopped in front of the store. Porter and Collins, clearly not thrilled with their drive north, slowly climbed out of the cab. Their muscles cramped and aching, it took both of them a moment to stand upright. But that was to be expected; what surprised Hultin was the bandages, one on Collins's forehead and another on Porter's hand.

"Hey, guys. Good ride?" Hultin asked, excited to see them and bring them up to speed on the grave site.

"If you call four hours of getting bounced around in that tin can a good ride, then yes, Johan," Collins said sarcastically. Roger Porter was already checking the supplies in the rear of the truck, making sure nothing was lost or damaged.

"What's with the bandages?" Hultin asked, remembering the last time he saw these two, Porter was chasing Collins into Nome, and apparently, he caught him.

"He hit me in the head with one of the fire extinguishers," Collins whined.

"After he bit my hand," protested Porter.

"You had me in a choke hold. What did you expect?"

"What the hell?" Hultin yelled above the fracas. "We're here for something so much more important than your bickering. I found the specimens we need. So let's get this truck unloaded and get going. We've got a six-mile walk ahead of us," Johan informed them. "Truce?" he asked both of them.

"Truce," they agreed.

Hultin, being the youngest, offered to carry the large fire extinguisher. He rigged a brace for it out of wood and rope, then slung it across his back. The recent storms had made the tundra even more soggy and spongy than usual. With every step, their feet sunk, sometimes as much as six inches into the muck. The suction created by the added weight they each carried caused them to struggle to free their feet and move forward. Grassy ridges dotted the landscape as well. Two to four feet high and five feet across, they added to the grind. The going was incredibly difficult, but surprisingly, nobody complained. The scientists were anxious to get to the grave.

Halfway to Brevig, exhaustion was becoming an issue.

"Johan, we gotta stop," Porter said, trying to fill his lungs with air. "I'm beat."

It took Hultin all the remaining energy he had left to reply. "Agreed."

He dropped to his knees, spraying mud on the other two. Johan was too tired to apologize, and it didn't matter anyway; their legs were already covered to the thigh with the disgustingly difficult sludge. Instead, he untied the sling holding the large fire extinguisher to his back and carefully slipped it off. Porter and Collins just sat down where they stood, holding their gear on their laps.

Fifteen silent minutes went by with all three men hanging their heads and breathing heavily while in exhaustive contemplation.

Hultin knew he would be able to make it, but he was concerned for his teammates who endured the long ride from Nome to Teller this morning. They had to be running on empty, he thought. He opened a canteen, took a drink, and passed it along.

Porter drank from the canteen while calculating the time and distance covered up until this point and computing how many more hours they had to walk, figuring in their fatigue and needed rest stops. *Did we get ourselves into something that's over our heads?* he wondered. *This situation is bordering on desperation right now and could take a turn for the worse at any time.* He wiped his mouth and passed the canteen.

This sucks, thought Collins, taking the canteen. *I'd rather have a beer.*

Collins screwed the cap back on the canteen and tossed it back to Porter, who didn't see it coming. He and Hultin just stared straight ahead.

"Heads up!" shouted Collins too late as the canteen bounced off the side of Porter's face and into the mud.

"Fucking asshole," Porter said, surprisingly softly while rubbing his jaw and shaking his head. He turned away again and looked to the horizon. Then Collins heard it too: the noise of an engine in the distance. Collins and Hultin stood, ankle deep in ooze, and watched it drive directly toward them. Porter remained seated, rubbing his sore face. It was a tractor driven by Otis Lee, the missionary. When Hultin told him of his plans to walk from Teller back to Brevig, Lee knew what they faced and decided to lend a hand. Behind the tractor, Lee had tied an aluminum flat-bottomed boat.

"You boys need a lift?" Lee jokingly shouted from about thirty yards away.

"Your timing is perfect, Otis!" Hultin yelled back above the massive tractor's engine.

Lee drove right by the three men, swung around, and stopped when the boat was in front of them. They carefully placed their backpacks, bags, and shovels into the boat and climbed aboard. Lee started up the tractor and towed the three mud-covered microbiologists in the aluminum boat through the sludge-filled tundra and back to Brevig.

It was decided that they were too worn out to head directly to the grave site. The smarter thing to do was to get a good night's sleep and start fresh in the morning. Otis Lee towed them to the Brevig schoolhouse, a one room building next to the mission where they inflated their air mattresses and lay down, too tired to even shower. Before falling asleep, Hultin told Porter and Collins of his flights of fancy, as he called them. As he recounted each takeoff and landing, the three laughed harder and harder at his incredible tale. Delirious from exhaustion and laughter, they passed out.

The following day, the weather finally cooperated. The cloudless sky allowed the sun to warm the grave, providing easy digging for the scientists who opened it to twenty-five feet long by seven feet wide. The young girl was the first removed from the grave and placed on tables that the Inuits built from wooden planks and sawhorses. Three more bodies were removed as well and placed alongside one another on the makeshift tables.

"Before we go any further, I think we should discuss what we're all thinking," said Collins.

"Go on," said Porter. He and Johan knew what was coming but listened anyway.

"We don't know what will happen when we open these bodies. We're hoping to find the cause of the worse epidemic in human history and hopefully, *hopefully* find a vaccine. But what if we cause another one by cutting into these corpses? What if the virus is waiting inside them? Waiting to be unleashed on the world again? We would be the cause."

Porter and Hultin didn't respond immediately. They had the same concern although had not spoken it aloud. Collins was right. There was no governing scientific body that had been consulted and then approved what was being attempted. Three microbiologists were given permission by a frightened village council to exhume the bodies of influenza victims in the middle of nowhere, Alaska. It had never been done before. There was no book to consult or research provided. They were writing the book.

"Otis, ask the Inuits to move back. At least fifty feet. Gary, we have our surgical masks and gloves. There's nothing more we can do to protect ourselves. Our instruments are sterilized, so we hopefully won't contaminate the samples. Let's do what we came here to do," Hultin said.

"I agree. There is a risk, but I believe it to be minimal," agreed Porter. "As long as we keep the samples frozen and get these bodies back in the ground quickly—" he stopped there. Not completely believing his own words but knowing he was not leaving this site without the samples.

Collins's look of concern acquiesced, and he took his position. Too late to turn back now, he figured. He felt better for bringing it up and having discussed it.

Hultin sliced through the thawing skin with his scalpel, revealing the ribs of the young girl and then stepped aside. Next, Porter stepped in with the rib cutters and cut through the frozen ribs. Hultin stepped back in with his scalpel, cut through the chest plate, and removed it, exposing the girl's frozen lungs. If the virus existed, this was where it had been hiding.

Hultin carefully and methodically cut a two-inch square out of each lung and turned to Collins, who held the opened thermos. After he placed the pieces of diseased lung into the thermos, Collins sprayed the dry ice from the fire extinguisher into it and then sealed it.

They repeated the process three more times with the three remaining bodies. When they were through, they returned the bodies to their resting place and, with the help of the Inuits, covered the grave. Before they packed up their equipment, they stood looking at the grave, the crosses, and each other.

"Should we say something?" asked Collins.

"Like what?" asked Porter.

"I don't know. A prayer maybe," replied Collins.

"It isn't necessary, gentlemen," interrupted Otis Lee. "We've prayed for these souls many times. Now we'll pray for your science and your skill. Let's get you back to Teller."

They repacked their equipment and placed it in the aluminum boat. Collins took special care to place the four thermoses into his backpack, then stepped into the boat with the other two scientists. The Inuits headed back into town. Otis started the tractor's engine, and they began their long trip back to Iowa City.

Jamouneau was waiting for them in Teller when they arrived. It was late evening, so they hurriedly transferred their gear from the boat to the Piper, thanked Otis Lee for all he had done, and they were off. Roger and Johan shared the back seat while Gary was stuffed into the small space behind that with the gear and shovels, his backpack containing the Brevig lung specimens held tightly to his chest.

After collecting their personal belongings in Nome, the flights continued with scheduled stops: Seattle, Salt Lake City, Kansas City, and then a short flight into Iowa City. Hultin held on to the backpack with the specimens the entire trip as Collins and Porter carried the four small fire extinguishers in two other backpacks. At each stop, the three would depart the plane and find a secluded area on the tarmac far away from the plane. Once they were convinced they were isolated, the small fire extinguishers were used to fill each thermos with fresh dry ice, keeping the specimens frozen for the following leg of the trip.

Back in Iowa City, Hultin resumed his role as team leader and began the experiments. He was assisted in the lab by Sally Whitney. She and Hultin worked under state-of-the-art conditions as a precaution should the flu virus be present. They wore masks, sterile gowns, and gloves and worked beneath a negative-pressure hood hung from the ceiling that swept up the air in the room into a pressurized duct that lead to industrial filters and then the building's exterior.

Hultin's techniques were also state-of-the-art. He began by grinding the lung tissue, suspending it in a salt solution, and then spinning it in a centrifuge to separate the virus from other unwanted debris. An antibiotic was added to kill any bacteria in the mixture, and since viruses are invulnerable to antibiotics, it would not threaten the experiment.

Next, he injected the fluid into fertilized chicken eggs. With a precise and delicate touch, Hultin cut and lifted a tiny square from the egg's shell. A needle containing what he hoped was liquid containing the 1918 influenza virus was poked through the thin membrane and into the white of the interior egg. For nearly two months, he and Sally Whitney performed the procedure on hundreds of eggs. Each morning, Porter, Collins, Whitney, and Hultin would begin their day in the lab in hopes of finding success.

However, each morning the eggs remained unchanged. The virus would not grow.

Disappointed but not defeated, they moved on to the next set experiments whereby tiny pieces of the Brevig lung tissue were injected into guinea pigs, white mice, and ferrets. Again, the flu refused to show itself. The experiments had failed, and Hultin was out of lung tissue.

Hultin and Whitney had nearly finished cleaning out the lab when a disappointed Roger Porter walked in.

"What do you think went wrong?" he asked.

"I've been racking my brain, going over each step since we exhumed the bodies. The samples were good when we took them and we kept them frozen the entire trip back. If there was influenza virus in those tissue samples, it should have grown in our lab."

"Perhaps there was no virus in the samples," Sally Whitney offered.

"No," Porter and Hultin said in unison.

"It was there. It's what killed those people. It was there," Porter said.

"Agreed. The virus had to have been dead before the bodies froze. It was there. It just died after the host did," suggested Hultin.

"If it's there and it's dead, there's nothing we can do," Porter said sympathetically but matter-of-factly. He turned and left the lab.

"Maybe, not *today*," Hultin said to his assistant, who tilted her head slightly with a quizzical look.

6

Best of Seven

Montreal

March 3, 1919

Newsy sat in the lobby of the Chateau Laurier Hotel, waiting patiently for Canadiens' general manager and part owner George Kennedy. The excessive opulence of the Ottawa hotel, alongside the famous Rideau Canal, made him feel uncomfortable. His humble beginnings had never left him, even though he had become one of the wealthiest and most recognizable people in Canada.

The Laurier resembled a French chateau; aptly named, he thought. Its exterior featured turrets and fine masonry that rivaled the Canadian Parliament building located across the street. The interior reflected the wealth and power of aristocracy. He imagined himself to be a duke or count, even a prince, since he was now as wealthy as royalty.

Two days earlier, he had led Montreal in a route of their playoff opponents, the Ottawa Senators, to take a commanding three games to none lead in the first-ever best-of-seven NHL playoff series. Lalonde scored five of the Canadiens' six goals, pulling them within one game of returning to the Stanley Cup Challenge Series.

Sitting there in the lavish surroundings, Newsy puffed his cigar, then blew the smoke onto the red-hot ambers at its end, his nose turned slightly toward the fabulous building's copper roof. Powerful senators and influential businessmen stopped in their tracks, overjoyed to say hello and shake the hand of the great Newsy Lalonde.

"Okay, it's done. I had to stop at three different banks, but I have the advance you asked for," George Kennedy said, sitting down next to Newsy. "And I'll say it again, I don't think it's right, you renegotiating your contract for next year before this season is even concluded. I thought you had more honor."

"You don't pay me for my honor, George, and people don't fill your arena for my honor. I play hockey—better than anyone else in the world. That's why you pay me, and that's why they come," Newsy said, taking the white envelope from Kennedy's outstretched hand. "Look at it this way, you have me signed up for another season. In a couple of weeks, after we beat the sissies from the western league for our second Stanley Cup Championship, we'll have the chance to win our third next season. They'll have to change its name to the Montreal Canadiens' Cup."

"Don't go counting chickens now, Newsy. I understand Nighbor is back for tonight's game, so let's not get overconfident," Kennedy feigned concern as best he could.

Newsy struggled to sit up and escape the oversized wingback chair. He doused his cigar in the crystal ashtray and slid the envelope into his coat pocket.

"Well, that is wonderful news, Georgie. Any idea why he missed the first three games?" he asked, finally freeing himself and standing up.

"Illness in the family is all I've been told. Nothing more than the papers have been reporting," responded Kennedy.

"Let's get down to the arena. I'd like to see him before the game," Newsy said, walking quickly toward the Laurier's massive front door.

Kennedy was two steps behind him, struggling to keep up. "Fine, you pay for the taxi."

Newsy slid the envelope out of his pocket and peeked in. "Can't do it. You didn't put anything smaller than a twenty in here. You must have a couple of loonies," he said with a smile.

"Fuck me!" Kennedy said, shaking his head.

Julius Francis "Frank" Nighbor was widely regarded as one of the best players in the game. At five feet nine inches tall and 160 pounds, the Pembroke Peach was physical, fearless, and dangerous with the puck. He had already won a Stanley Cup with the Vancouver Millionaires in 1915 and, two seasons later, tied Joe Malone for the NHL's scoring championship, scoring forty-one goals in nineteen games for Ottawa.

His legend continued to grow over the next decade. In 1924, he would capture the inaugural Hart Trophy as the league's Most Valuable Player. In 1925, Lady Byng, wife of the Canadian governor general, was so enamored with his game that she presented him with the first Lady Byng Trophy in honor of the "player adjudged to have exhibited the best type of sportsmanship and gentlemanly conduct combined with a high standard of playing ability." The following season, he won it again. Frank Nighbor was the centerpiece of the sport's first dynasty, winning four Stanley Cups in seven years for Ottawa during the 1920s. That dynasty may have begun in 1919 had Nighbor not missed the first three playoff games.

The Ottawa Senators tore up the NHL in the second half of the regular season. After Montreal won the first-half championship, the Canadiens struggled to a 3–5 record during the second half. Meanwhile, the Senators nearly ran the board, winning seven of their eight games, highlighted by Nighbor's scoring and playmaking abilities. Nighbor and Lalonde facing off for the NHL Championship was anticipated by the entire hockey world. Both were sixty-minute players. Both were highly skilled skaters with exquisite puck control. Both were generals on the ice. And when Nighbor traveled to Detroit to be with his ailing mother and sister prior to the start of the series, the entire hockey world was disappointed.

Nighbor had refused to see anyone prior to the game, so the first time the two superstars met was at center ice. Referee Dan Pulford raised his left hand and pointed at Senator goaltender Clint Benedict who waved back. Pulford turned to the opposite end of the ice, raised his right hand, and pointed at George Vezina, who nodded his head.

Pulford blew his whistle. Newsy Lalonde and Frank Nighbor glided to the center ice circle bent at the waist, their hands resting on their knees, clutching their sticks.

"Hey, Peach."

"Hey, Newsy."

"Glad to have you back."

"Thanks, Newsy. It's good to be back."

Pulford slammed the puck to the ice, and the two warriors' sticks instantly followed, battling for the rubber. Nighbor shifted his weight, pivoted his body, and lifted a shoulder into Newsy's jaw. The impact momentarily stunned Lalonde, enabling Nighbor to win the face-off.

With their captain back in the lineup, Ottawa played with confidence, control, and a fierce desire lacking in the first three games. They quickly jumped out to a 2–0 lead, with Nighbor providing the assists on both goals. However, it was his body checking that set the tone of the game from the opening face-off. Nighbor had developed and perfected the sweep check. When an opposing player advanced toward the Ottawa goal, Nighbor would artfully slide to the ice and dislodge the puck with a large looping sweep check of his stick. Tonight, however, Nighbor sent Canadiens flying into the boards with devastating body checks.

Time and again, the Canadiens rushed down the ice only to be flattened by the Senator captain, playing with a reckless abandon for his own health. Meanwhile, Benedict was enjoying his best game of the series, thwarting Lalonde, Malone, Hall, and the rest of the Canadiens when they did get past Nighbor.

By the third period, Lalonde's frustration was growing evident. Trailing 6–2 and time running down in game 4, Lalonde broke into the Senators' offensive zone behind their defense. His deadly wrist shot was once again deflected by the stick of Benedict and sailed over the chain-link fence and into the crowd. Play stopped as Pulford went to retrieve another puck from the scorer's table, so Newsy hustled to the Canadiens' bench.

"Give me the pouch," a winded Lalonde demanded.

"What?" asked an incredulous Odie Cleghorn from the bench.

"The pouch! Give it to me now!" Lalonde yelled.

Cleghorn reached behind the bench and handed Newsy the pouch of leaf-chewing tobacco that the substitutes enjoyed while watching the game. Newsy shoved his thumb and two fingers into the pouch and pulled out a large mound of chew, then shoved it into his cheek. Cleghorn and the three other Canadien subs chuckled at the lunacy of the moment. Joe Malone, who had come out of the game for a substitute, leaned over to Cleghorn when Newsy skated away and asked, "What the hell is he doing?"

"You got me. But I betcha it's gonna be fuckin' priceless," replied Cleghorn, not able to control his laughter even though the Canadiens were being embarrassed on the ice.

When play resumed, Newsy stayed high on his wing, never fully getting back into his defensive zone to help out. The game was decided, but Newsy intended to send a message, and Joe Hall knew it.

When an Ottawa shot ricocheted off Vezina's leg pad to Joe Hall, Newsy was already at full speed, leaving the Canadiens' defensive zone and into center ice. He split the two Senator defensemen and received a sharp pass from Hall just before the center ice line. Newsy had a clean breakaway to the Ottawa goal and this night's nemesis, Clint Benedict.

As he entered the Senators' zone, the crowd came to their feet, and Newsy slid the puck to his forehand for his much-feared wrist shot. Benedict confidently skated to an unmarked point on the ice ten feet in front of his net, hunched at the waist, glove-hand shoulder high, and his stick solidly on the ice between his skates. Then, he slowly skated backward, inching toward his goal, eyeing Newsy's every move and taking away any possible angle of open net.

Newsy was flying, coming in much faster than normal. Benedict slid backward quicker in order to compensate for Lalonde's velocity. When he got within five feet of Benedict, Newsy slammed on the brakes. Snow and ice flew from the blades of his skates, hitting Benedict in the chest. The two stood just a few feet apart, staring at each other for what seemed to be an eternity. The Senators' defensemen were still too far away to stop the shot that Newsy had not yet taken.

Then Benedict's look changed from confidence to confusion. Newsy's cheeks were slightly puffed, and he curled his lips and leaned over as if he were going to kiss the Ottawa goaltender. Instead, he squirted a mouthful of brown tobacco-laden spit into his eyes. The gooey liquid splattered off Benedict's face. Blinded, the goaltender dropped to his knees, his hands struggling to wipe away the thick soup that was burning his eyes. Newsy calmly lifted the puck over Benedict's crumpled body and into the Senators' net.

On the Montreal bench, Joe Malone grabbed Odie Cleghorn, and the two nearly fell on to the ice in hysterics. One Ottawa defenseman skated to his fallen goaltender. The other went right at Newsy who lifted his stick to the Senator's face, opening a large gash on his chin. Immediately, every player on the ice grabbed a player wearing a different-colored sweater, and the melee was on.

"I was just sending a message. We're the Montreal Canadiens, defending Stanley Cup Champions, and we're not going to stand being embarrassed," Newsy concluded.

The Montreal Star reporter had not stopped giggling since witnessing Newsy's unique goal over an hour earlier.

"Okay, Newsy. As always, thanks for taking the time. I'll see you back in Montreal," he said.

"Anytime, it's my pleasure."

They shook hands, and Newsy turned down the hallway toward the dressing rooms. As he approached the last turn to the main hallway under the arena, Newsy heard a number of voices and, surprisingly, laughter coming from around the corner. Newsy turned the corner to find both teams in the hallway drinking beer, undressing, and getting medical attention.

"How's the chin, Cameron?" Newsy asked the large Senator defenseman getting stitched up by the doctor. Newsy leaned in for a closer look. "Doesn't look too bad. You'll be fine for next game," he said, patting Cameron on the back, who lunged forward from Newsy's overzealous pats. The force pushed the doctor's needle slightly too far into the open wound. Cameron moaned and reached for Newsy who had walked away.

"Is that you, Newsy? You fuck!" asked Clint Benedict who was sitting on a bench between the two open dressing room doors. George Vezina sat beside him with a bucket of water and slowly poured it into his eyes. Benedict had his head tilted back and strained to keep his eyes open so the water could wash them out.

"No, it's George Kennedy," replied Newsy.

"Oh sorry, Mr. Kennedy."

Vezina suppressed a laugh and shook his head at Newsy who winked back and then continued down the hall to the Montreal dressing room where he found Joe Hall sitting with Frank Nighbor.

"And speak of the devil," Joe said as Newsy entered.

"What's up, boys?" asked Newsy, still smiling at fooling Benedict.

"I'll hop in the shower and let you two talk," Joe excused himself and grabbed a towel from the stack. *Quite abruptly,* thought Newsy.

Newsy sat down next to Nighbor who was still in full hockey gear.

"Nice win tonight, Peach," Newsy said breaking the ice. "You okay?"

"Well, first off, you can't be pulling anymore shenanigans on the ice. You practically blinded Benedict," Nighbor began.

"Agreed," Newsy replied, stifling a chuckle. The two warriors leaned forward together, as if on cue, and began untying their skates. "Sorry about your loss," Newsy offered. "Your mom, right?"

"Yeah. Influenza. My sister is bedridden with it now. Mom passed four days ago. I had to take care of the arrangements and all."

Newsy stopped undressing and leaned back, folding his arms as if to say, "Go ahead, I'll listen." Nighbor took a peek over his shoulder and continued.

"She was only forty-two. Nasty thing, this influenza. It seems like all of Detroit was sick while I was there. Anyway, like I said, she passed four days ago. I'm glad I got to spend some time with her before she died, though. She wasn't very awake, alert. But I think she knew I was there. At least, I hope she knew I was with her.

"You know what's funny? You think they'll be here forever. That they're never going to leave you. My dad died when I was young, so I never really got to know him. Mom did her best to make up for him. She was amazing, tender as well as tough when she had to be. I felt so helpless there, by her bed. Watching her. Watching what had become of her. What was left of her.

"And realizing that there was absolutely nothing I could do. After all the times she helped me and made me feel better. All the cuts, the bruises, colds, and hurt feelings—anything! She always made it better. And I just couldn't do that for her. She was such a good person. She didn't deserve this."

Newsy grabbed the back of his neck with a powerful hand, embracing his friend, trying in vain to ease some of the pain.

"Completely helpless," Nighbor continued, shaking his head side to side. "One thing a lot of people never knew about her is that she could really kick my ass. And she would. She was always concerned because Dad wasn't around, and me growing up in a house with just the two women, I wasn't as tough as I should be. Or maybe as tough as I could be. So she'd kick my ass. Not physically. She'd challenge me to man up. To play tough. It wasn't my game, so I endured a lot of speeches and even some ball-busting from her." He chuckled at the memory, but his pain was still evident.

Nighbor paused and gazed at Newsy who wore an expression few people ever saw on the hockey legend.

"She hadn't seen me play in quite a while. I think it's been a couple of years since she's come to one of my games. She couldn't take the time away from work, she said. So I decided this morning that I would play the game she always wanted to see me play. Physical. Tough. Tonight, I played for my mom. I know she was watching. From the best seats in the house." He looked to the ceiling. "I hope I made you proud tonight. And I'm sorry I couldn't do more for you," he said, choking back tears. He looked back down again.

"I love you, Mom."

Nighbor stood. He turned slowly and extended his hand to Newsy, who stood and pushed his hand aside and embraced him. "I'm sure you made her proud tonight," Newsy whispered in Nighbor's ear. "You made us all proud tonight, Frank." The entire dressing room had overheard their conversation. In this room full of brutally aggressive and violent professional hockey players, not one eye remained dry.

"Thanks, Newsy." He turned, wiping tears from his eyes. The Canadien players he walked past on the way out of the dressing room spoke soft words of congratulations to Frank, an enemy on the ice but a hurting comrade away from it. Nighbor just shook his head up and down, never looking up and shielding his eyes with his hand.

Three nights later on their home ice, the Montreal Canadiens defeated the Ottawa Senators, 4–2, winning the NHL series four games to one. The game's three stars were Newsy Lalonde, Joe Malone, and Frank Nighbor.

It was decided the Stanley Cup Championship would be played out west on the ice of the Pacific Coast Hockey League's champion. Vancouver and Seattle had not yet finished their series, but Montreal was headed west anyway. The ten-day trip crossing the dominion meant numerous train rides and connections. However, one player would not make the trip.

Offensive force Joe Malone had decided the amount of time away from his full-time job as an accountant was not worth the loss of money he would incur, so he remained in Montreal. A few days later, the Seattle Metropolitans were crowned PCHL champions and prepared to play the NHL Champions for Lord Stanley's Cup.

7

The Chain Reaction

Southern California

October 13, 1993

Kary Banks Mullis wiped the sleep from his eyes, still wondering if the call he just concluded was real or a dream. His history with hallucinogenic drugs provided experiences that should allow him to differentiate the two worlds, that of sleep as opposed to full consciousness. At times it seemed it may have further blurred the line for him, but those experiences also expanded his mind. *It let me see my mind*, he thought. *Some years earlier, it let me read the mind of my closest friend.*

"I can read your mind, Harry," I told him. "I'm only allowed into the front room, the reception area. But I'm in there."

"I'm in yours too," Harry had replied.

I walked away from the table we were sitting at, knowing that I had only had to stare into his eyes to reenter that place. I grabbed a couple of index cards and two pens and returned to Harry in my kitchen.

"Write the next word you are going to say, Harry."

That was just two scientists being scientists. We both wrote down a word and showed our cards to each other. It was the same word. We repeated it several times, and each time, we had written the same word. Fucking weird!

Mullis got out of bed and, clad only in his boxer shorts, performed the "just barely awake" stagger/walk to the bathroom. The mirror reflected an image that made him laugh. *What a mess*, he thought.

Perhaps the worse trip, as well as the most dangerous, was that time with Eric when I synthesized diethyltryptamine. Yeah, that was the worst. What was I thinking? Well, I wasn't thinking about the proper measurement, that's for sure.

He smiled, finished up his morning excretion, and grabbed for the toothbrush on the sink.

It had to be ten times the amount I wanted to ingest. I can still see Eric's face before I blacked out for the first time. What was the last thing I said to him? Something like "Don't take it, Eric!"

Mullis laughed again, drooling toothpaste down his chin. It bounced off the side of the sink and onto his boxers.

"What an idiot," he said aloud to the reflection smiling back at him.

And what a wild ride, fuck! I don't remember much, but I do remember that giant snake crawling out of my fireplace and then me beating it to death with a log. Oh wait, yeah, that was Eric's clarinet. And there was no snake.

A spray of toothpaste-laden spit hit the mirror. Laughing at himself, he wiped the mirror with his free hand, spreading the sticky goo around and causing his reflection to blur. *Appropriate,* he thought. *That's kind of how I remember that trip starting off with Eric sitting across from me in shock and disbelief. What a great guy and good friend. I think the happiest I had ever heard him was when they finally gave him his honorable discharge from the air force. "Psychiatric problems" was the diagnosis. I don't think it's a "psychiatric problem" if you don't want to help blow up the world.*

As a strategic air command pilot, Eric was part of a chain responsible for delivering nuclear weapons on target. He had one of two keys needed to arm the bombs on his aircraft. Talk about a huge responsibility, literally the weight of the world on his shoulders.

For two days, I didn't know where I was or who I was. He took care of me and brought me back from that doomed trip. Helped me find myself from the lost dark hold of the psychotic place I trapped myself in. It's funny. How people come in and out of your life. It's been years since I've seen Eric. For a time, we were as close as brothers, and now we rarely speak. Hardly ever anymore. That's really not funny, it's sad, he thought. *I'll clean the mirror later.*

It was nearly 7:00 a.m. now, and the call was becoming clearer to him. He played it over in his mind, at least what he thought he heard and said.

"Hello, is this Dr. Kary Mullis?"

"Yes."

"This is Dr. Carl Naeslund from the Nobel Institute in Stockholm. Congratulations, Dr. Mullis. I am pleased to tell you that you have been awarded the Nobel Prize."

"I'll take it," he said before hanging the phone back up.

"I'll take it"? I guess that's as good a response as any. I gotta call my mother. What a great birthday present this will make for her—if it's actually true and I actually got that call and I actually had that conversation. What did he say his name was? I heard him say the Karolinska Institute, so I know he was legit since that's the governing body for Nobel selection. Or did my subconscious just add that part? Shit! Fuck! Shit! He placed the phone back on to the receiver, not sure if he should call his mother just yet. The year before he was certain he'd win the prize. Especially after he spent an entire afternoon with that producer and his production crew from Sweden.

He had told Mullis that he always picked the winners correctly and had always done his television profiles ahead of time. *He was probably full of shit,* thought Mullis. *Probably had some insider information coming out of the institute in Sweden. That was a disappointment. I guess I fucked up his batting average.*

There was a knock at his door.

"Yo, brah, you ready?" Steve Judd yelled from the front porch.

Mullis grabbed his wet suit hanging in the foyer by the door and welcomed his surf buddy. "Hey, Steve. Yeah. I need a minute."

"Let's go, Mule, get dressed," he encouraged.

"I think I just won the Nobel Prize."

"You did. I heard it on the radio. Let's go for a surf," replied Judd with about as much interest as if they were discussing traffic on the 405.

Finally, confirmation. It wasn't a dream. "I'll take it."

"Unbelievable," Mullis said aloud and smiling at himself.

"It is, but so are the waves. Let's head out."

"Hold on, Steve. I have to call my mom."

Mullis grabbed the phone and started dialing his mother's number in South Carolina. *This will make a great birthday present,* he thought as he raised the receiver to his ear.

"Hello. Hello!" was being shouted at the other end of the line.

"Hello, who is this?"

"This is Jack Mallon of the Associated Press. Congratulations, Dr. Mullis, on winning the Nobel Prize. Can I have a few minutes of your time?"

"Ah sure. No wait. This isn't a good time. Let's set something up. I was just heading out."

"Okay, when would like to reschedule, Dr. Mullis?"

"Speak with my publicist."

"Can I have her name and number?"

Mullis placed the phone back down on the receiver. "Jesus, that was quick."

He picked the phone up again to call his mother, and this time, he listened for a dial tone first, but again, there was none.

"Hello?" he asked again.

"Hello. Dr. Mullis, this is Rob Newman from the UPI. Congratulations on winning the Nobel Prize."

Mullis hung the phone up again. He looked at Steve. "We gotta get outta here."

"That's what I've been preachin', brah," replied Steve. He wiped his mouth of the orange juice he just gulped from the container and placed it back in Mullis's refrigerator. "Get your wet suit on, I'll get your board and put it on the rack," he offered.

The phone rang again. Mullis hesitated, then answered. It was the local television station. They wanted to send a crew over immediately to interview him at his house.

"I need a couple of hours. I'm heading out and won't be back until later this morning."

"Where are you going, Dr. Mullis? Perhaps we can follow along and interview you there."

Shaking his head, Mullis was starting to feel squeezed. All he wanted to do was get into the water like he did nearly every morning with his buddies and ride a couple of waves to start the day and clear his mind.

"I'm going surfing," he said. *Fuck, why did I say that?*

As soon as the words were out of his mouth, he realized he wanted them back. Steve had returned from mounting Mullis's longboard on the top of his jeep and gave Mullis a look of "why did you just say that?" The San Diego area provided a multitude of good surf spots. Up until fifteen minutes ago, Mullis was just one of the hundreds of unknown surfers who started their day at their favorite spot. The Nobel Prize had changed that forever.

"That will make a great location to do the interview. The surfing Nobel Prize winner! Where can we meet you?" the reporter asked.

Mullis smiled.

"We'll be at Thirteenth Street in Del Mar."

"Perfect, Dr. Mullis. See you there."

"See you there."

He hung up the phone, turned to look at Steve, and in unison, they both said, "Tourmaline," and exchanged smiles and high fives, knowing that they just sent the news crew to the wrong beach.

"Awesome, Mule," Judd chuckled.

It was a fifteen-minute ride to Tourmaline. The car windows down, the warm San Diego air blowing through the Jeep felt refreshing, and a wave of successful satisfaction washed over Mullis. His bare feet on the dashboard, he could see the front end of his nine-foot-nine-inch surfboard protruding over the front of the jeep, Steve's shortboard's tip barely visible next to his. Suddenly, he was back where it all happened. Where the idea, the formula had come to him.

It was ten years earlier on a quiet stretch of Highway 128. Mile marker 46.58 and Jennifer was asleep in the front seat. It was late. That's when it hit me. How I could make it work. I pulled the car over and grabbed an old envelope that was in the glove compartment, searched for a pen, and started scribbling the formula for PCR. Others had worked on this problem before but couldn't get it done. Right there on that lonely stretch of highway, with my girlfriend sleeping next to me, I figured it out. A little while later, she would leave me. I had discovered one of the most important breakthroughs for science in the twentieth century, and she left me. I remember how lonely I felt. I should have been celebrating. People would know me the world over. I would be a guest lecturer in science labs at the University of East Bum Fuck, and they would ask me to say something brilliant to the undergrads, but it all seemed trivial in light of losing her.

The Jeep pulled into the small parking lot next to the beach. A half-dozen cars were already parked, and there were eight or ten people in the surf. Mullis's spirits immediately picked up. He forced Jennifer from his mind as he grabbed his longboard off the rack, reached behind him for his zipper handle, and zipped up his wet suit. Steve was already running into the surf break.

Mullis took three large steps into the water, dove on to his board, and without missing a beat, was paddling out to the lineup. Mullis realized he was smiling, and as a large wall of foam was about to wash over him, he rolled off the board, pulling it on top of him to let the wave continue. With another roll of the board, he was back on top of it. The sixty-degree water felt good against his face as he paddled out into the cool ocean.

In a couple of minutes, he was a hundred yards of shore and sitting up in the lineup. Steve had already told the other surfers about Mullis's morning, and they gave him a round of applause from atop their boards. The sun's severe angle turned the ocean into a golden liquid, and the scene seemed surreal. Mullis shook a couple of hands and thanked the boys, although none of them could ever comprehend what polymerase chain reaction was and how it had changed the sciences forever. *They probably couldn't even pronounce it,* he thought.

"I thought the Nobel Prize was for peace," a surfer questioned.

"Nah, they got a bunch of different categories. And our Mule is the winner in science," explained Judd.

A number of jokes were exchanged at each other's expense when they all noticed a beautiful set that had traveled thousands of miles across the open Pacific, just for them.

The Nobel Prize quickly became much less important in the face of these approaching waves. Two surfers lay down flat on their shortboards, dug into the ocean with their arms extended, and then hopped up on the first wave right when it started to break. It was a thing of beauty as they split in opposite directions, charging into the barrel and carving up and down the face of the wave toward the beach. The second wave was smaller, and Mullis knew the guys with the fun boards would wait for the third and final wave in the set, so he lay himself down on his board and started paddling to gain the appropriate speed. As the wave caught up to him, he placed both hands on the board beneath his chest, pushed up, and, in one motion, landed on his feet. He leaned his body weight to the right, and the board obeyed his command, cutting across the face of the wave. He let the power of the ocean grab on to the back of the board so he could walk to its front where he stood enjoying the sun, the ocean, and the approaching shoreline.

The ride was perfect, and as the wave lost its energy, Mullis skillfully let the wave finish its journey alone, hopped off in the shallows, and grabbed the board. The salt air, the cool breeze, the roar of waves crashing on the beach, a few seagulls screaming overhead, and the warming sun added to what had begun as a great day.

A few minutes later, he was paddling back to the lineup, again lost in his thoughts.

My coworkers at Cetus didn't take me seriously when I first described to them how to make PCR work. Well, most of them didn't, Ron Cook did. He shared my enthusiasm for the possibilities it presented. Others dismissed it. Ron told me I should quit Cetus, wait a while, and then write a patent for the formula and get rich on my historic breakthrough. Great suggestion but I had already discussed the formula with a number of people in the office at Cetus, and I felt that if I took his advice and this did work, they would have lawyers after me for the rest of my life. No one could have foreseen the amount of money this would generate. Hoffman-La Roche paid Cetus $300 million for the formula. I was about to win a $10,000 prize from the Nobel foundation. How foolish I was to think that if the formula worked big time, I would be amply rewarded by my employer. Fucking foolish!

The sun was higher in the sky, and the swells were coming in less frequently and with less force. The tide was rising, and that meant surf time this morning was coming to an end. Steve obviously thought the same thing as he finished another fine ride and paddled the last twenty yards to the beach. Mullis caught one final bunny wave and rode it to the edge of the beach. He unstrapped the Velcro leash from his ankle and walked up the beach to find Steve doing an interview with a news crew.

"So, Dr. Mullis, how did it feel this morning when you got the call?" the reporter asked.

"How did it feel?" Steve repeated. "Completely gnarly, brah. It's like waking up to find you're on top of the freakin' world, man. On top of Mount Everest looking down at the rest of civilization, and everyone else pales in comparison to my shining brilliance. That's how it feels to win the Nobel Prize, brah."

Mullis walked up behind Steve and dropped his longboard in the sand. It landed with a thud, and Steve turned to see his friend. They smiled at each other, and Steve turned back to the reporter. "Oh yeah, I just remembered. This is Dr. Mullis. My mistake," he said, and he walked away from the reporter who was frozen, still standing there with the microphone where Steve's mouth was a moment before.

After the real Nobel Prize winner finished the interview on the beach, they loaded up the surfboards and headed back to Mullis's house. The next several hours were nonstop, back-to-back interviews with print, television, and radio reporters. The news media ate it up. The surfing Nobel Prize chemist! Later on that afternoon, the calls finally stopped coming, and it was time to call Mom. Her reaction was typical. Extreme pride mixed with a number of "I told you so's" and suggestions of what to wear on his next round of interviews.

The party went on for two days with brief interludes of sleep, more appropriately, passing out for a few hours and then waking up and starting all over. With Mullis's home completely dry and mostly destroyed, he decided to end this party and begin another at his cabin in Mendocino, the wine country. The change of location would allow him to dry out on the ride north as well as share the celebration with friends and former coworkers at the other end of the state.

After sleeping for nearly ten hours, Kary Mullis woke up surprisingly refreshed. A quick shower and a few essentials thrown into an overnight bag took another twenty minutes and he was off.

It was late night, or early morning, depending on how one lived their life. For Mullis, time was just a measurement. The sun would begin to rise in two hours and the approximate six-hundred-mile ride would last another six after that. He fired up the 1964 and half Mustang convertible and pointed it north. A ride he was more than familiar with, Mullis could basically do it on autopilot, and his red relic seemed to be able to do it by itself.

The 405 up to Los Angeles was an uncharacteristic easy ride, probably because of the early hour. By the time the sun was up, Mullis was north of the city and gunning it through the valley where he crossed over to the 5. Ordinarily, he might have taken the PCH, Pacific Coast Highway, which is considered to be the most beautiful ride in the United States. *The winding coast road would add at least two or three hours to the trip, so I'll fly up the 5, get there quicker, and start the party again,* he reasoned.

North of San Francisco, he began to tire. A weird sensation came over his outstretched arms holding the steering wheel. They were tingling and numb. He pulled his right hand off the wheel and held it in front of his face. "Stop that," he said aloud in the howling wind. *A break. I need a break,* he thought.

The classic Mustang still could gallop. At eighty-five miles an hour, Mullis screamed under a sign that announced Cloverdale as the next set of exits. He selected Citrus Fair Drive as he always did and exited the freeway. Turning left at the traffic light, he crossed underneath the 101, drove a quarter mile to route 128, and turned right.

Warehouses and office buildings quickly turned into a nice but crowded residential neighborhood. After a few more minutes, the number of houses thinned, and the remaining houses grew in size and splendor. Then, they too became less frequent, and route 128 became a bucolic scene of rolling hills, tall green trees, and clean-crisp northern California air.

Five more miles and I'll stop. I promise.

He pulled off the shoulder at mile marker 46.58 as he had done too many times to remember. But that first time he could remember. Every detail, every moment, every thought. Most important were his thoughts.

Jennifer was asleep. My girlfriend and coworker that, looking back, was probably not the most brilliant combination, but at the time, I did love her and she loved me. I thought she did anyway.

Tragedy was just around the corner, but any relationship issues were pushed far back into the recesses of my mind. Even the succulent aroma of the blooming California buckeye peering in through Jennifer's open passenger window as if it were trying to listen to my thoughts couldn't break my concentration. It was warmer than usual, and my heart was racing. I realized I was sweating. I never sweat.

I knew how to do it! I could do it.

I grabbed the envelope and the pen from the glove compartment and started writing. The secrets of DNA had eluded the molecular science world since its discovery. Unlocking the secrets of this life-giving, life-changing strand of miracle would change all the rules of molecular biology. And I knew how to do it.

If I could locate a thousand sequences out of billions with one short piece of DNA, I could use another short piece to narrow the search. This one would be designed to bind to a sequence just down the chain from the first sequence I had found. It would scan over the thousand possibilities out of the first search to find just the one I wanted. And using the natural properties of DNA to replicate itself under certain conditions I could provide, I could make that sequence of DNA between the sites where the two short search strings landed reproduce the hell out of itself. In one replicative cycle, I could have two copies, and in two cycles, I could have four. In ten cycles, I could have 1,024. Twenty cycles would give me a million. Thirty cycles would give me a billion. And they would always be the same size. That was important. That was the almighty hallelujah! Clincher. Abundance and distinction were the two major problems in DNA chemistry, and I solved them both in one stroke. This simple technique would make as many copies as I wanted of any DNA sequence I chose, and everybody on earth who cared about DNA would want to use it. It would spread into every biology lab in the world. I would be famous. I would get the Nobel Prize.

I did get the Nobel Prize.

Time stood still as Mullis relived and reveled in his historic moment. His driver's seat leaning way back, he stared at the heavens with his hands folded behind his head. At that moment, he could not realize the full magnitude of his discovery. One that indeed changed science but may have had an even more important impact on law enforcement. In just a few months, his theory would play the central role for and against the prosecution of the most infamous defendant of the twentieth century, O. J. Simpson.

The brilliant sunny sky was giving way to one much more blue and becoming darker by the minute. As if in a trance, he hadn't even noticed the incredible sunset off to his left. In his mind, he was running over sequences, peptides, nucleotides, and oligonucleotides. He wore a smirk of extreme satisfaction, almost holy shit! on his face.

The process of amplifying DNA by the repeated reciprocal extension of two primers hybridized to the separate strands of a particular DNA sequence was mine. Someone else may have come along sooner or later and thought of PCR, but I did it first. And now I was a Nobel Prize winner. I've never been to Sweden. Perhaps I should get to Mendocino first.

He turned the key, and the Ford roared to life. He smiled. Pulling back on to route 128, he pushed the pedal to the floor and gravel flew into the buckeyes on the road's shoulder behind him. The wheels spun wildly until finally gripping the concrete. The car lurched forward, back wheels screaming and burning rubber into the pavement.

I wonder whatever happened to Jennifer, he thought.

Mullis purchased the cabin in 1975, during his Berkley days. Located along the Navarro River in Mendocino County, it was rustic and isolated. Driving the final twenty miles through the mountainous roads was the ultimate functional sobriety test. Only someone with a death wish would even consider driving this dangerous stretch with an ounce of alcohol in their system. Mullis was tired and desperately needed a bathroom, so he pushed the Mustang hard through the tight switchback turns toward relief.

Flipping the light switch on brought the rustic cabin to life. The distinct smell of aged wood always welcomed him, like a dear friend that was waiting for his return. He dropped the two bags of groceries he'd bought at the Safeway in Healdsburg off in the kitchen and grabbed the heavy flashlight he would need to answer nature's call, out in nature. The bathroom was located about fifty feet west of the cabin and down a slight hill. Most of Mullis's visitors thought this to be a horrible inconvenience and couldn't understand why he had never installed a john in the house. For Mullis, there was something communal about the custom-carved redwood seat in the dark. The sounds of owls in the valley below and the stars above made the necessary acts of bodily functions a more pleasurable experience. He walked down the three earthen steps and followed the path north for twenty feet when he noticed something that caused him to stop. At the far end of the path under a fir tree, there was something glowing.

There's no power out here, so whatever it was, it had to be battery operated, he thought. Startled, he felt his pulse rise and told himself to calm down as the scientist in him took over. He slowly took a couple of steps closer, expecting it to move, but the glowing shape just sat motionless. He was tired and probably still a little hungover from the two days of partying, but that wouldn't cause him to hallucinate now. He pointed his flashlight at the object, which made it glow brighter where the beam of light hit it. *Is someone playing a joke?* he wondered. He did a 360-degree sweep with his flashlight, revealing nothing but trees. He inched closer, more interested and intrigued than frightened. It began to take shape. About three feet tall, it looked like some kind of small animal sitting up on its hind legs. It was facing his direction, and its shifty little black eyes seemed to be looking right at him as Mullis approached to within just a couple of feet.

A raccoon. A glowing raccoon!

"Good evening, Doctor," the raccoon said.

"Hello," Mullis answered.

It was early morning, and Mullis was walking down the road toward his cabin. He had no idea how he had come to be here. Confusion was quickly turning to concern. He had no recollection of the night before. The last thing he could remember was that bizarre moment. He wondered if he had fallen, been hurt, and knocked out in the woods. But his clothes would certainly have been dirty and damp from the morning dew covering the ground. Instead, they were clean and dry. The last thing he could remember was pointing his flashlight at the glowing raccoon.

Did that actually happen? And where's my fucking flashlight?

It was as clear a memory as his early-morning brain allowed.

Yes. I remembered the little bastard and his courteous greeting. I remembered the way my flashlight looked on his already glowing face. Where the fuck is my flashlight? Mullis walked back to the cabin to find it exactly as he had left it the night before. The lights were on and the back door was open. The bags of groceries were still on the kitchen counter. The orange juice was warm and the ice cream had completely melted, proving further that he had been gone for several hours but where? The scientist in him was well aware of alien encounters people throughout the world claimed to have experienced. Without proof, however, Mullis was as skeptical as the next person. But something happened that was unexplainable and unbelievable, but it happened. He would have to keep this to himself. The press was having a field day with the surfing scientist angle, and this could tarnish not only his work but also the Nobel Prize itself. There would be no mention of glowing raccoons in Stockholm.

A few years later, Mullis received a call from his daughter, Louise. She had just returned home to Portland from a long weekend at his cabin with her fiancé and had to tell her father of the strange experience she had.

It was eerily similar to Mullis's. Upon arriving at the Mendocino cabin, she went down the hill to use the facilities. Three hours later, she was walking down the same hill Mullis found himself wandering.

"Did you see the glowing raccoon?" Mullis interrupted.

"The what? No. I don't remember anything. I walked out the back door, and the next thing I remember, I was walking down the hill, back to the cabin," Louise said.

Her fiancé was frantic. When he found her safe and uninjured, he was relieved but bewildered. For three hours, he searched the entire area around the cabin but found no sign of Louise. It was as if she just disappeared. And then reappeared.

For Kary Mullis, it was just another strange event in his extraordinary life. Mullis received the Nobel Prize for chemistry and had changed science forever. To this day, he continues working, surfing, and experiencing many uncommon occurrences, which provides entertaining content for his unique observations. However, the glowing raccoon will always remain a mystery.

"I wouldn't try to publish a scientific paper about it because I can't do any experiments. I can't make glowing raccoons appear. I can't buy them from a scientific supply store to study. I can't cause myself to be lost again for several hours. But I don't deny what happened. It's what science calls anecdotal because it only happened in a way that you can't reproduce.

But it happened."

8

Weird Science

London

November 1994

The small conference room had been transformed into somewhat of an operating theater by the two scientists from the University of London's Department of Molecular Genetics. It had taken months of requests, official letters, and a little arm-twisting, but the Royal Institute of Science had finally agreed to allow Dr. Russell Becker and his assistant Dr. Kenneth Allwood into their sprawling facility a few blocks from Piccadilly Circus in Downtown London. Dressed in surgical garb from their heads to their feet, Allwood, Becker, and the Royal Institute's representative, Jeffrey Grunther, waited quietly for the delivery of the glass jar containing the objects.

A small clean room had been hastily assembled just outside the conference room's only door. It was, in actuality, a tent made of plastic draping and pipes the scientists had brought with them. It was decided that the jar would be handed to Grunther in the clean room who, in turn, would carry it into the theater of operation, where they now waited. He was a senior member of the Department of Artifacts at the institute, and as such, Grunther was entrusted with observing the procedure. His job was to make sure Allwood and Becker did exactly what they had requested and agreed to do via the dozens of e-mails, letters, and finally, the executed contract exchanged between the two scientific institutes. Grunther was confident and comfortable playing the role but, being short and squat in stature, was uncomfortable wearing the surgical scrubs that were clearly too large, thanks to Becker.

"It's taking them bloody long enough, isn't it?" Allwood asked.

"Be patient, young Padawan," Becker responded, quoting from one of his favorite movies. "I'm sure they're performing some secret ceremony before moving it," he continued with a smirk. "Ah, it's Jeffrey, right?" he asked Grunther, turning his attention to the chubby man from the Royal Institute.

"That's right. Jeffrey Grunther."

"Well, Jeffrey Grunther, you may want to roll up the bottom of your knickers before they get here. Don't want you tripping over your scrubs and breaking the jar. That would ruin the day for all of us, I should imagine."

"Quite," Grunther responded as he bent over and did his best to roll up the pant legs that were at least ten inches too long and extremely baggy.

Allwood smirked and looked at Becker who winked back. "You did remember to bring the pitcher and fill it with water, didn't you?" Becker whispered to Allwood.

"Of course, it's under the table," Allwood responded still confused as to its purpose, but Becker always had his reasons.

"Excellent, Igor. You know, I could do something about that hump," Becker joked.

"Hump? What hump?" Allwood responded, slightly hunching over and dropping his left arm lower than his right arm, doing his best Marty Feldman impersonation from *Young Frankenstein*.

There was a knock at the door. Grunther stood upright, having just finished folding up his pant legs. He squared his shoulders, nodded to Becker and Allwood, and turned toward the door. He looked like a large meatball in an aqua green bag, and his pants squeaked between his chubby legs with each step, providing comedic audio to accompany the visual. Becker and Allwood squared their shoulders, looked at each other, and nodded in the same fashion Grunther had just done. Allwood stretched his right hand straight out from the shoulder, palm down in a Nazi salute, but Becker quickly slammed the arm back to Allwood's side. Then gave him a look of "What's wrong with you?"

A moment later, the door opened slowly, and Grunther reentered the room carrying a glass jar that was fourteen inches tall and eight inches in diameter. He held the jar in both hands and closed the door behind him with his foot. He stared at the jar, carefully stepping very slowly so as not to disturb its contents. The quick squeaking noise from a moment ago was replaced by a lower and slower hissing sound coming from Grunther's inner thighs. Becker just shook his head, hardly able to believe what Grunther looked and sounded like.

The Royal Institute's representative placed the jar down on the table. The liquid inside sloshed from side to side, and Grunther held his hands just off the jar as if that would make the liquid become still. He then slowly stood back up and took a half step away from the table as if to say "I have delivered what you requested."

Becker nodded at him and squared his shoulders again, mimicking Grunther's earlier actions. He leaned down and peered into the jar. The liquid filled the container about three-quarters to the top, and the pair of objects that was the focus of the room, as well as scientific inquiry for a century and a half, rested at the bottom, seemingly looking back at Becker, albeit in a drunken haze.

"All right then. Let's begin," Becker announced.

"Please, Doctor, be very careful," pleaded Grunther.

"Mr. Grunther, we are scientists, serious in our profession and trained to perform this procedure better than anyone else in the world. There is no cause for alarm. Masks on," he said, and all three men put on their surgical masks.

"Mr. Allwood!" Becker said authoritatively while removing the top to the jar.

"Yes, Doctor," Allwood snapped back.

"Hand me the grabby, squeezing, salad-prongy thingamajig," he commanded.

Allwood handed him the surgical instrument, trying to remain serious. Becker reached into the jar and removed one of the objects, carefully placing it into a flat steel pan on the table. The pan was six inches long by three wide and contained about one-fourth inch of formaldehyde at the bottom. All three of them leaned in for a closer look now that it had been removed from the cloudy liquid. Becker peered up at Grunther, who continued to gaze on the object in the pan.

"Boo," Becker said softly at Grunther.

Grunther snapped up and away, startled. Then he smirked with embarrassment.

"Sorry, Mr. Becker. It's just that the last time someone saw this without having to look through that bloody, foggy liquid was 151 years ago. It's quite a moving moment for me," said Grunther.

"It's all right, Mr. Grunther. I'm sure the handful of Royal Institute people standing outside that door right now would love to be in your shoes," Becker quipped.

"Actually, sir, it's more than twenty-five very nervous Royal Institute people standing outside that door right now," Grunther corrected.

"Right. Mr. Allwood, hand me the sharp silver cutting butter-knife-like utensil, please," Becker requested.

"The scalpel, sir," Allwood replied, slapping the scalpel into his hand.

Holding the object firmly but delicately so as not to damage it, Becker calmly sliced off a piece of it about half an inch wide by one inch long and as thin as a piece of newspaper. He grabbed the delicate slice with a tweezer and pulled a small jar from the padded steel briefcase on the table. The padding had holes cut into it the exact shape and size of the jars it carried. Allwood unscrewed the cap, and Becker dropped the slice into the liquid inside. Allwood quickly replaced the cap.

"Syringe, please, Kenny?" Becker asked.

"What's that?" Allwood responded with a smirk.

"I'll do the jokes. Syringe," Becker deadpanned.

Becker stuck the needle into the middle of the object in the pan and drew a small amount of fluid from it. He handed the syringe to Allwood, who carefully squeezed it into a smaller empty jar and then packed it away in the padded briefcase. Finished with the first object, he placed it back into the jar, took the second one out, and repeated the process. After finishing their work, Becker carefully put the lid on the large jar as Allwood packed up the briefcase.

Grunther breathed a sigh of relief now that it was all finished and the jar was sealed.

"See? I told you there was nothing to worry about," Becker said reassuringly.

Grunther smiled, thanked them for their professionalism and reached for the jar.

"Oh, we're not quite finished," Becker said as Grunther stopped in his tracks.

"We're not?" he asked.

"Just one more thing we need to do. Mr. Allwood, the pitcher of water, please," he requested.

Allwood reached under the table and handed the pitcher to Becker, still unsure of its purpose. Grunther tilted his head, and his face held a look of confusion and some concern. Becker held the pitcher with both hands under its bottom, just as Grunther had done with the jar when he entered the room, and slowly walked the ten feet to the door. Standing just alongside of it, he looked back over his shoulder at the other two men and then smiled. He lifted it over his head and let it drop to the floor while jumping away from the crash. The glass pitcher shattered, and the water splashed and sprayed his legs, the door, and the wall.

"Oh my god!" Becker shouted at the top of his lungs.

The door swung open, and twenty-five men and women pushed through the door, two at time, rushing in to the room to view the cataclysmic event that had just occurred. The Royal Institute of Science members' anger and dread turned to confusion when they saw, what appeared to be, the real jar containing John Dalton's eyes on the operating table in one piece. Becker shook his head, grinning, and then shook Grunther's hand firmly and sincerely. He turned and walked out of the conference room, broken glass crackling beneath his black dress shoes. Allwood grabbed the briefcase, nodded politely to Grunther, and followed Becker, leaving the smiling Grunther to deal with the Benny Hill-like scene.

Washington, DC

March 1995

The Armed Forces Institute of Pathology was located on the very border of our nation's capital city. The three-story building being devoid of any architectural substance was cold and bland even for a government building. Built at the height of the Cold War in the 1950s, its windowless walls were three-feet-thick steel-reinforced concrete. The reasoning for such a monstrosity to the aesthetic eye was safety and protection. The government planned on the early warning radar to alert the city of an incoming atomic attack. The location of the building was close enough to evacuate the president, his staff, and as many members of Congress as possible to this safe house. When it was discovered that the building would not withstand the blast of a hydrogen bomb, its blueprints were thankfully destroyed, and no other building was constructed in its likeliness.

Dr. Jeffrey Taubenberger was a microbiologist on a team with approximately twenty scientists at the institute who worked on various experiments, research, and government projects as directed. As scientists, they scoured medical and scientific journals to keep up with the latest news from this evolving field. Once a week, the group met during lunch in the conference room for an open discussion. Each scientist took turns leading the discussion on whatever subject they thought interesting enough to present to the group. Today it was Taubenberger's turn to lead.

The February 17, 1995, issue of *Science* had just arrived, and it contained a story that Taubenberger found fascinating about John Dalton's eyes. Born in 1766, Dalton was a famous chemist who was the first to suggest the atomic theory of matter: that all things were made up of tiny unseen particles called atoms. He was, in fact, so famous that until this day, the John Dalton Society exists to commemorate and celebrate this brilliant scientist's work and life. It wasn't Dalton's work that intrigued Taubenberger but rather his eyes. The article on page 984 featured a new procedure that unlocked the secret to Dalton's color blindness, something he suffered with his entire life and scientists had failed to understand.

Dalton and his brother suffered from a condition that caused him to confuse scarlet with green and pink with blue. In 1794, he mistakenly wore a red garment instead of the black required by his Quaker faith and was reprimanded by his fellow religious followers. Dalton was troubled very little by his Quaker brothers' chastising, but he was fascinated by its cause. Why did he and his brother see colors differently from the rest of the world, he wondered. He had many theories, but the only way to prove the cause conclusively was to cut out one of his eyes, a sacrifice not even this dedicated scientist was willing to make. On July 27, 1844, Dalton died. At his request, Dalton's assistant, Joseph Ransome, removed Dalton's eyes from his corpse. Dalton had asked Ransome to test his hypothesis that the liquid inside his eyes was shaded blue instead of clear like a normal eye. This would explain his problems of seeing red and green in the color spectrum.

Ransome fulfilled his promise to his mentor and friend that very day, carefully pouring the liquid into a glass, only to discover that the liquid was clear. Dalton's hypothesis was wrong. Next, Ransome cut a small hole in the back of Dalton's eye and peered through it. Again, the images were clear. Ransome could think of no other explanation other than Dalton possibly having a defect in the nerves from the eye to his brain. Out of options, he preserved the two eyeballs in a jar of formaldehyde, which are kept to this day at the Royal Institute of Science in London.

At the University of London, the Department of Molecular Genetics had been trying for months and had finally received permission from the Society to extract enough DNA from Dalton's preserved eyes and conduct experiments. They concluded that his condition was caused by deuteranopia, a form of color blindness because of the retina lacking the middle-wave photopigment, causing the subject to be unable to see the color green.

One hundred and fifty-one years after Dalton's death, the puzzle was finally solved, thanks to a revolutionary new procedure called polymerase chain reaction, PCR.

Taubenberger asked the group what other great mysteries from the past were waiting to be unlocked. If scientists at the University of London could solve this century-and-a-half-old question by researching and studying the DNA from a tiny piece of Dalton's eyes, what brilliant discoveries were waiting for the scientists at the Institute of Pathology, which contained millions of samples dating back to the Civil War? The group, which had listened quietly while eating their lunch, now perked up with enthusiasm. Suggestions poured out of their mouths along with pieces of their sandwiches and salads. By the end of lunch, they had yet to discover the project they searched for. However, the discussion didn't end when they left the conference room.

For days, suggestions were left via notes on Taubenberger's desk or mentioned while passing by coworkers in the hallways. Still, nothing intrigued his scientific curiosity.

Taubenberger and his lab technician of many years, Ann Reid, discussed the possibility of an important scientific project at every opportunity. Every time one of them suggested a subject, both agreed it wasn't what they were looking for. Then one afternoon, a coworker suggested the influenza virus of 1918.

It was perfect, thought Taubenberger. The deadly killer of hundreds of millions of people around the world at the turn of the century has never been solved. Taubenberger knew little of it other than what he had studied in school and that wasn't much. Reid had never heard of it. This was the project.

I'm not aware of anyone else working on it. We must have samples of people who died from the pandemic here in the archives. We can become famous for this research, his mind was running at a million miles per hour.

Immediately, Taubenberger went to his superiors and told them of the project he would like to launch. He explained the rational, the new science, and the good it could do. If they could find the virus in lung tissue stored at the Pathology Institute from a subject who died from influenza in 1918, they may be able to find the cause of the pandemic and, more importantly, possibly stop the next one. They agreed and approved the research project.

The first thing Reid and Taubenberger did was read Alfred Crosby's book *America's Forgotten Pandemic.* Their research begun, Reid studied and perfected the polymerase chain reaction. Ann Reid was the ideal person to perform the work since she had more experience working with tiny paraffin wax samples at the institute than any other technician. She had little experience with the PCR procedure but was a quick learner and studied endlessly how to do it perfectly and accurately. Taubenberger and Reid were ready. Now they needed to find samples containing the virus.

The institute's warehouse had moved a number of times since its founding during the Civil War and with good reason. Doctors from all over the country, indeed all over the world, sent samples for the institute to research and store all the time. The warehouse was currently located a few blocks from the institute. It was a climate-controlled, fireproof, state-of-the-art building, and every sample since 1917 was cataloged in the institute's computer system. *It was too good to be true,* thought Taubenberger. When he and Ann went to pick up their first samples for testing, he got a firsthand look at the warehouse, which closely resembled the one where the Ark of the Covenant was stored at the end of *Raiders of the Lost Ark.* Taubenberger had requested the warehouse to provide a list of lung samples from young adults in their twenties or thirties who had died in a matter of days after becoming ill with virus. The computer generated a list of seventy samples fitting that description. Taubenberger selected the six samples he felt were most likely to contain the virus. He and Reid each picked three names, got their bearings using signs on the walls and computer printout maps in their hands, and went off in different directions in the massive warehouse. The first name Taubenberger selected was Pvt. Roscoe Vaughn. Within moments of separating from Ann, they were a hundred yards apart and still walking farther away from each other. *The inside of the warehouse had to be several acres in size,* he thought. *It's fairly dust free, which means their air-purification system is a good one. Not good enough to keep out the mice,* he thought, noticing one struggling to escape glue paper at his feet.

Taubenberger knelt to get a closer look at this tiny struggle for life. Its back legs were stuck in the glue, but its front legs were free and they reached just beyond the sticky paper. Using its front legs only, the tiny mouse was dragging the one-foot square paper down the hallway, desperately struggling toward some unknown and totally useless destination. Just its will to survive pushing it forward, trying to stay one step ahead of the death that was its certain and unyielding fate.

"Found my first sample!" Reid yelled from what seemed to be a mile away.

Taubenberger stood up and continued on his way toward his first sample. He turned left off the main hallway and down the aisle that contained the spectrum of numbers in which his sample was located. He found the proper shelf and checked the number again on the computer page against the numbers on the boxes. Walking toward his right, following the progressing numbers, he finally stopped. He looked at the number on the box and then at the number on the sheet in his hand. This was it.

He pulled the box off the shelf, pulled on surgical gloves, and opened the lid. There was no dramatic music or cool sound FX as there was in *Raiders* the first time the ark was opened; however, he paused for just a second when he realized that the last time this box was opened was probably 1918. He gently thumbed through the well-stored wax samples of human organs containing a variety of diseases until he came to the proper number. Sliding it out, Taubenberger wondered if this sample from a young man who died in September 1918 at Camp Jackson in South Carolina still contained the deadly killer. And if so, could he find it?

"Hello, Private Vaughn," Taubenberger said to the paraffin wax and slipped it into a plastic bag.

Ann Reid got to work immediately on the samples. Unfortunately for her, the work was nothing like the excitement and pulsating action of science in television or the movies. The work was tedious and slow. The paraffin wax blocks retrieved from the warehouse that contained the lung samples were the size of a thumbnail. Reid's first step was to slice a sheet from the sample by hand using a sharp razor-like tool. Each sheet she sliced was one cell thick. After many further steps using chemicals, centrifuges, solvents, test tubes, and finally PCR, the virus should appear on a fifteen-by-seventeen-inch piece of x-ray film as black splotches. That is, of course, if the samples were from people who actually died from the virus, if the virus cells were still present in the samples, if the samples weren't contaminated during storage, or since then, if, if, if . . .

Time and again, she repeated the process, only to find the x-ray film blank. Negative. The virus wasn't there or they were doing something wrong. It was frustrating. For eighteen months, Ann worked with the samples. While she was meeting with failure each time, Taubenberger continued his research into the virus. He learned that the virus's unique nature caused the onset of other illnesses, mainly pneumonia, which was the cause of death in many victims. Healthy young adults died within days of acquiring the virus because one lung shut down rapidly because of the incredibly quick advance of pneumonia. Had this occurred slower, the other lung could help the body recover, but it was so fast and so violent that it shocked the body to the point that other major organs would just shut down. He needed to find the lung of a virus-infected victim that did not show signs of pneumonia. Roscoe Vaughn's information suggested just that.

The paperwork accompanying Vaughn's sample stated a Dr. K. P. Hegeforth performed the autopsy on Private Vaughn nearly eighty years earlier. His attention to detail was remarkable, considering it was wartime and an epidemic had broken out. Then Taubenberger realized that it had not broken out yet. If a doctor at such a large army base had this much time to autopsy the lungs and write such clear, precise notes, Vaughn may have been one of the first to die of the disease. In his paperwork, Hegeforth noted he was surprised to find one of Vaughn's lungs so ravaged by pneumonia while the other lung had not even a trace. This was Taubenberger's *Ark of the Covenant*. Vaughn's non–pneumonia-infected lung must contain the influenza virus.

Reid had set aside Vaughn's samples, assuming if one lung tested negative, then both would. Taubenberger explained to Reid his theory. She started work on Vaughn's non-pneumonia lung, trying to locate the matrix cell. A few weeks later, Reid was nearing the end of the long process of isolating the tiny lung sample from the young doughboy. The brain of the virus, the matrix cell, directs the virus to reproduce in its host as well as creates the chemical mutations of the virus. If Reid could find this matrix cell and use it as a fishhook, they should be able to reproduce the rest of the virus from the pieces of DNA they would extract from Vaughn's lung. But that was later. Right now, she only wanted to find proof that the virus existed in the sample so she placed a fifteen-by-seventeen-inch piece of x-ray film over the top of Vaughn's prepared lung sample and went home for the night. If Taubenberger's theory was correct and if she had performed the process properly and if the virus was still stored in the paraffin-encased piece of lung from 1918, then she should see the black splotches on the x-ray film in the morning. If . . .

Ann Reid didn't understand why, but she had a good feeling the next morning. Driving to the institute, she thought the entire process through in her mind, beginning with slicing the paraffin wax to the last procedure of adding the enzyme. Every step carefully replayed time and again, while driving the crowded streets of Washington. It had to work. *This was it,* she thought. She rushed into the drab-looking building, changed into her lab gear, and went straight to her table. She took a deep breath and lifted the x-ray film off the dish. She held it up to the light and stared at something she couldn't believe. There were black splotches on the x-ray film. She rushed out of the lab and up to Taubenberger's office on the third floor, unable to contain her excitement. She burst into his office with the film and saw her boss on the phone.

"Hang up," she managed to say, out of breath.

"Call ya right back," Taubenberger said into the phone. "What is it?"

Handing him the x-ray, she proclaimed, "The 1918 influenza virus!"

He held it up to the light and saw the black splotches and started to laugh and yell at the same time. He dropped the film on his desk, grabbed Ann by the hands, and they half-jumped, half-danced around his office, celebrating their first step in unlocking the secret of mankind's deadliest killer.

9

Etched in Silver, Forever

Seattle, Washington

March 30, 1919

After four games of the Stanley Cup Challenge Series, the Seattle Millionaires led the Montreal Canadiens two games to one with game 4 ending in a tie. Professional hockey in the West Coast league featured great skaters and exquisite playmaking, which differed vastly from the physical NHL.

Each league employed different rules as well, the most noticeable being the sixth skater in the PCHL: seven players on the ice, including the goaltender. NHL teams skated five players out, plus the goalie. To compensate for the difference, the cup trustees decided to switch the rules each game, starting with the PCHL rules for game 1.

The Canadiens were overmatched from the outset. The large hostile crowd added to the confusion of the sixth skater on the ice for the visitors. John McDonald, usually one of the three Canadien subs, was added as the team's sixth skater but never got into the flow of the game because he couldn't figure out where to go on the ice without getting in the way of his Canadien teammates. The Seattle fans enjoyed the best collisions during the game, which were those between McDonald and his unsuspecting Canadien teammates. Seattle blasted Montreal 7–0, much to the delight of the partisan American crowd.

Playing under NHL rules, game 2 took on a completely different appearance as Newsy scored all four Canadien goals and Joe Hall provided the fireworks in a 4–2 victory. Leading 3–0 in the second period, Hall inadvertently cracked his stick over the head of Seattle forward Cully Wilson. With Wilson lying on the ice bleeding from Hall's handiwork, defenseman Roy Rickey charged at Hall with two hands on his stick like a baseball player. Just before he was able to deliver retribution on Hall's noggin, Odie Cleghorn's flying tackle drove the Seattle player on to the ice, and the two combatants slid into the sideboards with a loud thud. The teams squared off, and fists were flying; everyone engaged, except for Hall who helped Cully to his feet and led him over to the Seattle bench to get stitched up. A bizarre scene played out as players from both teams pummeled their opponents with fists and sticks, while the person who started the melee, Joe Hall, was holding Wilson upright as the team doctor stitched his head. Ten minutes later, order was restored, and the teams lined up for the ensuing face-off in the Canadiens' end of the ice. The puck was sent behind Vezina's net where Hall stopped it and was about to make his move when Cully Wilson threw his body into Hall, driving him into the end boards with a devastating body check. Hall bounced back up, dropped his gloves, and Wilson did the same, finally getting their opportunity at the fight they had just missed out on. Hall landed a number of punches to Wilson's face, and he crumbled to the ice again. Holding the collar to Wilson's sweater, Hall loaded up for the final punch but realized Wilson was finished and just let go of the sweater. The referees stepped in and ended the carnage. The series was tied 1–1.

PCHL rules returned for game 3, and Seattle's Frank Foyston matched Newsy's goal output in the previous game as well as adding an assist on another goal during the 7–2 Seattle route.

Two days later, the greatest match ever played on the West Coast took place on Seattle's outdoor ice stadium. Playing under NHL rules again, the game was physically brutal but featured incredible skating, stick handling, scoring opportunities, and goaltending. After sixty minutes of regulation and twenty minutes of overtime, the sun had started to set, and ice conditions had become so poor that the game was called a tie, ending 0–0.

Four days after that historic game, the fifth game was to be played. On the morning of March 30, the Canadiens were still tired and sore. An extra day to recover didn't help Montreal as much as manager George Kennedy had hoped it would, so he decided to give his weary club a break and cancel the morning skate. They would need all the strength they could muster as once again, the Canadiens would be chasing the Millionaires around the ice under PCHL rules.

Two blocks from the stadium, George Washington Elementary School was in session. Newsy realized his coaching wasn't having the impact he'd hoped for on the Canadiens under the PCHL rules. Confusion still reigned when they added the extra skater, so Newsy made a quick stop at the school before arriving early for the game.

When the rest of the Canadiens entered the visitor's dressing room, they were surprised to see Lalonde standing by a blackboard that contained a lopsided hockey rink drawn on it.

"Ha! Going to teach us math today, Newsy?" Odie Cleghorn jokingly asked.

"Sit down, boys. School is in session. We have to play West Coast-style hockey if we're going to defend the cup. This," Newsy said, turning to the blackboard and pounding the chalk on the odd shape, "is the ice surface."

"Looks more like your crooked head," interrupted one of the Canadiens, which caused the rest of the team to giggle.

"That's fuckin' enough!" yelled Joe Hall. "Newsy's right. We're not fuckin' playing under fuckin' NHL rules tonight fuckin' again, and we're going to get our fuckin' asses kicked in if we can't figure out their fuckin' system. Now shut the fuck up and pay fuckin' attention."

No one laughed now as Joe turned back toward Newsy and motioned with his head and hand to continue. Joe Hall was a miserable person before every game, but tonight, his misery was reaching new levels, even for Joe. For the next two hours, Newsy drew the plays and schemes on the blackboard that Seattle had successfully used against the Canadiens. Chalk dust filled the air and floated to the floor in the cramped room as Newsy used X's and O's to explain what Seattle was doing and how Montreal had to counter it. The lecture turned into a confident discussion with multiple players offering ideas on how to defend and beat the Western style. Most of the Canadiens started to dress, but the defensive pair of Hall and Corbeau continued to draw angles and lines on the blackboard, strategizing how to shut down the high-flying Millionaires while they dressed. Lalonde, Pitre, Cleghorn, Berlinquette, Couture, and McDonald finally had their uniforms on and were using pucks on the floor to represent players on the ice and further their game plan with the extra skater. Vezina sat in the corner in full goaltending gear with his head back against the wall and his eyes closed.

They had discussed and strategized for so long, the Canadiens had missed most of the pregame skate. Before leaving the dressing room, Newsy addressed the team.

"Boys, this is a big one tonight. And I don't just mean because we have to play under PCHL rules again. That certainly is going to make climbing the mountain much more difficult. We have to win tonight, or we lose the cup. We can't look ahead. We can't assume we're going to play well enough to win tonight. We have to put our hearts, our health, and our courage on the line and leave it on the ice. There is no tomorrow if we lose this game. We lose the cup.

"Think about what we talked about in here. Yes, their rules are different, and that extra skater is new to us. But it's hockey. And the Montreal Canadiens are the best hockey team. Forget the rules. Forget their players. Forget the crowd. We are the better team.

"The Montreal Canadiens. Defending Stanley Cup Champions. Tonight, boys, we need to play like it. And after we win this game, we'll look forward to the next one. Then we'll talk about having our names etched on that thing again. Then we'll talk about walking together for the rest of our lives as back-to-back Stanley Cup champions and how all our children and our children's children will be able to read our names on that cup forever.

"Not now. Not tonight. Everyone take a knee."

The nine men rose in unison and knelt with one knee. They bowed their heads as Joe Hall performed the ritual he had done prior to every game since arriving in the trade to the Canadiens. He recited the Lord's Prayer. The rest of the players joined.

When they finally got to the ice, the crowd booed vigorously as the Canadiens took two quick laps around their end of the ice, attempting to quickly become accustomed to the playing surface.

The game started off badly for the Canadiens who seemed to be on their way to being routed again. Losing 3–0 early on, something suddenly clicked. They could see what Seattle was doing as if the chalkboard had come to life on the ice in front of them. All they had to do was apply what they discussed before the game. They did.

Lalonde scored twice, quickly, in the second period to pull Montreal to within a goal, 3–2. From then on, the end-to-end skating was interrupted only by violent collisions. With just four minutes remaining in the game, McDonald, the sixth skater for the Canadiens, appropriately scored the tying goal. Regulation ended 3–3, and both teams skated to the benches for the five-minute respite before overtime began. Both teams were feeling the physical effects of the second overtime in three games, especially Joe Hall who rested on the boards. His entire body seemed to be limp.

"You okay, Joe?" Newsy asked.

"Just tired. I can't seem to catch my breath," Hall's response was interrupted by uncontrollable coughs.

"Can you go?" Newsy asked.

"Yeah. Of course, I can," Joe said, finally standing up straight and turning to Newsy.

Hall's face was flush-red, and his ears seemed to have turned a different color, gray and ashen. He continued to cough while putting his gloves back on his hands. He reached for his stick as the referee blew his whistle to start OT.

The first five minutes of the extra period featured ruthless hitting at center ice as both teams tried to send a message that they were not about to back down. A wrist shot from Newsy was deflected high over the netting and play stopped. As the two teams lined up for the face-off, Newsy checked to make sure all his teammates were in their proper positions. Hall was bent over at his waist with his stick on his knees and his head drooping. Newsy skated over to his friend.

The ref blew a loud blast from his whistle. "Come on, Newsy!"

"Just a second," he responded. "Joe? You okay?"

"I can't . . . I can't . . ." he dropped to one knee.

Newsy grabbed him by the arm and pulled him to his feet. "It's okay. Let's get you to the bench," Newsy said, helping his teammate.

Newsy skated Hall to the Canadiens' bench while the Seattle fans booed and heckled their antagonist. Kennedy and Cleghorn helped him onto the bench as the rest of the Canadiens skated over to see what was wrong with their star defenseman.

Hall dropped to the bench hard and leaned over with his elbows resting on his knees. "I can't breathe" was all he could manage between coughs.

"Odie, you're in. Me and Pitre will move to defense, and Corbeau and Cleghorn move to forwards. Let's go, boys," Newsy said very matter-of-factly while Kennedy summoned for the doctor.

For the next ten minutes, the action remained almost exclusively in the Seattle end as Lalonde and Didier Pitre were impregnable on defense. With just 4:03 left in overtime, Odie Cleghorn scored the winning goal for the Canadiens. The entire team rushed the hero of game 5, hugging and patting him on the head. The series was tied, and the Canadiens knew they would hold the advantage for the deciding game 6 with NHL rules being employed. Joe Hall remained on the bench, unable to do much more than smile, so the Canadiens skated to him to join in the celebration. Hall stood at the bench, holding on to the boards. The Canadiens were still celebrating as they approached him when Hall coughed violently, spraying a red foam on to the boards and the ice. Then he collapsed.

10

New Doors (Same as the Old Doors)

Washington, DC

Spring 1997

The thrill and celebration of two years earlier was now a distant memory for Ann Reid and Jeffrey Taubenberger. They had been successful in finding the matrix gene that had eluded them for a year and a half in Pvt. Roscoe Vaughn's lung sample, only to be disappointed by the trail ending there.

Scientifically, Reid and Taubenberger had made incredible strides toward finding the killer flu virus. Locating the matrix gene in a sample housed in the institute's warehouse for eighty years was a modern miracle. They had combined painstaking patience working through the new processes of PCR with creative detective work, thereby bringing the secrets of the virus closer to discovery. The most terrifying part of the discovery was how closely the virus resembled the H5N1 bird flu currently mutating in several regions around the globe.

Their most disheartening discovery was that there was just not enough DNA left in the Vaughn sample to recreate the virus. They had glimpsed at a piece of the deadliest killer in history, only to have the trail go cold.

Taubenberger was disappointed but still dedicated, especially since they had gotten so close. He and Reid carefully searched every piece of Vaughn's remaining lung sample for more DNA, to no avail. He went back to the Army's Pathological Warehouse to search for more samples, and hope sprung anew when the computer revealed the lung samples of a Pvt. James Downs stored there. Downs had died just two hours before Vaughn and featured very similar symptoms. However, both of his lung samples were saturated with pneumonia-like conditions, and the virus was simply not present.

Taubenberger knew the science had worked. It was the samples that were flawed. Preserving and storing lung samples had changed very little since Vaughn and Downs had died, so to continue looking through the warehouse for paraffin-encased lung samples was probably not going to move the project forward. He needed samples from bodies that were frozen soon after death. Not an easy task since in 1918, during the worse pandemic in human history, bodies piled up in morgues, then churches, and finally alleys and streets. Death overwhelmed the medical community *and* the coroners. Constructing coffins suddenly became a prosperous business. It was a prehistoric time in the practice of medicine and the caring for decomposing bodies compared to present day. But the effectiveness and worldwide destructive power of this virus would also provide the next opportunity to track it down.

Scientists believe that an estimated one hundred million people perished from the virus in 1918 and 1919, and some accounts speculated the number of dead could be double that. Incredibly, it struck nearly every corner of the globe at practically the same time and most disturbing was its deadly effectiveness against a usually healthy and immune demographic. Young people in their twenties and thirties were the hardest hit, becoming ill and dying at an alarming speed. In his research, Taubenberger had read how villages in remote, isolated parts of the northern hemisphere were almost completely wiped out. This was his next target. If people from those remote villages were buried shortly after death in the frozen ground, there may be lung samples that have not deteriorated, still there, waiting for him. Permafrost was the key. Ground that was permanently frozen and undisturbed since the pandemic could contain the samples Taubenberger and Reid needed to continue their search.

It was time to go public and get the word out to the scientific community. While Taubenberger wrote the article for *Science* magazine describing what they had accomplished and what they were searching for next, Reid searched for the areas where permafrost existed to cross-reference with burial grounds. To their amazement, two scientific research teams were currently looking for the exact same thing. One group was well financed and staffed with world-class scientists from England, Canada, and the United States. The team of medical geologists and microbiologists were led by Kirsty Duncan, a world-renowned medical geographer from the University of Toronto. She had planned the expedition for four years and was now on location in Norway at the grave site of seven young miners who died from the 1918 flu. The other team had been bogged down for months with official requests to search and dig in the northern territories of Canada and was going nowhere. As Taubenberger delivered his paper to *Science*, word came from the Norwegian team that they had found the site, but the permafrost had melted several times over the years during thaws and the decomposed bodies held no worthy samples. Another dead end.

Undeterred, Taubenberger continued his research. He studied old medical journals and newspaper accounts leading up to the outbreak in 1918. They contained stories about smaller isolated outbreaks around the world for years preceding the catastrophic pandemic. Time and again, the flu would reappear, and each time, it became a more efficient killer, circumstances eerily similar to what was going on at the end of the twentieth century and the start of the twenty-first. H5N1, well-known to viral scientists the world over, was becoming more familiar to the public masses. Avian flu had caused panic several times during the 1990s when it mutated and spread from birds to humans. Millions of poultry were destroyed each time an outbreak occurred, successfully containing the virus. The H5N1 virus is a deadly killer: swift, efficient, and there is no vaccine to defend humans. As of yet, there had been no human-to-human transfer of the virus, but scientists feared that day was not far off. Taubenberger knew the question wasn't "if that occurred" but rather "when?" Influenza history had a pattern of repeating approximately every one hundred years, and Taubenberger knew the key to stopping another pandemic was in finding DNA from a 1918 victim, unlocking the virus code, and creating a vaccine. The key was finding a 1918 flu victim buried in permafrost.

Alpine County, California

Spring 1997

It was a massive undertaking but still a labor of love. Building an exact replica of the fourteenth-century Norwegian Harbor home by hand had taken over four decades, but every notch, nail, and timber had been carved out of the California woods and assembled by Johan Hultin.

That love of labor could be traced back to his childhood and can be attributed to Hultin's stepfather, Dr. Carl Naeslund. When Johan was ten years old, his parents divorced. His mother remarried Naeslund and moved Johan to Sweden, where they began their new lives with Carl and his son. Naeslund was a well-known professor of medicine at the Karolinska Institute in Stockholm, which selected the Nobel Prize winners. Four years earlier, as chairman of the committee that chose the Nobel Prize for science, it was Naeslund who had the brief and bizarre call with Dr. Kary Mullis, abruptly ending with Mullis saying, "I'll take it."

At such a young and impressionable age, Hultin was in need of a father figure, and Naeslund filled the role. Hultin was fascinated by Naeslund's abilities in science and woodworking. Young Johan and Naeslund's biological son helped their father build a new home on the outskirts of Stockholm. The beautiful structure was Mediterranean in appearance, featuring an indoor pond and garden, which grew palm and fig trees, and so impressed the royal family of Sweden that years later, they bought the home for one of the royal princes.

When he was fifteen, Johan helped Naeslund build their summer home on the Baltic Sea. It was during this time with his stepfather that he developed his passion for microbiology, adventure, and carpentry, which influenced the rest of his life and kept him coming back to the California woods for nearly half a century to finish his cabin.

"I've asked myself, what is the satisfaction in this house? It's not to own it or use it, but it's in the building process, to see the house coming out of my hands," he explained to friends.

Dr. Hultin's hands had taken part in building many important and revolutionary projects throughout his storied career. He retired a dozen years earlier from his job as forensic pathologist in three major San Francisco hospitals, but he was so much more: respected scientist, inventor, automobile safety designer, mountain climber, and obviously, carpenter. The young man who left Sweden in 1949 to "attend medical school and see the world" had led an incredibly successful and exciting life. With his seventy-third birthday just a week away, he still lived his life by his credo: "Never quit."

He had first seen the Vastveitloftet as a child in Norway and immediately became fascinated by this ancient Norwegian structure. Its appearance was both odd and beautiful, but the structure's practical defenses explained the oddity. The smaller first level provides defenses from nature and intruders, supporting the larger second living area off the ground. Even the entrance is difficult to breach.

The house was raised, sitting on crisscrossing logs, keeping it safe from flooding and making access up to the door over the uneven stone steps burdensome for unwelcomed strangers. Once inside the first floor, a winding hallway leads uninvited guests through a maze before finally reaching the stairs to ascend to the second floor, which would afford the inhabitants time to prepare their defense. Originally constructed at Vastveit in Telemarken, Norway, this unique combination of beautiful craftsmanship and practical defenses is now housed in a museum in Sweden.

For half a century, Hultin toiled at his pet project when he wasn't skiing the twenty-five-thousand-foot peak of Mastagh Ata in China or receiving grants from the US Department of Transportation to establish and oversee the Automotive Safety Engineering Department at the Stanford Research Institute. Now nearly finished, Hultin and his second wife Eileen spent quiet time during his retirement in the rolling California hills forty miles outside the hamlet of Arnold while he perfected the final touches on the cabin.

In the clearing behind the structure, Hultin was working on the cabin's door, which was laid across two sawhorses. It was the third time he had attempted to build the door, finding it difficult to match with modern tools what the original builder had accomplished over five hundred years earlier. Hultin toiled in the early morning sun, its warmth just beginning to chase away the damp chill in the air and the dew on the ground.

"How's it going, honey?" Eileen said, startling her carpenter husband.

"Better. I think I have it this time. Did you eat breakfast?" he asked.

"Of course, dear." She leaned over and kissed his head. "I'm going to drive down to town to pick up the mail and a few other things. Do you need anything?"

"Just the Norwegian bastard who built the original door to show me what I'm doing wrong," he said with more than a hint of frustration.

"Can't help you with that, but I'm sure you'll figure it out. You always do. I'll be back in a couple of hours. Don't hurt yourself," she reminded him again.

Eileen made the trip back to Arnold twice a week for mail, groceries, and other essentials. Two weeks earlier, Hultin's *Science* magazine was part of her delivery. While he tried to work a difficult tongue into its groove on the door, he thought back to that moment. Settling down to read his favorite periodical with a cup of green tea, he thumbed through the pages until he came upon an article that captured his attention entirely. It was written by a Dr. Jeffrey Taubenberger from the US Army's Pathological Department and explained, in great detail, his project of researching the virus associated with the 1918 influenza pandemic. He read the article carefully, absorbing each step described by this young scientist on the other side of the continent.

Of course! What a brilliant idea to retrieve the lung samples from the army's warehouse, he thought. As he read on, he was disappointed to learn of Taubenberger's and Reid's dead end: the lack of DNA to retrieve the strand for PCR to reproduce it. *But they got close,* he thought. *They need lung samples from people who died and were quickly buried in permafrost. I've done this. I know where they are, and I can go back to Alaska and get the samples Taubenberger and Reid so desperately need.*

Hultin had read about the polymerase chain reaction a few years earlier and knew this was the process that could unlock the secrets of mankind's deadliest killer. Now here was a scientist who put that process into practice and had actually looked at the virus. Something Hultin was unable to do in 1951. Science had finally progressed to a point where it enabled its practitioners the chance to work with tiny samples of genetic code and, more importantly, reproduce them.

Immediately, Hultin sat down to write a letter to Taubenberger. But it would have to be crafted very carefully. How was he to tell the world's leading authority on the 1918 flu virus that he knew where victims were buried in Alaskan permafrost, that he knew how to retrieve the lung samples, and that at seventy-two years old, would make the trip alone in order to keep it quiet should anything go wrong? *What could go wrong?* he thought. *How about the possibility of unleashing the most lethal organism in the history of man back on humanity? No, that couldn't happen. It didn't in 1951. The disease was dead. If it didn't happen then, it wouldn't happen now. But would Taubenberger believe me? Would I believe me if I were him? Probably not,* he thought. The letter would have to be written with enough information from his first trip but not appear overly aggressive.

Hultin's third attempt at the letter finally seemed professional and sane enough that Taubenberger wouldn't think he was a lunatic. With just enough information about his expedition forty-six years earlier and the resulting failure in his lab, he thought Taubenberger's interest and scientific curiosity may cause him to respond.

The tongue in the door's plank snapped in his hand before it had come to rest in the groove. Hultin stood upright and looked with disgust at his latest failure. He picked the nearly finished door up off the sawhorses, walked to the edge of the clearing, and tossed it on the remains of the first two attempts as well as material from his first two attempts at building the chimney, which was thankfully finished and functioning. He continued over to his lumber pile, picked up a number of planks, and prepared to start over. Never quit.

Eileen's car could be heard pulling down the quarter-mile-long dirt lane to the cabin as he lay what he hoped would be the beginning of the final door on the sawhorses. She jumped out of the car and ran around the back of the cabin. Eileen wasn't prone to such emotional and physical displays, which concerned her husband.

"Eileen, everything okay?" he asked.

Handing him an envelope and speaking through excited breaths, she managed to say, "Look at what came in the mail. I know you've been waiting for this, so I didn't even do any shopping. I just hopped in the car and drove straight back."

Hultin took the envelope and read the return address. It was from the Armed Forces Institute of Pathology in Washington, DC. He looked up at his wife and smiled a faint smile, not wanting to be too excited and therefore too disappointed if the contents contained a generic letter of "thanks for your interest, but we're not in need of your help at this time." He opened the envelope and pulled out the letter. Eileen watched his expression change from concern to a faint smile and then a large grin.

"He's fascinated by what I wrote to him, blah, blah, blah, and wants me to call him as soon as possible at the number below," he said, skimming through Taubenberger's letter and realizing he had not provided his phone number in the original correspondence. "What time is it on the East Coast?" he asked Eileen.

She checked her watch. "It's 8:35 a.m. here, so 11:35 a.m. in Washington," she told him.

"Let's give Dr. Taubenberger a shout, shall we?" he asked with confidence.

A life full of astonishing achievement with one glaring near miss was about to be offered the opportunity to finally accomplish that which had eluded him. Hultin had waited for this day since his failure in the lab forty-six years earlier. Now he tried to calm himself as he hurried into the cabin to retrieve his cell phone. The door to the cabin will have to wait. Another more important door had just opened.

"Hello, Dr. Taubenberger's office."

"Hello, Dr. Jeffrey Taubenberger, please," Hultin requested with authority while sitting down in the same chair in which he read Taubenberger's *Science* magazine article a week earlier.

"Who may I tell him is calling?" asked the young female voice at the other end of the line.

"Tell him it's Dr. Johan Hultin."

"Can you spell that, please?"

He did.

"Please hold," she said.

Hultin's heart raced. A few moments passed when he heard someone pick up the phone.

"This is Taubenberger."

"Dr. Taubenberger, this is Dr. Johan Hultin. I'm calling in response to your letter."

"Yes, yes! Dr. Hultin, please hold on for just a second."

The line went quiet again.

Taubenberger put me on hold. He sounded excited to hear from me. Why did he put me on hold? That was strange.

"Hello, Dr. Hultin?" the voice sounded different this time. "Sorry to put you on hold, I have you on speaker, and I'm with Dr. Ann Reid who's helping me on this project," he said.

"Good morning, Dr. Reid. Nice to meet you both."

"Good morning, Dr. Hultin. The pleasure is ours," Reid responded.

"Thank you for taking the time to reach out to us. We're excited to speak with you and very impressed with your previous trip and what you accomplished. Can you be more specific than you were in your letter? Where exactly did you find the frozen bodies?" asked Taubenberger, both as a scientific inquiry and a test of validity.

"Of course, the bodies were found near a small village on the Bering Sea called Brevig. It's just north of Nome, about seventy miles north if I remember correctly," Hultin went on and explained the location in more detail. At the other end of the call, Reid had laid out her geological map of Alaska on Taubenberger's desk, and as soon as Brevig was mentioned, they confirmed that the area did, in fact, contain permafrost. Perhaps Dr. Hultin was the miracle they needed.

"Yes, we're familiar with Brevig, Dr. Hultin," interrupted Taubenberger. "The corpses, can you describe their condition for us?"

"Well, in 1951, they were in pretty damn, uh, darn good condition," Hultin went on to describe the bodies in detailed medical terminology, impressing Taubenberger and Reid. Hultin did know his stuff and was indeed legitimate.

"Dr. Hultin, how quickly can you get your team together and return to the site?" asked Taubenberger, trying to contain his excitement. He and Reid were hoping Hultin would be able to assemble his team, raise the funds he would need through scientific grants and, if need be, supported by Taubenberger's budget, and make the trek back to Alaska in the next three months. A difficult schedule to request knowing that the trip to the seven miner's grave site in Norway took years to plan, months to execute, and cost hundreds of thousands of dollars before ending in disappointment. This was too good to be true, and Taubenberger didn't want to push the old man on the phone.

"My team? You're speaking to my team. I can't go next week because it's my birthday, but I could probably go the following week. I just have to take care of a couple of personal things," Hultin said, looking at Eileen as if to say, "Okay with you?" Eileen's expressions rarely hid her emotions, and now her face revealed frustration and disappointment.

At the other end of the call, there was nothing said in response. Reid and Taubenberger could not believe what they had just heard.

"Hello?" Hultin asked.

"Ah yes. That timing should work for us as well. Do you need anything from us, Dr. Hultin? Any help at all?" Taubenberger said.

"No, I don't think so. The only thing I would request is that we keep this quiet. I read all about the expedition to Norway. A lot of press about nothing and too much controversy over the risk of finding and then releasing the disease again. Let's try to avoid all that. I know the disease is dead, but just in case any unforeseen phenomenon occurs, you won't be tied to my expedition in any way. It will just be the three of us who know about this. I don't think we want the embarrassment of finding the permafrost in Alaska has thawed like in Norway. I'll call you back if anything changes, but expect the samples in about three to four weeks. That is, of course, if all goes well."

"Of course, Dr. Hultin. We're here for you if anything comes up. Keep us informed as best you can and good luck," Taubenberger responded. He pushed the Speaker button on the phone and it went dead.

"What do you think?" asked Reid.

"Well, his credentials are impressive, and he seems legitimate. He also seems willing and able to do this. By himself! I guess we just wait three to four weeks and see what shows up," Taubenberger said, more hopeful than confident.

"I thought we agreed that you were done with this, Johan," Eileen said, using his proper first name as she always did when she was unable to hide her emotions.

"We did and I *am* done with mountain climbing and all my other adventures. But this is different. This is something I have to do. It's something that has clawed at me since I failed the first time," he said, staring at his cell phone in disbelief. He looked up at Eileen standing over him with her arms folded, then stood and embraced her. She firmly hugged him back. "Think of it as a rugged scientific excursion. My last one. I have to do this," he whispered into her ear.

"I know you do. I knew it since you read that article. I just hate the thought of you walking out that door again," Eileen commiserated.

Two weeks later

"Go get your things together. I have a couple of things to take care of outside that will take me a few minutes, and I'll meet you at the car," he said excitedly.

Eileen kissed him on his cheek and turned to the kitchen. She wanted to straighten up that room before gathering her overnight bag and bathroom essentials. Her slow disappointed walk was much different from Hultin's, who hustled out of the door to the backyard. He grabbed the wood from his fourth attempt at the door off the sawhorses and lay them on the ground next to the cabin for protection from the elements. Standing there for a moment, he realized that perhaps he should throw them back on to the lumber pile since he was just starting over. *What am I doing?* he thought. *This door is no longer the priority of the moment.* He chuckled with nervous excitement, packed up tools, and went running back into the house.

Eileen had already moved on to the bedroom, and the kitchen was his to rummage through, thankfully. After placing his tool belt by the kitchen door, he slowly and quietly opened a drawer in the kitchen's cabinet, listening for but not hearing approaching footsteps. He found and then grabbed the scissors. Holding them up, he studied them closely. *Too small*, he thought and put them back.

Next, he went through the knife drawer and inspected the inventory, but none would do the job he needed to do in the Alaskan wilderness. He looked around the kitchen, but nothing here was going to suffice. Then it hit him. Hultin hurried back out of the kitchen door, across the yard to Eileen's gardening shed. He ducked down to accommodate for the height of the small building and stepped inside after checking his trail. Confident that Eileen had not seen him, he surveyed the large assortment of tools.

Boy, she could start her own botanical gardens with this stuff, he thought.

He reached for the pruning shears hanging on pegs in the wall. They were obviously very new. The blades were still oiled and well over a foot long. The wooden handles were smooth, strong, and clean. It took a little strength to open them, and when he closed the shears shut again, the smooth sharp steel of the edges sliding over each other made a metallic sound that was music to Hultin's ears.

These are perfect, he thought. *I've got to get these out of here without her noticing.* He opened the door and peeked from the shed, back toward the cabin.

Eileen must still be in the house.

He slipped out of the shed and carefully closed its door so as not to make a sound, as a child, looking for Christmas presents in their parents' closet a week before the holiday. In his head, he could hear the theme song from one of his favorite TV shows from the seventies, *Hawaii Five-O*. He hummed along very softly. "I've got the pruning shears, Shteve."

What was the Hawaiian detective's name? he wondered. *That's not very important right now. Stay focused!* he told himself.

He hurried across the backyard toward the car out front. The seventy-two-year-old held the pruning shears by their blades in his left hand and searched his pants and coat pocket for his keys with his right. Both were empty. Still hustling, he switched the shears to his right hand, but he was closer to the cabin than he realized. The handles bumped off the side of the cabin with a thud, became free of his grip, and then landed on some rocks with a *ping*.

"Shit!" he said softly, turning to go back the two steps and retrieve the shears while glancing at the bedroom window two floors above his head. His left hand had found his keys in his pants pocket, and as he stooped to pick up the shears with his right hand, he dropped the keys. "Goddamn it!" He picked up the keys and calculated the time he had remaining before Eileen would be outside. There wasn't much time left, he realized, if any at all. He shoved the shears up the front of his jacket to hide them in case Eileen was ahead of her usual packing schedule. Running was now out of the question.

If I trip, I could impale myself on the shears, and Taubenberger would not be happy with the news that the old fool he asked to retrieve lung samples that hold the key to the worse pandemic in human history had to be postponed because of stupidity, he thought.

He walked quickly and cautiously, while newspaper headlines flashed through his mind: World Waits While Noted Scientist Recovers from Near-Fatal Pruning Accident.

Chin-ho. That was his name!

"Shteve, we've got your man, Shteve."

"Roger Chin, McGarrett out."

"Shteve, we've got the pruning shears!"

He finally arrived at the car with still no sign of Eileen. He opened the trunk of the car. A wool blanket kept for emergencies waited for him, and he buried the pruning shears in the back of the trunk under the unfolded blanket.

"What are you doing?" asked Eileen, suddenly behind him with the luggage.

"Just straightening the trunk, waiting for you," he said as innocently as possible. "Did you lock the door?" he asked, grabbing the bags.

Eileen's expression supplied the answer, but she responded anyway. "Of course. I don't know why you're knocking yourself out with that door you're building. The one that's there is perfectly fine," she said.

It worked, if Eileen had caught him sneaking her new pruning shears out of the shed, he had distracted her with another one of his obvious questions that annoyed her. "Honey, that door is from Home Depot. It's temporary. I don't think they had Home Depots in Norway during the fifteenth century."

Eileen's expression now read "No shit, Sherlock."

"Knock your socks off, honey," she said, shaking her head and patting him on the cheek. She started for the passenger door. Hultin beat her to the spot as he always did, opening it and helping her into the car. He closed the door behind her, and his face lit up as that child's would on Christmas morning. He nearly danced around the back of the car on his way to the driver's seat. "All set to go?" he asked.

"Just drive carefully. We're in no rush," she said.

He started the engine. *I* am, he thought.

11

Recovery?

April 1, 1919

James Tower Hospital was located in the Central District of Seattle, one of the most ethnically diverse neighborhoods in the United States. It was a fifteen-block walk from the hotel the Canadiens called home for the past three weeks. That walk seemed to take Newsy around the world inside this one city. Nearly every block had its own distinct culture, language, and aromas. Simply crossing the street, he stepped out of Chinatown and into the Jewish neighborhood. A few blocks later, he crossed through the Japanese, Negro, and the Dutch neighborhoods.

Newsy had made this trip to visit his friend the day before but was shocked and saddened by Joe Hall's appearance. He lay unconscious, curled up in a fetal position, coughing and spewing the red-frothy slime Newsy first saw the day of his daughter's birth. Jack McDonald had returned from the hospital to the hotel with word of a near-miraculous recovery of their Canadien teammate. Newsy quickly finished his lunch in the hotel restaurant and hurried to see for himself. Along the way, he had the good fortune of passing a general store. He stopped in to purchase liquor, root beer, and a ball of yarn.

Two blocks from the hospital, Newsy slipped the bottle of root beer into his pocket and then opened his trench coat. While keeping his brisk pace, he ripped a six-foot length of yarn off the ball he had just bought. He doubled the yarn up, making it stronger, then tied a knot about a foot from one end, creating a loop. The other end he tied tightly around the neck of the whiskey bottle. He slid his left arm out of his coat and then slid the loop up his arm and over his shoulder. The bottle now hung alongside his rib cage. Sliding his arm back into the coat, he climbed the twelve white stairs to James Tower Hospital, buttoned his coat, and concealed his present.

Newsy approached the nurse's desk just inside the impressive doorway and announced that he was returning to Joe Hall's room. The nurse did not immediately respond but rather just stared Newsy up and down. The six bottles of confiscated liquor sitting next to the papers she had been working on explained her reaction.

"Another teammate, I presume?" she asked.

"Yes, ma'am. Newsy Lalonde. Can I see him? I'm told his condition has improved greatly. I was here yesterday," Newsy went on excitedly.

The nurse was disinterested. "Give me the bottle," she stood and demanded, reaching her right hand out to receive it.

"Excuse me?" Newsy responded, acting as best he could to appear offended.

"The bottle. Give it to me. Liquor is not permitted on hospital grounds. You and your teammates should know better."

Newsy pulled his hands out of his coat pockets. "Miss Nurse, I have no liquor. I apologize for the behavior of my teammates, but I must say, if you know my reputation—"

"Empty the pockets, Mr. Lalonde," she interrupted. "I know who you are and your reputation. I can read, which is more than I can say for your teammates," she said, motioning to a sign on the wall behind her prohibiting alcohol.

Newsy pulled the bottle of root beer out of one pocket and turned the other inside out, revealing only lint and a copy of the score sheet from the previous game. "Is root beer prohibited as well?" he asked.

"Open your jacket, please," she continued, unimpressed. Newsy responded by tilting his head, incredulous and insulted by the request. "Open your jacket, Mr. Lalonde," she repeated.

Newsy adroitly unbuttoned the coat. Once done, he pushed the sides of the coat straight back, making sure the bottle would remain hidden inside the folded coat. A clear view of Newsy's entire body was provided to the nurse who was finally satisfied and a little embarrassed.

"Thank you. I'm sorry if I've insulted you, but we can't have people breaking the rules. You're going to walk straight down the hallway to the stairs on the left. Third floor, turn right, and you'll find Mr. Hall in the third door on the right," she directed.

He grabbed the root beer off her desk. "Thank you, nurse. I was here last night so I can confirm your explicit directions. You have a lovely day," he said semi-sarcastically, pulled his coat closed, and turned down the hall. When he got to the third floor, another nurse who sat behind a small desk greeted him.

"May I help you?" she asked.

"I'm here to see Joe Hall. Don't get up, I know where I'm going. I was here last night."

"Sir," she stopped him. "If you're going to visit with Mr. Hall, you must put this on," she continued as she stood up, holding a surgical mask outstretched to him. Newsy looked at her, and again, his thoughts flashed back to the hospital in Montreal filled with young dying soldiers.

"Thank you," he managed to reply. *Could this be the same thing?* he wondered. He knew the answer.

When Newsy visited Joe the day before, he sat quietly, watching his teammate labor over every breath. It pained him to sit there, helplessly, speaking to this unconscious man who was once his most hated rival and the toughest man in the NHL. Now Joe Hall was his best friend. *Life is funny that way*, he thought. *Twists and turns, opponents become teammates, assholes become good friends. And now Joe's sick. My friend is sick.* He put the mask over his nose and mouth and tied it behind his head. Nodding another thanks to the nurse, he continued down the hall to Joe's room and then turned back. "Can you bring us six glasses with ice, please?" he requested, showing her the forty-ounce bottle of root beer.

"Of course, right away, Mr. Lalonde," she replied.

"Thank you," he said and turned again toward Joe's room.

As he approached, Newsy heard the sound of muffled laughter coming from inside the closed hospital room. The usual ball-busting was underway. Newsy stopped just outside the door and listened to the good time being had inside.

"Fuck you, it was a clean goal. I had him beat all the way and knew I could go 5-hole," Odie Cleghorn, said referring to his game 5 winning goal scored between the opposing goaltender's skates.

"Clegger, you got lucky, admit it," Billy Couture needled. "Holmes was exhausted!" he continued while lying flat on his back near the door. Couture had played all season with a staggering pain in his back that was only alleviated when he lay on a hardwood floor for hours.

"It did seem like we had the puck for about a week during that overtime," added Didier Pitre.

"So it was inevitable. At some point, the goal was going to happen. You just happened to take the last shot, Clegger," continued Couture.

"Kiss my fuckin' ass, Billy," Cleghorn responded, lifting his foot as if he were going to step on Couture's face.

"Make it bare, Clegger. Look, I'm puckering! Have a seat right here," teased Couture, pointing to his chin. "By the way, did any of your parents' children live?" he continued, adding the usual extra dig that caused the entire room to explode in laughter. Cleghorn put his foot back on the floor and reached for his belt buckle and started taking down his pants in an attempt to call Couture's bluff.

"Enough! I'm not well enough for that! Pull your trousers up, you fucking asshole," Hall ordered Cleghorn, laughing and still fighting a small cough. "If I see that ass, I'll have a relapse!" Laughter filled the small room again. The door swung open, and Newsy joined the fracas.

"Hey, boys!" he shouted over the laughter.

"Newsy!" they shouted in return.

"Where ya been, Lalonde?" asked George Kennedy.

Newsy surveyed the room then landed his attention on Hall, the only one not wearing a mask on his face. He was astonished at his teammate's improvement. "McDonald gave me the good news about our pal Joe here while I was having lunch. I came over immediately to see for myself. Saints alive, Joe. You look so much better. What happened?" Newsy asked.

"Chalk it up to good, clean livin'," Hall said, which ignited another round of laughter.

"Bullshit!" said Couture.

"Fuckin' good clean livin', yeah right!" followed Didier.

"It's amazing his dick hasn't fallen off from all that good, clean' livin'," Kennedy chimed in. More hardy laughter followed the unusual dig from the Canadiens' manager who did his best to fit into a situation he clearly wasn't comfortable with. The players rarely spent time like this with their boss, but the unusual circumstances and Joe's surprisingly quick recovery permitted the two cultures to mix.

"The nurse said some people are fighting off the influenza. Guess I'm just one of the lucky ones," Joe said a little more seriously.

The nurse from the third-floor station walked in, carrying a tray of six tall glasses with various levels of ice in each one. The nurse didn't see Couture, still lying near the door flat on his back, his outstretched feet pointing straight up. Her left foot caught Billy's right foot, and she started to go down. Newsy, still standing near the door, grabbed the nurse with his left hand and the tray of glasses with his right, saving Joe Hall from an icy bath.

"Goddamn, that was close! Nice save, Newsy!" exclaimed Hall, sitting up and coughing.

"Better save than any Georgie Vezina made last night. Damn straight," added Didier.

"Sorry, ma'am. I didn't see you come into the room," said Couture, getting up off the floor.

"It's quite all right. No harm done. But, gentlemen, you have to hold it down. There are other patients on this floor, and you're disturbing them," the nurse insisted. "I'll be at my station if you need anything else," she said and turned to leave the room.

"Thank you, nurse," said Hall. "Billy, why do you always have to lie in the exact wrong place with those big fucking feet of yours?" he continued. "I didn't even know you were down there."

"What the hell, Joe? Did you think one of the boys was a ventriloquist?" asked Couture. "'I'll be at my station if you need anything else,'" Couture repeated, impersonating the nurse. "I need something else, a new back and some hot wild sex," he said, turning back to the room full of teammates. They all smirked and shook their heads in disgust.

"What the fuck is ventral-la, ventrill-of-kiss?" asked Hall.

"Ventriloquist," corrected Couture. "It's someone who can . . . oh, never fuckin' mind. Newsy, what's with the ice?"

"I thought we'd toast to Joe's health and the Montreal Canadiens who stand on the eve of another Stanley Cup Championship," said Lalonde.

"Here, here!" responded the room.

"You can't toast with root beer, Newsy. I know you don't drink, but the rest of us will lose our membership to the Sloppy Drunk Society if we toast with that shit," said Didier, pointing to the bottle of pop Newsy had placed on the table next to Joe.

Hall smiled and nodded. "Gotta agree with Didds, Newsy. Even in my condition, I won't toast with that shit," he said.

"Ah darn," said Newsy, feigning insult and disappointment. "That's why I brought this with me!" he exclaimed and opened up his coat to reveal the bottle tied to his shoulder.

The room erupted in euphoria and then quickly settled down when Hall scolded them. "Shhhhhh. Shut the fuck up. What's wrong with you, assholes? Newsy," he said, turning to Lalonde and holding the bottle of whiskey while Newsy untied it from his shoulder. "This is why you are the greatest hockey player to ever put on a pair of skates!" Hall proclaimed.

The others in the room did their best to stifle their amusement. Unable to hold everything in, Odie Cleghorn shot a puff of snot out of his nose that landed in Hall's lap.

"What the fuck, Clegger?" Hall whispered with disgust. "Give him the fuckin' soda pop! Fuckin' shithead."

Hall opened the bottle of whiskey while Newsy worked on the bottle of root beer. They filled five glasses with alcohol and one with root beer. Newsy took the root beer, allowing Cleghorn to enjoy the good stuff with his teammates. Then they raised their glasses.

"To Joe Hall and his speedy recovery," Newsy began.

"To Joe's health and the Canadiens' victory," followed Kennedy.

"To my fucking game-winning goal," added Cleghorn.

"To tired goalies," said Couture and then turned to Cleghorn. "Dick head."

"Blow me, Billy."

"Stop acting like a fuckin' ass plug, Clegs."

"I'm not acting!" More muffled laughter.

They all pulled their masks down and chugged the half-full glasses, wiped their mouths with their shirt sleeves, almost in unison, then extended their glasses for more. None of them put their masks back on. A half-hour later, the root beer bottle was nearly three-quarters full. The bottle of whiskey was empty.

"All right, boys, it's getting late," observed Newsy. "Joe, take the boys over to the rink for a short skate. Let's work out the soreness and the whiskey, just some light drills," he ordered.

"You coming, Newsy?" asked Kennedy.

"Nah. I'll stay with the Bad Man a little longer. I'll see you boys later for dinner. Hotel restaurant? Six o'clock?" he asked, which meant that was where and when they should all be if they wanted to eat.

"Sure thing, Newsy," said Kennedy. They all took turns shaking Hall's hand, rubbing his head, or punching his shoulder. Each man, however, looked him seriously in the eyes and told him to get better and that they needed him tomorrow night. *If my condition doesn't get any worse, I'll definitely play,* thought Hall. *Even at 50 percent, I'm the best defenseman in the game.*

"Have a good skate, boys. See you at dinner," called Newsy as his teammates were leaving the room.

Couture waited at the door for Cleghorn to leave and stuck his foot out just in time. Cleghorn tripped out the door, stumbled two steps and, just as he was about to regain his balance, barreled into a nurse walking by with a large silver tray of glass bottles. Cleghorn and the nurse disappeared from Hall's and Newsy's view, but they heard the tray hit the floor followed by an explosion of broken glass. Couture's eyes widened, and his mouth formed a small *O* as he turned to look at Hall and Newsy. Couture covered his eyes with his hand and stifled a laugh. Calming himself, he stepped out of Hall's room and closed the door, but before it swung shut, his ball-busting continued, "What the hell did you do, Clegger, you clumsy bastard? Are you okay, ma'am?"

"See you boys tomorrow on the ice!" Hall said, hiding a laugh.

Newsy grabbed the chair Cleghorn had been sitting in, wiped off the whiskey Odie had spilled on it, and pulled it closer to the side of the bed to speak with Joe. Hall was propped up by a small mountain of pillows. The nurses had a two-pillow minimum per patient, so Hall's teammates stole pillows from other rooms while those patients were asleep.

"What's up, Newsy? You okay?" asked Joe.

"Oh yeah. Yeah. You just put a little scare into me. Last night, when I was here it seemed . . .," he trailed off.

Joe sensed his friend was struggling so he tried to help him. "Wait a second. You were here last night? After visiting hours? No wonder my ass is sore today," he said and chuckled.

Newsy smiled in return. Not his usual response to one of Joe's inappropriate jokes but Newsy seemed preoccupied.

"Newsy, come on. That's a good one I just got over on you," Hall continued.

"Good one, Joe."

"Listen, pal, I'm going to be fine. I'll be on the ice tomorrow. I promise you that. We'll kick the shit outta those girlie figure skaters and party all the way back to Montreal with the Stanley Cup."

Newsy smiled. "I think I've had enough of your partying on trains. I almost crapped my pants in New York a few months ago. Remember that?"

"You kidding?" Hall asked, chuckling. "Nervous Newsy! Fuck, that was funny. Remember those customs assholes? They had that young couple down to their skivvies in the next car. She was still in her fuckin' wedding dress! Going to the Big Apple for their honeymoon, I suppose. The new missus had a nice pair, if I remember correctly," said Joe, distracting himself. "Poor kids. I wonder what they did with 'em after they found the liquor on 'em."

"Probably drank the liquor and detained them a few hours to teach them a lesson," said Newsy.

"How many bottles did you have in your coat, do you think?" asked Hall.

"How many? Who knows? The damn coat was weighing me down. I think I was hunched over. Could you really hear the bottles clanging together?"

"Oh yeah. But that's why we gave them to you to hold. We knew the customs boys wouldn't bother you. I don't know if its respect or fear, but we knew they'd just wave you on."

"Probably a little of both," admitted Lalonde. He paused and then looked Hall in the eye.

"How you feeling, Joe, seriously?" he asked.

"Better, much better, Newsy. Why? Don't I look better?"

"No, no, you do. One hundred percent better," Lalonde said and leaned forward in his chair but didn't make eye contact. "I'm sure it's nothing, and I'm making a bigger deal out of it than I should," he said and then paused, searching for the right words. "The day you and I visited Iona and Laurene in the hospital, the day she was born? You and George left early. I kissed Iona and the baby good night, and when I left the room, you were gone."

"I remember. George took me for drinks and to find me a place to stay. Is everything all right with the girls?" asked Hall.

"Iona and Laurene are fine. When I left them and couldn't find the two of you, I wandered down the wrong hallway on my way out. There was this room, a large room, with so many of them."

"So many what, Newsy? Who? Now you're spookin' me," Hall said, becoming concerned.

"Young men. Military men. Just back from the war. Lying in cots one after the other after the next. Coughing and gasping for air."

He turned his head and looked Joe in the eye. "Just like you were last night. The nurse in Montreal said it was influenza and that most of them would be dead a few days later. When I saw you cough up the blood and heard you breathing last night, if it could be called that, it reminded me of those boys in Montreal.

"But it can't be the same thing, right, Joe? At least not the same kind or you wouldn't have recovered this way," he said with a slight smile, seemingly talking himself out of his concern.

"Sure doesn't seem like the same thing. And even if it was, Newsy, it's not gonna stop Bad Man Joe Hall. I'm too fuckin' tough for any pussy influenza crap. Look at me! I'm getting better every minute, and you can bet your ass that I'll be pullin' on my Canadien's sweater tomorrow night and followin' you on to the ice to kick the shit outta those girls," Hall said with 100 percent certainty.

Newsy slapped Hall firmly on his near shoulder. "Agreed, Bad Man. We're back to NHL rules tomorrow night, but we can't take them lightly. We have to stick to our game and pound them for sixty minutes." Newsy leaned back in his chair, propped his feet up on Joe's hospital bed, and clasped his hands behind his head, his mind turning to the upcoming final hockey game of the season.

"I may not be able to go the entire sixty, Newsy, but I'll be out there giving it my all as long as I can. You know that," Hall promised.

Lalonde nodded in agreement. Both men sat silently for a long moment when Joe asked a question that took Newsy by complete surprise. "Have you written Iona?"

Newsy's thoughts turned from the championship game strategy to Hall's bizarre inquiry.

"Yes, of course, I have," Newsy managed to reply, hoping his lie would not be noticed. "Why would you ask me that?"

"Come on, Newsy. I think I know you pretty well. I've seen what's been going on with you two. You hardly talk about Iona at all anymore. Everything is Laurene this and Laurene that. I'm not saying there's anything wrong with that—don't get me wrong. But you and Iona, you just seem like something's different. After the last Ottawa game I saw you together, I can't remember the last time I saw that and you didn't look comfortable. I don't think you were arguing and I can't say for sure what it was, but something was different. And after tomorrow, you're going home, and there won't be any more hockey to distract you. To keep that physical distance between you two. So before that happens, do you want to talk about whatever it is?"

There was another long pause between the two friends. Newsy thought about discussing it, *but that's not what men do, is it?* he wondered. *If I can't talk to Joe about it, there's really nobody left on God's green earth to talk with.* He unfolded his hands and leaned forward in his chair. He scratched the top of his head and leaned back again before starting the uncomfortable conversation.

"Do you know . . . did I ever tell you the story how we met?" Newsy asked.

Joe shook his head no and slid his butt up the bed, sitting up. To his surprise, Joe's plea had worked, and Newsy was going to share something personal about himself for the first time.

"It was the first game of last season, we were playing the Toronto Arenas at home. We were hungry, motivated, and dedicated to winning back the Stanley Cup at all costs. The previous year we'd lost in the finals, so we were a determined bunch.

"The Jubilee was buzzing that night, even during the warm-up skate. Our fans were as hungry as we were and, brother, were they letting the Toronto players know that they were going to be in for a long night.

"I was standing near center ice watching the Toronto warm-up, you know, figuring out some matchups, seeing who may have been favoring a leg or arm, looking for weaknesses as usual. That's when I saw her. She walked behind the Toronto goaltender and up the bench side of the arena toward our bench." While he spoke, Newsy pointed and followed an imaginary route as if he were watching her for the first time that very moment.

"Her hair caught my eye first. It was waist-long and seemed to glimmer under the arena lights. It was so beautiful. When she turned the corner and walked toward me, my heart nearly stopped. I realized I had lost focus on the game that was moments away from starting, and I didn't even care. Doesn't sound like Newsy Lalonde, does it, Joe?"

"Sounds like a man in love," Hall said sympathetically. He couldn't help but smile at his best friend's heart-opening story. He'd never heard Newsy, or any other man for that matter, speak like this.

"I was. As she continued walking, her face came into view. Her dark-brown almond-shaped eyes and that ridiculous button nose were almost too good to be true. And it just kept getting better, the closer she came. The cute cleft in her chin and then it happened. The friend she was walking with must have said something funny and she smiled. It was the perfect smile. It seemed to brighten the entire arena," Newsy said, shaking his head in wonderment.

"And?" Joe asked, leading Newsy on.

"And what?" asked Newsy.

"And how did you meet her?" His inflection made his point.

"They sat a couple of rows behind our bench. I later found out the friend she was with was a dedicated Canadiens fan. We named our daughter after her, Laurene. Iona knew very little about hockey and even less about me. She actually didn't want to go to the game that night."

"Are you going to get to the meeting part sometime tonight for fuck's sake?"

Embarrassed, Newsy smirked and continued, "I grabbed a pack of that new chewing gum, Wrigley's, off the bench and leaned into the crowd. I introduced myself to Laurene, who covered her mouth with both hands and tried to hold in some kind of high-pitched shriek. Unsuccessfully, I may add."

"Of course, the great Newsy Lalonde just spoke to her. She probably shit herself," said Hall only half-mockingly.

"Anyway, with Laurene in shock—"

"And her reaction to you signaling to Iona that you are some kind of god," Joe interrupted.

"Do you want to hear this or not?"

"Sorry."

"Allow the god to finish, please. I pulled a piece of gum out of the pack and asked Iona to chew it for me and let me know when the sweetness was gone. She looked at me as if I had two heads, but she agreed."

"Yeah, that Wrigley's is too fuckin' sweet. Only a child would chew that crap during a—" Joe stopped in midthought. "I'm sorry. Continue."

"I finished my warm-up skate, and just before the game, I looked back at Iona and asked her if it's ready. She smirked, still chewing of course, and shook her head yes. I waved for her to come down to the bench. By this time, the entire team was watching and wondering what was going on. Iona didn't hesitate. Like she couldn't care less who was watching, and by this point, it must have been the entire arena. She walked down the two steps from her seat, reached into her mouth, and pulled out that piece of chewed wet gum. She stood there for a moment, holding it between her fingers." Newsy held out his hand with his forefinger and thumb pressed together. "I leaned in and took it from her hand with my mouth."

"You?" Joe asked, incredulously.

"Yep," Newsy said with pride.

"Wow! That's so out of character for you. If someone else told me this story, I'd tell 'em to fuck off," Joe said with amazement.

"Agreed. If someone told me this story about me, I wouldn't believe it either, but it happened just like that. The next game, every single player on the team had a pack of Wrigley's chewing gum with them on the bench while they surveyed the crowd," Newsy continued with a smile.

"Did you say anything? How did you two finally talk?" Hall asked.

"I asked her to wait for me after the game. Laurene was only too happy to oblige, of course. I took the two of them out for a cup of coffee, and two months later, Iona and I were married." His expression seemed to change on the last word, which didn't go unnoticed by Joe.

"I remember reading about it in the paper. I gotta admit, I felt sorry for the woman marrying you. Kinda quick, wasn't it?"

"It may have been. Since little Laurene was born, our relationship has changed. No, that's not exactly true. It was changing before Laurene. I've fallen out of love, Joe. Or maybe I've fallen out of lust. She took my breath away that night at the Jubilee Arena. We started dating, and the next thing I knew, there was a wedding being planned. It's like I was watching it happen to someone else and I wanted to tell them it was all happening too fast, but I couldn't. I didn't. The press, the fans, my teammates all told me it was a great thing. So I went along for the ride.

"And it was great. But over time, that feeling began to fade. I know she still loves me and I still love her, just not the same way. And now we have Laurene in our lives, and to me, that's nothing short of a miracle."

"I know, Newsy. I see you with her, and it's the sweetest thing I've ever seen. I always think back to our wars on the ice, the stitches, broken bones, and then I see you with your daughter and it's like you're a different person. Someone I'm seeing for the first time. It's not the person I knew before. I guess I never knew you other than being the person I hated on the ice."

Newsy smiled. "The feeling was mutual, Joe, believe me."

"Oh, I know. I have the scars to prove it," he said, and they both laughed.

"Me too," said Newsy.

"Divorce?" asked Hall, almost suggesting it.

"Out of the question, Joe. My religion doesn't allow it, and I would never do that to my daughter. No, I'm in it for the duration and so is Iona. I can't say it was all a big mistake. Laurene makes that impossible to believe. But Iona and I have become distant. Even standing a couple of feet from each other in our home, we're distant. We don't argue and we're always civil, but it's not a marriage. It's something else. Something I'll live with for the rest of my life."

Game Day

April 2, 1919

He was a poor sleeper for as long as he could remember. As soon as he lay down in bed, his mind would start racing, regardless of how tired his body was. Newsy had grown accustomed to spending at least an hour each night thinking of what needed to be done, having entire conversations in his mind, rehearsing pregame speeches, or worrying about events that would never happen prior to falling off to sleep. But last night was different. A soreness had crept into his body during the night that kept his sleep shallow at best. He awoke to the sun pouring in through the hotel window. He was late for the team's game-day breakfast.

He rolled on to his side and sat up at the edge of the uncomfortable bed, shaking his head from side to side trying to free himself of the cobwebs that remained and caused his head to ache. He splashed water into his face from the bowl on the dresser, which only helped his mind focus on the searing pain in his joints. Something was obviously wrong.

After dressing, he made his way down the four flights of stairs, back to the hotel restaurant, where only hours earlier, he enjoyed dinner and laughs with his teammates. George Vezina and Bert Corbeau were already seated at the table, enjoying breakfast.

"Good morning, boys," Newsy mustered.

"Good morning, Newsy," responded Vezina.

"You look like shit," said Corbeau, stating the obvious.

"Thanks, Bert! Didn't sleep too well as usual," Newsy said, waving the waitress over.

Jack McDonald appeared next, looking worse than Newsy. He sat down at the large round table on the far side from the other three.

"Fuck me, I feel like shit," he said, placing his elbows on the table and dropping his head into his hands.

"What do you feel like?" asked Lalonde.

"Achy and tired, just like shit," answered McDonald, adding a cough.

Newsy's heart skipped a beat. Realizing he shared the same symptoms, he stood up. "Where's the rest of the boys?" he asked no one in particular.

"I guess they're still in bed," said Corbeau. "Where else could they be?"

Newsy pushed his chair back and headed to the hotel's front desk. The man behind the front desk was in his twenties, wore wire-framed glasses, and had pristine black hair. Newsy grabbed the pen from the registry and ripped a page out of the back of the book and started to write feverishly.

"Sir, is something wrong? May I be of assistance?" the hotel clerk asked. Newsy did not look up until he finished writing.

"I need you to go to the rooms of these four men and wake them immediately, please," he urgently asked.

"Does this have anything to do with what happened last night?" the clerk asked.

"What happened last night?"

"One of the guests became ill and had to be rushed to the hospital."

"Which guest? What was the name?" Newsy asked, his heart rate rising along with his voice. The clerk looked through the registry for the notation and found it.

"Kennedy. George Kennedy," the clerk said, hoping that would calm the guest in front of him down.

"Oh my god!" Newsy said, dropping his head. His shoulders suddenly felt heavy, and his eyes had trouble focusing. He pointed at the piece of paper he had just handed the clerk. "Write the room number beside each name on that list, quickly!" He stepped back into the restaurant while the clerk searched the room list.

"George, Bert, Jack! We have a problem," he yelled into the restaurant and turned back to the front desk. His three teammates arrived there a moment later.

"Here you are, sir. Can I ask what this is about?" the clerk said, handing back the list. Newsy did not respond. Instead, he turned to his teammates and gave them each a name and a room number.

The horse had been running as hard as it could for most of the twenty-two blocks to James Tower Hospital, stopping only when traffic demanded her to. Pulling the carriage of eight passengers plus the driver was more than the filly had ever pulled before, and when the reins tightened, she leaned backward with all her weight to stop the forward momentum but the carriage pushed her another fifteen feet passed the steps to the hospital, her hooves grinding against the gravel street.

"We're here!" the driver yelled and the carriage door swung open. They had paired off into twos so that the people who were sick were helped out of the carriage and up the stairs by a healthier teammate.

First, Vezina stepped out and reached back, grabbing Didier Pitre who stumbled feet-first to the ground. Next, Corbeau helped Couture out. McDonald struggled himself but found the strength to grab and help Louis Berlinquette. Finally, Newsy stepped out and literally caught Odie Cleghorn from falling face-first into the street. Arm in arm, they climbed the stairs to the hospital door, looking like a battered army which had been through a devastating battle.

Newsy knew they were in for the toughest fight of their lives.

12

Back to Brevig

Brevig, Alaska

August 19, 1997

Forty-six years after his first visit, Hultin was back in Brevig. The trip to get here was as distinctly different as the village he once knew. The proud and hardworking community had been replaced by despondent, unemployed people on the dole. The oil of Prudhoe Bay provided the United States with an abundant supply of power and the people of Alaska with a $1,800 per person, per year government check. The oil money, combined with their government welfare checks, created unusually large families with numerous children and parents who did nothing for a living. The situation surprised and saddened Hultin. But he couldn't dwell on it. His was a mission of historic proportions for microbiology and one that nearly no one knew about, including the villagers.

Brian Crockett had been in Brevig for almost a decade. At forty-four years of age, the bespectacled missionary was the current pastor of the Lutheran church. Hultin had called him before departing but didn't say why he was coming. Crockett was waiting in his office when Hultin arrived late in the morning. The two men shook hands, and Crockett offered Hultin a chair. Hultin set his small piece of leather luggage next to the old wooden chair and sat down.

"Can I get you anything? A cup of tea or coffee? Water?" Crockett politely offered.

"No, thank you. I'm just fine, Mr. Crockett."

"Brian. Please call me Brian," the pastor requested.

"Then you can call me Johan. Let me get directly to the point of why I'm here."

"Please do, Johan. We don't get many visitors," said Crockett.

"This is not my first trip to Brevig, which apparently makes me unique. In 1951, I came here to retrieve lung samples from people buried in the mass grave on the hill just outside of town. The villagers were kind enough to give me permission to exhume the grave. The reason for this morbidly odd request is quite important and historic," Hultin explained.

Crockett had been sitting behind his relic of a desk, leaning back with his hands clasped behind his head. At the mention of the grave exhumation, he leaned forward, his old chair creaking loudly as if it would drop the slender man to the floor. He placed his elbows on the desk and folded his hands under his chin with both index fingers extending straight upward over his mouth and lightly touching the bridge his nose. Hultin had his full attention.

"Are you familiar with the flu epidemic of 1918?" Hultin asked.

"Of course," Crockett responded with confidence and apathy. "It's as much a part of Brevig's history as any event. It nearly wiped out this entire village. I understand that you exhumed the people who died from the flu?"

Hultin nodded yes.

"Why? Why the people of Brevig?"

"Let me take a step back. I'm working with the leading scientist on the subject of this flu, a Dr. Jeffrey Taubenberger. You see, we are in need of lung samples from the victims who died of the flu, but eighty years ago, forensic medicine had not yet been practiced. Just a few years ago, in his search for samples, Dr. Taubenberger utilized the army's Pathological Warehouse, where he works and was able to find two lung samples from two young men who died from the 1918 flu. Unfortunately, the warehouse in which they were stored was not refrigerated. The samples were locked in wax, the standard method for the time and still practiced today, but hardly the quality we need for our research."

Hultin unzipped the leather bag at his feet and reached inside as he spoke. He felt the few pieces of clothing he had brought, pushed aside the pruning shears, then found the folder, and continued.

"My theory, one which is shared by Dr. Taubenberger, is that we need frozen tissues to study. Tissues recovered from bodies frozen not long after the victim's demise. In 1951, I theorized that the virus may be found in people who lived in extreme northern environments, were buried quickly in permafrost, and if the permafrost had stayed true to its name and not melted, it quite possibly could still exist there. I successfully found those samples in the exhumed bodies from the grave here in Brevig. The permafrost had kept the bodies frozen so that the tissues did not deteriorate, unlike those in Dr. Taubenberger's wax samples." He opened the folder and took out three documents and pushed one across the desk to Crockett. "This is a picture of Otis Lee. He was the missionary in 1951."

Crockett studied the picture, recognizing one of his predecessors and realized the other younger man in the picture was the very man sitting across his desk. He stared at Hultin a moment longer whose shoulder-length white hair and beard made him look every bit his seventy-two years. Hultin pushed his wire-framed glasses back up the bridge of his nose with one hand and slid several pieces of paper across the desk with the other.

"He's the man I first contacted then as well. Mr. Lee helped me gain the villagers' trust and then their permission. These are a few of my correspondences with Mr. Lee. The top one I wrote to explain why I was coming, and his response letter is beneath that. The others are copies of letters we exchanged afterward. In them, I explain my unsuccessful experiments of recreating or regrowing the virus, which caused the 1918 flu. It was there, I saw it. However, I just couldn't get it to grow again.

"And so I have returned, asking once again this very delicate and very personal request of the people of Brevig. I do this now because science has progressed to the point where we can rebuild the DNA from the virus's genes. It's a very exciting time in science. This very eccentric, but a brilliant scientist, Mullis I believe his name was, developed a process called PCR, polymerase—" He stopped himself hearing the enthusiasm in his explanation. Realizing his inappropriateness, he cleared his throat, resettled in his chair, and continued more sincerely.

"Mr. Crockett, Brian," he corrected himself. "This flu bug will return. That, we are fairly certain of. You are correct in your knowledge of Brevig's history. Seventy-two of the eighty inhabitants perished from the flu in 1918. It also killed perhaps as many as a hundred million people around the world. There was no way to stop it then, and there is no way to stop it now. Not without first finding the original strain of the virus, growing it, analyzing it, and developing a vaccine. And I believe the virus that is in that grave on the hill holds the secret to stopping the next pandemic," he said, pointing out the window to Crockett's office.

Hultin looked out of the window and noticed for the first time that the two white crosses that marked the grave were no longer there.

Hultin slowly stood, never breaking his gaze out of the window. As he walked toward it, he kept his hand raised, pointing out the window.

"The grave?" he began to ask.

Crockett was still studying the pictures and the letters Hultin had provided. He was convinced the story and the science this man just shared was true. Without looking up, he responded, "It's still there. The markers were lost a number of years ago during a storm. You know the Bering Sea," he suggested. "That's some story you just told me, Johan. And I wish I could give you permission to continue on your journey, but I can't," he said, standing and handing the pile of documents back to Hultin, who turned from the window, expecting more assistance than what was forthcoming.

"But I can take you to the person who can help you get permission," Crockett said with a smile.

Hultin's face turned from a disappointed intensity to a smile as well. "Lead the way, Brian."

Rita Olanna was short in stature as were most Inupiat Eskimos. Barely five feet tall, she had shoulder-length gray hair, which contained a framing of white around her round friendly face. Her smooth dark skin hid the number of years she had lived in this foreboding place along the sea. Her home was simple and small like the others here. But it was well kept and clean. Rita was the village elder, who still possessed pride in herself, her home, and her community.

Hultin had been in Brevig for a little over a half-hour. Meeting with Rita was an important step, and he was pleased with his progress. Hultin sat directly across from her, studying her face as he retold the same story he had just told Crockett, with even more sympathy this time. Rita listened politely, but her expression never changed. Nor did she interrupt Hultin to ask a question or offer an observation. Hultin had no idea if he was succeeding.

When he finished, Rita stood up without saying a word and turned her back. Hultin looked at Crockett, who seemed as puzzled as he was. After walking to the bookshelf behind her chair, Rita returned to her seat and opened the large photo album she held on her lap. She slowly and meticulously turned several pages, making sure none of the old pictures fell out of the book. When she had come to the proper page, she spun the book around so it faced her visitors. Hultin leaned forward and helped her slide the book off her lap. He held it in between them so everyone could see. Rita slowly leaned forward, placed her right index finger on a picture, and poked it three times before sitting back in her chair. Hultin pulled the book onto his lap and studied the picture.

"That's my grandmother," she began with a voice full of subtle strength. Staring back and forth between the two men, she continued, "She's been dead for many years now. When she was eight years old, a terrible sickness came to our village. People got sick and died very quickly. One morning, my grandmother woke up to find something strange. Her mother was not in the kitchen cooking the family breakfast. So she looked in her parents' bedroom and found them still asleep. She crawled into bed with them, but when she hugged her mother, she found she was cold and would not wake up. It was the same with her father. My grandmother lay there all day, knowing that her world had just drastically changed, but she clung to her old life for as long as she could. She was one of the eight people who survived the terrible disease, my grandmother," she concluded her story by looking down at her hands briefly before looking at Hultin.

"I remember you, Mr. Hultin. We both have aged well, would you agree?" she asked, smiling.

Hultin smiled back. "Yes, we have, Mrs. Olanna."

"If you can find this disease, this flu, in our ancestors and make medicine to stop it from ever returning, I will get you the permission of the others," she offered.

Hultin was almost dumbfounded. His trip was going better than he could have possibly dreamed. He kept his emotions in check. "We will do our very best, Mrs. Olanna," he said with respect.

"Good then. Will you require help? I have four very strong grandsons," she offered.

Now Hultin could not help but smile. The last time he had to dig the grave by himself, painstaking, backbreaking work. Now he would have the help of four young men. "That would be most kind. Yes, I would welcome their help. Thank you," he said and bent over to shake Rita's hand.

Crockett drove Hultin back to the church's school, which would double as Hultin's deluxe accommodations while in Brevig. It was heated, featured four air mattresses, and had a small kitchen, which was available for the three guests.

Hultin met his bunkmates upon their return to the school. The two men were clearly not locals as both were well over six feet tall, clean-shaven, with short haircuts and clean clothes containing a technology logo on the front left chest and across the back. The men exchanged hellos and began to chat while Hultin inflated his bed. One of the men explained they had been in Brevig for four days and were leaving earlier than expected. They were packing their bags happily while explaining how they had completed the installation of Brevig's first satellite dish two days ahead of schedule. Their tests successful, they were leaving that afternoon. Hultin stopped what he was doing and slowly turned to the two men who were hurriedly making their escape.

"Satellite dish?" Hultin nervously asked.

"Yep. It's powered up, calibrated, and seeing the bird, so we're outta here!" was the reply. "How long you here for, buddy?"

"Oh, probably not much longer than you, boys," replied Hultin, trying to be as vague and coy as possible. "Is the satellite dish for transmitting or receiving?" he asked.

"Receiving and connecting this place to the rest of the world. What possible interest would anyone have transmitting from Brevig?" one technician responded, not trying to conceal his amusement. The chitchat continued while the satellite boys finished packing. Excited to escape this place that they clearly weren't thrilled about, they decided to walk to the airport instead of waiting for their ride. A few minutes later, Hultin shook both of their hands, and off they went.

A satellite dish installed the same day I arrive. Karma, thought Hultin. "Karma," he said again to himself. He chuckled and shook his head. The trip was going well beyond his greatest expectations. *Coincidence, not karma,* he thought. *Nobody but Taubenberger, his assistant, my wife, and now a couple of people in Brevig know why I'm here. I could be on vacation. I could be visiting family. I could be here to dig up an eighty-year-old grave, looking for the virus that produced the deadliest influenza pandemic in human history so we could reconstruct its DNA and find a vaccine.* He smiled again.

Coincidence!

"Good news, Mr. Hultin!" Crockett announced as he burst in the door and was surprised to see that the two men he was going to drive to the airport had already vacated. He shook his shoulders as if to say "oh well" and continued, "You have your permission. Only took Rita a couple of minutes. I assumed you wanted to begin immediately, so I informed her grandsons to meet you on the hilltop in thirty minutes. Pickaxes and shovels in hand." He smiled a proud smile.

"Thank you, Brian, and please call me Johan. That is great news. I'd love to report this to my friends back east. Do you have a fax machine?" he asked.

"Yes, of course, Johan. Wouldn't you rather use the phone?" Crockett asked.

"Actually, I'd prefer the fax. It's cheaper and quicker and I don't have to waste time with niceties. I can get right to work," he explained. The real reason was security. The less he and Taubenberger communicated over open phone lines the better, he thought.

"Arrived this morning, easy trip. Met with village elder. Received permission to dig. Starting this afternoon. Sleeping on air mattress on school floor. You owe me nice stay at DC Four Seasons Hotel!" Taubenberger read aloud, almost not believing the words he was seeing on the fax in his hands and hearing come out of his mouth. Ann giggled incredulously at the complete ridiculousness that she had just heard. This seventy-two-year-old man was two weeks into his journey, and he was starting to dig this afternoon! They exchanged "can you believe it?" smiles and got back to finishing their lab work. It was late on the East Coast, and the two scientists were tired. The news from Brevig, Alaska, gave them a second wind of hope and excitement. What news of progress would Hultin share with them tomorrow? They concentrated on finishing their tasks in the lab, trying to conceal their excited anticipation. This was still a long shot, they thought. The permafrost could have thawed over the decades; the bodies may have deteriorated beyond usefulness to their cause; a thousand things could still go wrong.

Ann and Jeffery finished their work and hung their lab coats on the hooks in the corner of the room.

"Do you think he'll find them?" Ann asked with concern but also a touch of excitement.

"He's gotten this far."

"And so quickly," she added for Jeffery, who was thinking the same thing.

Taubenberger smiled. "Let's keep our fingers crossed and wait for tomorrow's fax. Good night, Ann. See you in the morning," he said, patting her on the shoulder.

"You bet your ass you will!" She smiled.

August 20, 1997

Hultin awoke refreshed and anxious to get back to the grave. He slept better than he thought he would. The air mattress was more than comfortable, and the blankets and pillow provided by Crockett made for a pleasant night's rest. The cool morning Alaskan air, combined with his anticipation of successfully finding preserved lung samples, shook his cobwebs quickly. Five minutes later, he had washed his face, brushed his teeth, and dressed for the day's work at the grave site. Crockett arrived with a breakfast of fresh coffee, toast, and smoked salmon caught in a nearby river. Hultin wished for a New York bagel, some cream cheese, and a slice of onion to go along with his salmon but only expressed appreciation at Crockett's kindness. He quickly made a salmon sandwich, poured some coffee into a Styrofoam cup, grabbed his overnight bag, and thanked his host again before heading up the hill.

Hultin had agreed to meet his four young helpers as early as possible. He felt it inappropriate to set a time since they were volunteers and not day laborers. Whenever they cared to arrive would be the start of the workday. Hultin wished he could remember their names, but they said them so quickly, Hultin didn't have time to commit them to memory. That, along with his relief and gratitude that he would have young strong workers digging this time, had distracted him. For all he knew, they were Bruce, Donald, Muhammad, and Isaac. Climbing the hill to the grave, he thought about how he had spent the day before referring to them as "buddy," "pal," and "young man" in an attempt to cover his impoliteness. They didn't seem to mind or care. Their work kept them busy, and the skill and speed at which they removed the layers of earth impressed Hultin. Living in this frozen landscape had taught the indigenous how to use pick and shovel and remove layers of the permafrost quickly. Each piece was one foot wide by two feet long and three inches thick. Once removed, the boys carefully placed and stacked the pieces of earth in a system that would allow the pieces to be returned in the proper order and location when they were through. Hultin wondered if this was a process handed down by generations or just discussed ahead of time to show honor and respect to those buried here. Either way, it was an efficient system, and after removing the top layer of unfrozen sod, the work progressed with impressive speed.

Hultin arrived at the grave site just before 8:00 a.m. The sun's warming August heat was welcomed, but the temperature couldn't be above forty-five degrees. He reviewed the work from the previous day. He had instructed the four young men to stand where they believed the four corners of the grave were. It was difficult for him to be precise since the white crosses no longer marked the site. He then instructed the digging to begin in the same location he believed he had dug in 1951. The hole was now a little over three feet deep and was twenty-five feet long by four feet wide. A fine day's work performed by Rita Olanna's grandsons. He had finished his sandwich and was draining the last of the coffee from his cup when he turned back toward the town of Brevig, framed against the Bering Sea. His gaze dropped to the bottom of the sloping hill in front of him and a large smile appeared on his face. There were four figures climbing the hill with shovels and picks thrown over the shoulders. It was obvious the four men were talking, one shoved another, and the other two could be heard laughing even at this distance at the top of the hill. Hultin was surprised to see them, but he was also thrilled they were returning to work so early.

"Good morning, Dr. Hultin," the eldest said as he neared the top of the hill.

"Good morning, boys!" Hultin nearly shouted. "Up and at 'em early, huh? I like that! Did you boys eat?"

"Yes, sir, we're ready to get back to the job."

"Then let's not waste another minute," Hultin said and turned to allow the boys access to the grave. The other three tipped their heads and softly said, "Mornin'" as they walked past their seventy-two-year-old leader. Hultin threw the coffee cup into one of the five-gallon buckets and placed his hands on his hips. He wished he had a fedora, visualizing in his mind the digging scene from *Raiders of the Lost Ark* where Indiana Jones watches his minions closely as they searched for the Well of Souls.

The boys got right to work and, with Hultin directing them, made impressive progress. Within a couple of hours, the hole was nearing six feet deep. One of the young men swung his pick to wedge another sheet of frozen ground out of the hole and the pick made a sound that up until now had not been heard. He spun around and looked at Hultin, making sure not to move the pick from its spot. His expression was part scared and part excited. He realized his steel pick had struck human bone and didn't know if he should continue or run out of the hole, screaming. Hultin smirked and climbed down into the hole. The three other boys moved in even before Hultin arrived and carefully removed the piece of frozen earth with their hands. There lay a partially covered human skeleton. One of the young men gasped but quickly recovered and shook his head, acknowledging that he was fine and embarrassed by his reaction. Hultin patted him on the back as he crossed by and squatted over the victim of the 1918 epidemic. He felt excited and saddened at the same time. This was the right place, and they were indeed digging in the grave. However, there was no soft tissue left on this victim. Just bones and frozen dirt. Hultin's heart sank as did his head but just for a moment. He stood without saying a word and climbed back out of the grave.

Standing above it now, he held his arms out to his side, remembering where the boys stood marking the four corners of the grave the day before. He folded his arms and stood staring at the hole. A minute later, he turned toward town, trying to remember and realign his dig from forty-seven years earlier. He shook his head up and down and then from side to side. The four boys had been watching him and now turned to one another as if to ask, "What the hell is he doing?"

As he turned back to the hole and his diggers, he said, "We're in the right place, boys. I believe we have been digging in the same spot that I dug when I was here last. At least, I'm hoping that's the reason for the decayed body you just uncovered. We need to begin working north," he said and pointed to his left. "I believe if we start working in this direction, we'll find the bodies that I need to work with."

The four young filthy men climbed from the hole and moved around it to the north side and started the process again without complaining. The work seemed to go even quicker with one side of the grave excavated. Hultin opened his bag and pulled out the file that contained pictures and his hand-drawn sketches of the area from 1951. He held the pictures up to the western horizon and surveyed the town, comparing the still frame to the scenic expanse in front of him. *It sure looks like the exact same angle,* he thought. *The Bering Sea seems a little closer, but the town is in the same place. They must have found one of the original bodies that I uncovered years before,* he thought. It was now just after ten in the morning and the boys were hard at work, expanding the hole northward.

By noon, they were nearing the depth of their original hole, and more skeletons were being unearthed. Each time, Hultin carefully cleared the frozen dirt away from the decayed body and inspected what lay before them. Each time, he was disappointed. No soft tissue remained on the remains of four unfortunate souls. While Hultin worked with the exposed bones, the boys continued to dig toward the north. The stench of the decaying bodies was overwhelming, but he was accustomed to it in his work. He was surprised that the boys never complained about the uniquely obscene odor.

Hultin was becoming worried, almost horrified. The skeletons before him were more than the number he exposed in 1951. He remained confident for the first three discoveries, but now his confidence was waning. *What if the permafrost had indeed melted since I was here last? I may be desecrating these people's remains for nothing.* Science and nature were battling once again, as it has for thousands of years, and it appeared that nature just might win this round. He couldn't believe it. He wouldn't believe it. He stood up, relieving his aching knees, and pushed those thoughts aside. There was too much at stake here. Science had finally progressed to a point in which the samples, he alone was able to find, could be analyzed with the latest technology and processed. Hultin had waited years for this moment. Since that failure in his Iowa lab, his patience had been tested. Patience that was forced to last for decades in anticipation of returning to this site and retrieving more samples that just might save humanity from the looming epidemic. An epidemic that many scientists agreed would return. The deadly process of mutating viruses had already begun.

They would press on. They had to.

The work had slowed during the afternoon. The young men's bodies were tiring as was their spirit. It showed in their faces and with every swing of a pick and shovel. Their hard work was yielding no results, and they began to think that this might go on until the entire grave had been exposed and for no good reason. Their hearts were becoming heavy as were their tools.

Hultin needed a break from the site. He needed to clear his mind, so a half-hour earlier, he walked back to town to get sandwiches and drinks for his hardworking boys. He had hoped to be finished by now, but the digging and searching continued unsuccessfully. The walk up the long sloping hill drained him. Or perhaps, it was the fear of failure on this desolate Alaskan hilltop. He was feeling the weight of his predicament on his shoulders while he climbed the final few steps to the hill's peak. Something immediately caught his attention. There was a lack of sound coming from the hole. As he approached, he wondered if his help had given up and returned to town while he was gone, but that all changed as he got closer and heard their voices. They sat alongside three newly exposed bodies.

The starving boys climbed from the hole and immediately accepted the sandwiches and cold drinks Hultin had hauled up to the site. They excitedly thanked him and began devouring the food. Hultin barely responded, never taking his gaze off the bottom of the freshly dug pit. There, in the northernmost part of the opening, were three bodies. Out of the three new remains, two of them were badly decomposed, but they contained more soft tissue than the first four skeletons. There was ample skin, hair at the top of the skull, fingernails, and even the ripped remains of their clothes. He realized that these two bodies had remained frozen longer than the first four victims because they were in permafrost that he had not disturbed in 1951. But his attention quickly turned to the body in between them. This one seemed to be preserved nearly perfectly since burial. There was plenty of soft tissue. In fact, unlike all the other remains, no bones were visible at all. Her preservation was so good that it was easily deduced that the body was that of a woman's.

On his knees alongside her, Hultin inspected the remains closely. Yes, this was it. This is what he had come for. The remains were perfect, but he couldn't help but remain perplexed. He grabbed one of the buckets from the bottom of the pit, turned it upside down, and sat it on. Above him, the four diggers enjoyed their lunch and the realization they had found what Dr. Hultin had come here for. They talked, congratulated, and smiled at each other, food falling from their proud faces. But why wasn't Hultin happier?

"Is everything all right, Dr. Hultin? Is that what you were looking for?" the oldest asked.

"Hmm? Oh yes. Everything is perfect, great! I'm just wondering how this happened," he responded.

"How what happened?"

"Well, the remains of the woman in the middle are almost pristine, perfect for my purposes. But she is surrounded by two corpses that have deteriorated very badly. They are much more advanced than she is, and yet, she lies between them."

Hultin shook his head and realized what he had failed to figure out up until now. The woman in the middle was obese. Even by today's fast-food standards, she would have been immense. Her body fat must have frozen after burial and that provided another layer of protection from the warmer seasons.

"I got it, boys. She's fat," he explained.

"She sure as hell is, Doc!" said the youngest Olanna, which brought a look of disdain from his brother.

"Show respect" was the short lecture, and it was all that was needed.

"No, I mean her large girth probably protected her soft tissue. All the extra fat in her body froze and made her more resilient to the thawing earth around her," he explained. "Can one of you please hand me down my bag? It's right over there." He pointed out where he had left it for them.

Hultin grabbed the bag from the young man above him on the edge of the grave and placed it on the overturned bucket. There was no need to remove the body. The boys' work provided enough room to perform his tasks where she lay. He opened the bag and spread a small blanket on the bottom of the pit next to the body. Next, he pulled out a small surgical kit, his wife's pruning shears, and the four bottles containing chemical preservatives that Taubenberger had overnighted to him after their first conversation. These bottles were for transporting the samples back to Taubenberger.

The boys were finished with their lunch now and stood at the top of the grave, watching Hultin's every move. He grabbed a scalpel from the surgical kit, leaned over the body, but stopped just before making an incision. He sat back, his mind was racing back to a similar scientific discovery.

On November 24, 1974, paleoanthropologist Donald Johanson discovered the skeleton of a hominid in Hadar, Ethiopia. The 3.2-million-year-old discovery rocked the scientific world as it was later discovered that these remains were the first known member of *Australopithecus afarensis*. Johanson's girlfriend suggested calling the three-foot-tall biped Lucy after the Beatles' "Lucy in the Sky with Diamonds." Later at their camp, Johanson's team celebrated the find, already knowing the uniqueness of Lucy as the song played on an eight-track stereo long into the night. Hultin thought about that historic discovery as he sat at the bottom of this grave about to cut into a woman who died nearly eighty years earlier. *Lucy,* he thought, *was appropriate for her as well.* Not because of the Beatles but more for the Latin word *lux,* which in English meant "light." Hopefully, Lucy would shed light on the killer virus from 1918 and help Dr. Taubenberger and his crew learn its deadly secrets.

The scalpel slid through Lucy's abdomen. Hultin expertly cut a large *I* into her and peeled back the thawing skin, exposing her ribs. Next, he reached for the pruning shears and cut through the ribs closest to her two lungs. When finished, he wiped the shears clean and placed them back in his bag, hoping that he could return them without his wife realizing they were gone or what they had been used for. The lungs were incredibly preserved as were all her vital organs. But it was the lungs that would contain the virus, and that's where he focused. He cut two small pieces out of one lung and placed each one into their own bottles. He then cut two pieces from the other lung and repeated the procedure with the bottles. Hultin checked each of the caps multiple times. After reassuring himself they would not open until arriving in Washington, DC, he closed up Lucy's incision and repacked his bag.

Standing up and surveying the grave, he said, "We're done here, boys. Let's close it back up."

Hultin helped for about fifteen minutes but soon realized he was only getting in the way. The young men knew where each piece of permafrost went and were better off doing it by themselves. Hultin offered to buy the boys dinner when they finished and excused himself. He walked just fifteen or twenty feet toward town, then stopped and turned to look back at the grave. Realizing there was one more job to perform, he hurried down the hill.

Brian Crockett was in his office when Hultin knocked on the door. "Come in. It's open."

"Good evening, Brian," said Hultin, covered with dirt from head to toe.

Crockett smirked at the sight of this man in his seventh decade of life looking like a boy who was just out playing in the yard.

"How did it go today?" Crockett asked.

"A tremendous day, Brian. Just tremendous. I found what I came for, and my work here is finished, except for one final deed," he announced. "With the permission of you and your neighbors, I'd like to replace the crosses that stood marking the grave site when I was here last."

"That is a very noble gesture, Johan. I'm sure there would be no objection," replied Crockett. "Can I help you? I have some four by four studs in the back."

"That would be perfect. Where can I buy some white paint?"

"No need, I'll donate that as well."

The two men went quickly to work. It was nearing six o'clock in the evening when they began, and by six thirty, they were done. One cross was nearly ten feet tall, and the other was slightly more than six feet. Hultin and Crockett agreed they would place the markers the next morning. After returning home, Hultin paid for two bronze plaques to be commissioned. One was to be placed on the horizontal part of the cross, and it read, "The following seventy-two Inupiat Eskimos are interred in this common grave. Pray, honor, and remember these villagers who lost their lives during the short span of five days in the influenza epidemic. November 16–20, 1918." The other plaque would be attached to the vertical part of the cross just beneath the first plaque. It contained the names of each villager, including Lucy Lyons, Postmaster Brevig, and the woman who would shed light on this pandemic eight decades after her death. The following September, Hultin returned to Brevig and affixed the plaques to the larger cross facing the town of Brevig and the Bering Sea.

The fax machine was moved to Taubenberger's lab so that it was never out of earshot. The previous night, no faxes came across, and the two scientists left work feeling concerned and disappointed.

Neither Ann nor Jeffrey slept much that night, so both arrived early. The sun had not yet risen on the East Coast, and the streets were eerily quiet for the capital of the free world. A couple of minutes after 5:00 a.m., they had donned their lab coats when the fax machine sprang to life. A couple of robotic sounding pings were followed by something inside the machine aligning itself for printing, they had no idea what. Next, paper could be heard feeding in to the spools followed by the sound of their fax machine printing, which was like music to their ears. It had to be Hultin. *Who else would be faxing this early?* they thought. They both rushed to the machine waiting for what felt like an eternity for it to reveal the contents of its transmission.

The paper spit out on to the tray, and Hultin grabbed it. He read aloud, "Found Lucy. Samples are stored and safe. Leaving tomorrow and will send samples back while en route. Took my team out for dinner."

"His team?" they both asked in unison. Then they hugged. This crazy old man had been able to accomplish, by himself, in just a few weeks what others had failed to do after years of preparation, research, and globe-trotting, as well as enormous amounts of money.

Taubenberger and Reid didn't know it now, but they would later learn that Hultin's entire trip cost just $3,200. He gave $900 to his assistants at the grave site to split among one another, which was most of his remaining cash. The rest was spent on his flight, parking at the airport, and the cost to send the samples back east.

Hultin realized the value of the samples he was bringing back to the lower forty-eight states. They could not be replaced since no one had successfully found a permafrost grave in a town decimated by the 1918 influenza, except him. And he couldn't ask the people of Brevig if he could come back and try again because he lost the samples. It was out of the question. These samples had to be kept safe and had to be delivered to Taubenberger.

The airlines could not know he was once again carrying samples that contained lung samples from a diseased body that died from the deadliest pandemic in human history. He hid them in his carry-on bag, and at his stop in Portland, while changing planes, he found a post office in the airport. He packed two of the tubes in separate boxes and stuffed the boxes with what he learned was called packing peanuts to keep them safe during travel. He sent one overnight and, the other, a second-day delivery. Upon his return to San Francisco a few hours later, he stopped first at a UPS store, packed a tube into a box, and sent that for overnight delivery. Next, he stopped at a FedEx location, packed the last tube, and sent it on its way as well.

He drove home tired from his experiences but euphoric in the knowledge of what he had accomplished. He knew at least one of the four boxes would be delivered. Sending them separately with multiple carriers would ensure that. It was now up to Taubenberger and his team. The samples contained the virus, he was sure of it. Everyone in that grave had died from the disease in those five horrible days. It was there. It had to be. Taubenberger would find it.

He dropped his bag on the couch, kissed Eileen, and told her he needed a hot shower and headed straight upstairs for the bathroom.

"You look exhausted. I'll bring your bag upstairs and unpack for you, sweetheart," she offered.

"You're too kind, dear. Thank you," Hultin mumbled, walking ahead of his wife to the second floor.

He reached the top of the stairs and turned left into the bathroom while she continued ten more feet down the corridor to the master bedroom. He closed the door behind him and turned on the water in the shower. It would take a minute for the hot water to leave the water heater in the basement and make its way to the shower on the second floor. He closed the lid to the toilet and sat down to wait. He was tired, but it was such a good tired. His pride swelled, knowing that in a lifetime filled with wonderful contributions for society, this may just be his greatest.

"Shit!" he said under his breath while hopping off the toilet and opening the bathroom door in one motion, his exhausted body suddenly and instantly springing back to life because of the thought that had just crossed his mind. He hoped against all possible hope that he could get there in time. He rushed down the hallway to the bedroom. He knew he was running, but the door wasn't getting any closer. It seemed to move away from him. *I must run faster,* he thought. *I have to get there before—*

Time sped up now and flew by until he slammed to a stop in the master bedroom. As if on cue, Eileen turned around to face her frantic husband holding her pruning shears in her hands. Her expression was one of confusion that was quickly becoming annoyance as she tilted her head to the side in the manner he had come to fear.

"Why are these in your bag, dear?" she asked with a large amount of disdain in her voice and holding the shears up for him to see.

Breathing hard from his short sprint down the hall, he looked at his wife, inhaled deeply, and raised his hands, palms up in preparation for delivering his best excuse and fairy tale he ever came up with. He opened his mouth, but all that came out was "Shit." He shook his head and turned back to the bathroom, not even bothering to offer any explanation.

The following day, three of the tubes arrived at Taubenberger's lab in Washington, DC. He and Ann could not believe what they held in their hands. They immediately went to work preparing the samples for their work and did not stop, working through the night on Lucy's lungs. The next day, the final package arrived via two-day delivery from Portland. The delivery services were four for four, and Taubenberger had enough lung tissue to keep him busy for years. Hultin had begun his trip just six days earlier, and remarkably, Taubenberger and Reid had four pristine lung samples from a Brevig woman who died seventy-nine years earlier because of the influenza epidemic in their lab. Within one week, they had proof of the influenza virus present in Lucy's lungs.

An incredible set of circumstances, scientific advances, and determined people had aligned, connected, and worked toward this single goal. A small group of brilliantly talented people who possessed unique skills and knowledge that few others possessed had united, revealing one of mankind's deadliest and most sought-after killers.

Taubenberger's first call was to Hultin to inform him that they had succeeded. They had found fragments of the virus's genes and were preparing their attempt at recreating the gene's DNA sequence using the polymerase chain reaction theory. Hultin was ecstatic at the news. Even though he had convinced himself that the virus would be present in the lung samples, it still moved him to tears to hear Taubenberger report the success in the lab.

Nearly five decades after his own failure, Hultin was part of the team that succeeded in finding the 1918 influenza virus. Immediately upon hanging up, Hultin called Brian Crockett to inform him of their success. He asked that the good news be relayed to Rita Olanna, her grandsons, and the rest of the village. Brevig, Alaska, would become renowned the world over as the location that successfully supplied the infected samples for microbiologists to study in hopes of preventing the next pandemic.

The clock continued to tick.

13

Migrating to Thailand

Thailand

September 2004

Pranee Sodchuen had always wanted a better life for her daughter Sakuntala than the one she had endured herself. The first nine years of Pranee's life were spent in an orphanage near Kamphaeng Phet, where she learned to take care of herself and how to read people quickly. She had an uncanny ability to see people for whom and what they were, cutting out the cancerous types and sharing her sweetness and zest for life with those she knew to be true and caring friends. Only once had she been wronged; however, even something great came from her misplaced trust and love. At fourteen, she gave her heart to the young man she believed was the true love of her life. Their torrid romance lasted just a few months and ended when Pranee became pregnant. He was nineteen and decided he had more living to do before settling down with a family. He moved away from Kamphaeng Phet, leaving behind Pranee and their unborn child.

Sakuntala was the village's child. Everyone loved the beautiful girl whose eyes sparkled and face lit up with an infectious happiness, no matter if she was saying hello to her best friend or a perfect stranger on the street. People felt better when they were with Sakuntala. Her personality was irresistible at a very early age, and her belly laugh was as well-known as her long brown hair. She made everyone she met feel special and happy. Pranee realized her unusual gifts as an infant. Everyone loved babysitting for her, and that allowed Pranee to work multiple, although menial, jobs and make enough money to rent an apartment in a good school district where Sakuntala excelled. Theirs was a comfortable existence, and with the help of their more than supportive neighbors and friends watching Sakuntala, Pranee was able to become a part-time student at nearby Naresuan University in Phitasnulok, Thailand. The schedule was difficult for both mother and daughter, but they knew they were building a better life and sacrificed time together toward that goal. It took Pranee nearly six years to finish college and earn her degree in language studies and business. Upon graduation, she applied for a job with GE Capital Ltd. in Bangkok. And thanks to her near-perfect English, the American company that financed auto loans, credit cards, personal loans, and business loans hired her after her second interview.

Since the Asian investment boom of the 1980s and 1990s, Bangkok had become the political, social, and economic center of Thailand, Indochina, and Southeast Asia. Its stunning new skyscrapers, mixing with ancient parks and temples below, gave the city a unique and awe-inspiring skyline. The business boom offered new and potentially lucrative careers to an area of the world that was enjoying its first taste of modern economic expansion. Bangkok was the tip of the economic sword for Southeast Asia, and Pranee Sodchuen was lured by the opportunity it offered.

GE Capital was not one of the larger banking businesses in town, but that didn't matter to Pranee. One of the greatest perks of her job was telling everyone that she worked in the Sathorn's Robot Building, where GE rented the top two floors also known as the robot's shoulders. The fifteen-story building actually looked like a giant robot complete with giant bolts on the sides of the building, a head with two giant eyes, and two antennas at the top looking like, well, two robot antennas, according to Pranee. The other great perk was working as an assistant to an American loan officer. He intrigued, entertained, and puzzled her. She found it difficult to understand the confidence and optimism the Americans possessed, and her boss possessed more than most. Even on what she perceived to be difficult days in the Stock Exchange of Thailand, her boss always exuded the same cheery, upbeat attitude.

America must be a wonderful place, full of happy people who whistle and sing most of the day, like my boss, she imagined.

Pranee shared a small apartment with three other GE assistants on the outskirts of Bangkok just a few blocks from the massive thirty-five-acre Chatuchak Weekend Market, which was adjacent to her train stop on the Bangkok Metro Blue Line, ironically, the Kamphaeng Phet Metro Station. Pranee traveled home at least twice a month to visit Sakuntala who was now eleven years old and lived with her aunt, Pranee's sister, Pranom. It was difficult being apart for such long periods; however, Pranee knew her daughter was well taken care of and loved by her sister and their friends and neighbors.

Pranee had been saving money in her three years as assistant at GE to rent her own apartment so she could move Pranom and Sakuntala to Bangkok. Sakuntala was anxious to move away from Kamphaeng Phet where the schools were no longer challenging for her, and most of the streets were still unpaved and featured free-range poultry living among the villagers. Her few visits to her mother in Bangkok thrilled and amazed her. She was entering that age where the separation of mother and daughter was not healthy for either. She needed her mother as her body and her personality were rapidly changing. There were so many questions to ask, triumphs to share, and boys to talk about with her mother. The move and their dream were a few weeks away from becoming a reality. It was late Sunday night, and Pranee was feeling especially sad because she could not travel home for the second weekend in a row to see her daughter. Sakuntala was mature and strong that morning when they spoke on the phone, but Pranee knew her daughter well. She could hear it in her voice. The time was not passing quick enough for mother and daughter to be reunited permanently.

Pranee had finally finished all the paperwork for her apartment and had picked out the clothes she would wear for work in the morning. Her plan was to get up early to stop at the bank before work and get the teller's check for the two-month rent deposit she would drop off at the realtor's office that afternoon. The phone rang, and Pranee's roommate told her it was her sister.

"Hi, Pranom. It's late. Why are you still up?" Pranee nervously asked. There was no response for a long moment.

"Pranom? Are you there?" she asked.

"There's something wrong with Sakuntala. We're taking her to the hospital now. I think you should come home," replied Pranom, her voice full of fear.

"What is it? Did she get hurt? What happened?" asked Pranee. *She was fine when I left,* she thought. Pranee's mind was jump-started by her sister's tone. She was overtaken with horrified concern just as every parent was when they receive this news.

"She's got a fever, and I can't get her to wake up. I gave her some tea and put her to bed a few hours ago. When I checked on her, I couldn't wake her up. I don't know what's wrong, and I'm scared, Pranee. Please hurry," begged Pranom.

"I'm on my way" was all she said and hung up the phone.

The trains were no longer running this time of night, so she woke up her other roommate who had access to a boyfriend's car and explained the situation.

"Let me put some clothes on" was the response. Two hours later, she arrived at the hospital in Kamphaeng Phet. Pranom met her and wrapped her arms around her sister.

"I'm sorry. I didn't know what else to do. The doctor is still in with her," explained Pranom.

A nurse walked by, and Pranee grabbed her by the arm.

"My daughter was brought here by my sister," she said, nodding at Pranom. "Her name is Sakuntala Sodchuen. Can I see her?" she pleaded.

"Of course, Mrs. Sodchuen, follow me." She pulled the frantic woman's hand off her bicep and grabbed Pranee by the elbow, leading her through two doors and down a short corridor. A young doctor stepped out of a patient's room on their left and the nurse motioned with her head as if to say that was her room and that's her doctor.

Pranee ran the last ten yards to the doctor, who was checking paperwork on a clipboard. She looked into the room and saw her daughter lying in bed.

"Doctor, that's my daughter. Sakuntala Sodchuen. Is she okay?"

"She's resting comfortably, Mrs. Sodchuen. Come on, I'll take you inside to see her," the doctor said in what Pranee perceived as an unusually comforting manner. Perhaps this was not as serious as she thought. She prayed. They stepped into Sakuntala's room as the doctor explained the situation.

"We believe she's been infected with dengue fever. She's running a temperature of 104 degrees and she's dehydrated, so we started an IV to rehydrate her and we'll keep her here overnight to monitor her. I'm sure she'll be better by morning," he assured her.

"Dengue fever. I've heard of it, but I'm not sure I know what that means," said Pranee, beginning to calm down for the first time in hours.

"It's transmitted by mosquitoes and very common this time of year. The symptoms could last as long as a week, but your daughter is young and healthy so I'm confident she'll fight it off. It seems to have hit her especially hard and quick so I don't want to take any chances tonight. She may become ill, vomiting and a rash are common symptoms. It's the dehydration, however, that I'm concerned about, so we'll just keep her overnight and you can probably pick her up in the morning," said the confident doctor.

Pranee was rubbing her daughter's head with her left hand and softly touching the IV needle in the incredibly thin arm with her right hand. She felt an overwhelming sense of guilt for leaving her daughter and was not going to do that again.

"No, Doctor. I believe I'll stay here with her tonight. I'm not leaving," she said with an air of absoluteness. The doctor knew there was no point in arguing.

"Of course, Mrs. Sodchuen. I'll have a nurse bring you a pillow and some blankets to make you more comfortable," he said. "She's going to be fine. We've had dozens of dengue cases since August, and it's not contagious so you are welcome to stay. We know how to treat it, and I'm confident that you will see improvement after a good night's rest. I'll check back with you in a few hours. You try to get some rest as well," he continued.

"Thank you, Doctor," Pranee managed. His confidence had calmed her, but the look on her face was still that of a mother with the love, guilt, and concern over a sick child.

When the morning arrived, Pranee woke up to the sound of her daughter experiencing coughing fits. Sakuntala was not yet awake, but her tiny body convulsed with each round of coughing that seemed to rock Pranee's very being. She rushed out into the hallway and asked a nurse to step in to her daughter's room. The nurse turned on the light inside the still semidark room and grabbed Sakuntala's wrist with her right hand and checked her watch with her left.

"Sakuntala? Honey, can you hear me? Sakuntala?" she asked calmly but became concerned by the raised pulse she was counting. "I'll be right back," she said and left the room.

For the rest of the morning, doctors and nurses took turns checking on the young child's condition, which was not improving as expected. They seemed surprised but remained confident that she soon would. Every other case of dengue fever had followed a specific course except for this one. They discussed the severity of the young girl's symptoms but theorized that every patient was different, and perhaps Sakuntala just needed more time to recover and fight off the initial shock to her system.

Pranee remained at her daughter's bedside throughout the day. Pranom had gone home to get her niece's favorite books, stuffed animals, and pajamas and returned with them to the hospital. The two sisters carefully slipped the red pajamas on to Sakuntala. Her body seemed even more tiny and frail than usual. By evening, the coughing fits seemed to come farther apart. Each time the child started to cough, Pranee wrapped her arms around her daughter, holding her tight to her chest. She would whisper in her daughter's ear, "That's it baby. Get it all out. Mommy is here, and I'm not leaving you."

And as Sakuntala's body would calm down at the end of another series of violent coughs, Pranee would pray with everything she had inside of her that her baby would not suffer through it again. But it didn't work. Within minutes, her body would heave up again, nearly lifting off the hospital bed, and Pranee would grab her child in her arms. "It's okay, baby. I'm here."

Tuesday morning brought more concern and new symptoms. Sakuntala's color had become ashen and gray with large purple blotches appearing on her ears, hands, and feet. The doctors expected a rash but had never seen one like this from dengue fever. They continued their treatment, and Pranee continued comforting and praying for her child who still had not regained consciousness.

That night, a nurse on her rounds slowly opened the door to Sakuntala's room. It was dark, but she was able to see the silhouette of Pranee sleeping in bed alongside her sick daughter. At first, she thought about not disturbing them since it was the first time in several days that mother and daughter were both sleeping peacefully, but her professionalism got the better of her and she quietly entered the room. Sakuntala was curled into a fetal position, facing her mother who held the child's head to her chest. The nurse reached for Sakuntala's wrist as she had dozens of times over the previous days, but something was different. *The bedding seemed moist, but that couldn't be,* she thought. She turned on the light above the bed and her heart skipped a beat. As if on cue, Sakuntala provided the cause of the dampness when she coughed and sprayed a pinkish foamy froth over the bed, herself, and her mother. Pranee woke up, not realizing yet where she was or what was going on. She had hoped it was all just a bad dream, but reality hit her hard, snapping her back to full consciousness. There was bloody froth covering everything, including herself and her daughter. Sakuntala coughed again, spraying more of the frothy pink around the bed, and Pranee let out a harrowing scream. Doctors and nurses came running into the room, each and every one of them shocked at the scene in front of them.

Two of the nurses quickly put on surgical gloves and helped Pranee from the bed. She fought them and screamed louder. Finally composing herself enough to yell, "What's wrong with my baby? Oh god! Sakuntala! Sakuntala!"

Pranom and the nurses pulled Pranee from the room and down the hall to another room. A doctor came in to first retrieve some of the bloody liquid covering her and then to administer a sedative to the hysterical mother. Pranom stood in the corner, tears flowing down her face and her hands covering her mouth.

When Pranee woke up two hours later, she was groggy, thirsty, and her head was pounding. Pranom held her hand and rubbed her head.

Pranee sat up in the bed.

"Where's Sakuntala? Is she okay?"

"The doctors are in with her. They've cleaned her up and moved her to another room," Pranom said through bloodshot teary eyes.

"I have to go to her," Pranee said, getting up out of the hospital bed. Her head pounded, but she was determined. She walked out of the room with Pranom following close behind.

"Mrs. Sodchuen, come with me. Your daughter is right down the hall."

A nurse wearing plastic gloves and a surgical mask covering her mouth and nose intercepted the frantic mother, grabbed Pranee by the arm, and led her toward her daughter's new room.

Two doctors and a nurse wearing the same surgical garb were in deep discussion by Sakuntala's bed. They turned when Pranee entered the room, and one of the doctors helped her into a chair next to her child. Sakuntala's bed was clean now. Her red pajamas were also cleaned and neatly folded on the table next to the bed. Thick white towels lay across her chest and alongside her tiny frail body that struggled for every breath. Pranee kissed her forehead and lay down on the bed, pulling her daughter close. The doctors did not have to tell her the situation.

"Sakuntala? I know you can hear Mommy," she whispered into the child's ear. She cleared a couple of pieces of hair from Sakuntala's face and kissed her cheek. "I'm here with you. And I'm not leaving you again, ever.

"I want you to know something. You've always made Mommy so very proud of you. Everything you do and everything you are brings joy to Mommy's life. You're an angel who blessed Mommy with happiness from the moment you were born. I couldn't love you anymore than I do, no one ever could."

The child purred and shifted in the bed next to Pranee as if reacting to her mother's tender words.

"I'm here, baby. I love you so, so much. I'm here."

The cough started small and weak but then exploded with another spray of pink foam. Sakuntala's head lifted off the bed and then dropped back to the pillow, her life escaping with a final few gasps.

Pranee whimpered, still holding her daughter. "Oh, Sakuntala. Please come back. Don't leave me. Not yet. Not now. Mommy loves you, baby. Please don't leave me," she whimpered and then broke down sobbing while clutching her lifeless child in her arms.

The doctors allowed her stay there for several moments before moving around the bed to help Pranee up. They had more work to do. She whimpered softly without raising her head. Her body felt limp as if her own spirit was taken, but something else caught the doctor's attention. Pranee's skin was hot to the touch. She was burning up with a temperature. The doctor asked the nurse for assistance, and they moved her into an adjoining room.

Sakuntala's body was moved to the hospital morgue where an autopsy was performed. Samples from the vital organs, skin, and blood were taken for further study and then the body was cremated as was typical protocol for people dying of infectious diseases. It was an extremely rare occurrence. Very few people died from dengue fever and even more uncommon was the transmission between two people. Protocol also demanded the local doctors to alert the World Health Organization, who in turn contacted several other leading health authorities, including the Centers for Disease Control. Within minutes of receiving the information at the CDC, an alert was sent back to the originating hospital as well as the Thai government. This did not appear to be dengue fever.

It was Wednesday morning in Washington, DC, when the call came from Geneva, Switzerland. Dr. Kumara Rai of the WHO was calling the person she believed to be the leading authority on H5N1. After exchanging pleasantries, Dr. Rai got right to the point. She described in great medical detail the facts provided by the local doctors in Kamphaeng Phet. Then, she conveyed her concern.

"The symptoms point to an influenza virus, not dengue fever. I believe Sakuntala was misdiagnosed. Either H1N1 or H5N1, I'm not sure which. But I believe the more likely strain was avian," Dr. Rai reasoned.

"The symptoms certainly point to influenza, but I'm interested in why you believe it to be avian," Taubenberger said. "What makes you think it couldn't be H1N1?"

"I spoke to the aunt, a woman named Pranom. Sakuntala lived with her about one hundred kilometers north of Bangkok, where her mother lived and worked. The mother, Pranee, had not been home in several weeks. Sakuntala became ill Sunday night. Her mother was driven directly from Bangkok to the hospital where Sakuntala was being treated.

"Pranom and Sakuntala lived in the village of Kamphaeng Phet, a fairly large village where free-range chicken farming is common. It is my belief or, more precisely, my theory that Sakuntala was infected with H5N1 by a diseased chicken in Kamphaeng Phet. Since her mother traveled straight to the hosp—"

Taubenberger stopped listening as his mind jumped ahead to where Dr. Rai was obviously going. *Transmission of the H5N1 virus from human to human,* he thought.

"First thing we have to do is see her blood work," Taubenberger insisted. "And I need to get samples of both of her lungs as quickly as possible," he continued.

"I'll do my best to send you samples of both, Doctor. Samples are already on board a Thai medical jet to the CDC in Atlanta. I'll ask them to send reports of their findings immediately to you, as well as any samples they can spare. We've dispatched an emergency response crew to the hospital in Kamphaeng Phet. Let's keep a line open between us, Dr. Taubenberger. Any information you think important to share with the WHO, please call me directly."

"Of course, Dr. Rai. We'll be in touch." He hung up the phone. Ann Reid had come into his office halfway through the conversation and was sitting across the desk from him.

"Her reasoning is sound," Ann said matter-of-factly.

"It is, I agree. And it's not like Dr. Rai to jump to conclusions without reviewing and confirming all the facts several times," Taubenberger said.

"She also sounds concerned. Out of character for someone in her position, no?" Reid wondered.

Taubenberger sat, shaking his head up and down in agreement, the same concern was obvious on his face.

Sakuntala Sodchuen died on September 8, 2004, because of complications from H5N1 while her mother lay in critical condition with similar symptoms. A massive army of volunteers wearing protective plastic bags over flip-flops, surgical gloves, and masks went into action the following day. Under the supervision of government agencies, tens of millions of chickens throughout the country were destroyed. It was a devastating blow to the billion-dollar-a-year Thai poultry business, but Deputy Prime Minister Chaturon Chaisang understood the dangers of the alternative.

"If we have to spend billions, we will," he announced at a press conference. "The priorities now are to protect humans from the disease and minimize the chances of more chickens being infected."

The second part of his announcement would be the more difficult part to accomplish. Medical researchers had been coordinating with other sciences studying the spread of H5N1. It was theorized that migratory birds may be having an impact on the world's collective health. The research indicated that the virus was mutating in these wild birds that traveled specific routes around the globe, following migration patterns dating back thousands of years. When the wild flocks stopped to feed and rest, the virus was spread to domesticated fowl in the villages of Southeast Asia where chickens roamed the streets and shared pens in neighboring yards. Presently, there was little that could be done to stop the migration of millions of wild birds, so destroying the poultry believed to be infected on the ground was the logical defense. Taubenberger believed it was a strong theory and could explain how Sakuntala could have caught the disease. It also could explain how millions of people around the world in 1918 became terribly ill with the same form of influenza at almost the exact same time. If migrating birds were the cause of the original epidemic, it could happen again. *It could be happening right now*, he thought.

On September 20, Pranee Sodchuen passed away from complications related to the H5N1 virus. Samples of her lungs were sent to Taubenberger's department at the US Armed Forces Institute of Pathology. Eight people had died of the same strain in Thailand. Five others were infected but survived.

Pranom Thongchan was one of the survivors.

14

A Frightening Success

Washington, DC

October 6, 2005

*"This is huge, huge, huge," said John Oxford, a professor of virology
at St. Bartholomew's and the Royal London Hospital who was not
part of the research team. "It's a huge breakthrough to be able to put
a searchlight on a virus that killed 100 million people. I can't think
of anything bigger that's happened in virology for many years."*
—*New York Times*, October 6, 2005

The headline read "Experts Unlock Clues to Spread of 1918 Flu Virus."
Science reporter Gina Kolata's article detailed the historic and near-
miraculous breakthrough by Taubenberger's team at the US Armed
Forces Institute of Pathology. It had taken nearly ten years, but
Taubenberger, Reid, and the rest of their small team had finally pieced
together this viral jigsaw puzzle. During the decade, while the virus
begrudgingly revealed its secrets, the team had published the first five
of the eight gene sequences that made up the virus. The final three
sequences were half of the virus's total DNA length and had finally
been extracted. Taubenberger's discovery was being printed in two of
the most influential and respected science magazines that very day. The
journals *Nature* and *Science* both featured stories about the history of
Taubenberger's microbiological investigation, the unlikely participants

that contributed to the success, as well as the final three gene sequences, of the 1918 killer flu virus.

"It's a landmark," the *Nature* article quoted Penn State University virologist Eddie Holmes. "Not only is this the first time this has been done for any ancient pathogen, but it also deals with the agent of the most important disease pandemic in human history."

The medical and scientific worlds applauded the Team Taubenberger achievement. However, those were not the only communities whose attention had been captured.

Washington, DC

October 7, 2005

Taubenberger sat at his desk, rubbing his chin and staring out the window. He had been receiving congratulatory calls and e-mails since the news of his discovery was printed the day before and enjoying his scientific celebrity status until the call he had received ten minutes earlier. That call came from the White House and informed Taubenberger that a car was being sent to his office and his participation in a late morning meeting was urgently requested. "Urgently requested," he replayed the phrasing in his mind. That sure sounds like a polite way to say, "Get your ass over here now." He was asked to prepare a presentation with additional details of the report that appeared the day before in *Nature*, *Science*, the *New York Times*, and many other newspapers across the United States and around the world.

These types of reports and articles rarely stirred this type of response, he thought. *I guess we woke a few people up.*

The knock on his open door startled him. The two young men in dark suits and communication devices in their ears did not help calm his nerves.

They sent the Secret Service, he thought. *Okay, stay calm.*

"Dr. Jeffrey Taubenberger?" asked one of the men.

"Yes."

"I'm Special Agent Ken Cavanagh, and this is Special Agent Tony Ponturo. Are you ready to go?" Cavanagh asked with efficiency.

No small talk, just straight to business. They were here with a purpose, and that was to transport Taubenberger back to the White House. Taubenberger was still unaware of who he was meeting with but realized it must be someone of importance if they're sending the Secret Service.

"Ah sure, just let me grab my coat and my briefcase," he said, moving around his office.

"I'll take that for you, sir," said Ponturo, grabbing the briefcase from Taubenberger's hand.

"That's not necessary, agent. I'm perfectly capable of carrying—"

"Standard procedure, sir," interrupted the Secret Service agent, opening the case and checking its contents.

Taubenberger left his office flanked by the two agents. Their walk was quick and determined. Ann Reid intercepted them at the building's exit.

"Agent Cavanagh, I need a minute with my associate," he requested.

The agent just nodded and took a few steps away.

"Do you have everything you need?" she asked.

"Yes. Interesting escorts they sent, don't you think?"

"Very. Do you know who you're meeting with?"

"At first, I assumed some lower-level administration type. But now I'm not so sure."

"Well, if you meet Condoleezza Rice, get me her autograph, will you?" Reid asked, smiling and brushing lint off Taubenberger's jacket. "Oh, and remember to tell me what she's wearing!"

"I doubt I'm meeting with the secretary of state, Ann."

"Doctor? Please, we're on a schedule," Cavanagh pointed out.

"See ya later," Taubenberger said and continued on his way with his escort.

"Good luck," Reid called after her boss.

He waved his hand goodbye and gave a thumbs-up without turning around.

The black SUV pulled up to the front gates of the White House. Taubenberger had been here once before, but as part of the White House tour, he did not enter the front gate. After the guard checked the ID with the computer in the gatehouse, he returned Taubenberger's driver's license with a plastic Visitor's Pass.

"Have a nice day, Dr. Taubenberger," the guard said through the SUV's window, and the gate opened.

"Thank you," Taubenberger said, clipping the pass on to the breast pocket of his sport coat.

The car pulled up to the front of the White House and stopped. A member of the White House press department hustled down the stairs to meet him, shook his hand, and grabbed Taubenberger's briefcase from the SUV. The young man's name escaped Taubenberger, who was in awe as he climbed the world-famous steps toward the most powerful building on the planet. He studied the marble steps, thick columns, and the enormous light hanging above them. He stopped and looked back at the White House lawn from the top step, a view very few citizens ever experience.

"Dr. Taubenberger, this way, please," said the press aide.

Taubenberger emptied his pockets into the small plastic bowl and stepped through the metal detector inside the White House. A large African-American man opened his briefcase and carefully searched every inch of it while Taubenberger took his personal belongings from the plastic bowl and returned them to several pockets. Once finished, the security guard closed the briefcase and handed it back.

"Thank you, Dr. Taubenberger. Have a nice day," he said.

Taubenberger checked the Visitor's Pass but did not see his name on it. He smiled politely and continued down several hallways, walking past rooms he had only seen on TV. They walked past several people he recognized from the news, and Taubenberger couldn't help but stare. The press aide stopped at an unusually small elevator door. While they waited for the door to open, Taubenberger continued taking in every sight and smell of his unique visit. He glanced at the wall next to the elevator's door. The wallpaper was dark but warm, giving the first home a feeling of power and importance. It appeared to have a raised pattern on it, but Taubenberger couldn't be sure in this light. He reached up and ran his finger across the wallpaper, satisfying his curiosity.

"Please don't touch anything in the White House, Dr. Taubenberger," said the Secret Service agent, who appeared seemingly out of thin air.

He pulled his hand back quickly and stuck it in his pocket.

"I, I, uh, I'm sorry," he replied and turned to the aide in hopes he wasn't in any trouble. "Why does everyone know my name?" he asked when the elevator door opened.

"This way, Dr. Taubenberger," the aide said with a smirk, holding the door and allowing the doctor to step in first but not before taking several quick glances searching for the location of the Secret Service agent who had disappeared. There were no buttons inside the elevator.

The walls were smooth and metallic, and Taubenberger could see the warped reflection of the aide and himself in them. There was a light above and a dark piece of plastic in the corner that Taubenberger assumed covered a camera. The elevator must run directly between two floors, he thought. There was no noticeable movement by the elevator, but the doors opened and they stepped out into a much colder hallway. The warm colors and stately charm of the White House were gone. This hallway was well lit, and the white walls gave the appearance of a hospital to its visitor.

"Dr. Taubenberger. Thank you for coming on such short notice," said the woman walking down the hallway with an important stride to greet him.

"No problem at all, Madam Secretary," he stuttered in response to Condoleezza Rice. *Blue blazer and knee-length skirt, white button-down blouse, USA flag brooch pin*, he said to himself. *That's a power suit worn by a powerful woman*, he thought. They shook hands, and she pointed down the hall from the direction she had just come. "We've been waiting for you. The meeting is going to start any minute so if you will come with me," she said, leading him down the hallway to the double steel doors with no doorknobs.

When they were just a couple of feet away, the doors slid open, disappearing into the walls and then closed behind them after they entered the room.

The conference room was large with a table in its center that looked to be thirty feet long and eight feet wide. The dark wood of the table was matched by the dark leather of the twenty or so expensive chairs circling it. The far wall opposite the door he just entered contained a dark piece of glass nearly as long as the room and three feet in height. The other three walls were covered with large wooden panels approximately three feet square in size. His first impression of the room was that of extreme power and secrecy. Taubenberger wondered what other kind of meetings were held in this room beneath the White House. He had no idea that the room was located five stories below street level and featured beyond state-of-the-art security measures so that no one could hear or see what took place inside it.

Secretary Rice walked to the far side of the table after pointing out Taubenberger's chair to him, which became obvious after the fact since there was a white name tag with his name on it three feet from the table's edge. He noticed the other three name tags in front of the chairs next to his, recognizing all the names. The three people, who were talking in the corner when Taubenberger came in, made their way over to him. He knew each of them well, professionally and personally.

"Hello again, Dr. Taubenberger," said Phillip Campbell, editor-in-chief of *Nature* magazine as he reached out with his right hand and shook Taubenberger's. "It seems your historic findings caught the attention of our government," he continued.

"Indeed. Do you have any idea why we've been asked to come here?" Taubenberger nervously inquired.

Campbell shook his head. "No, but I think we're going to find out very shortly."

"Congratulations, Jeffrey," said Dr. Richard Ebright, not as welcoming as Campbell. The bacteriologist from Rutgers University in New Jersey was a well-known and respected scientist whose views did not always align with Taubenberger's.

"Thank you, Richard. It's good to see you again. Hello, Barbara," Taubenberger said to the third person approaching him.

Barbara Hatch-Rosenberg's reputation as a conspiracy theorist was well documented throughout the scientific community. Her aggressive pursuit of the 2001 anthrax attack following the 9/11 terrorist attacks had focused the national media and security authorities on an innocent scientist in the United States and pressured the FBI relentlessly and mistakenly to arrest Dr. Steven J. Hatfill. Her theories were based on innuendo and rumors, but her dogged and very public pursuit never waned. In the years since, the government agreed to settle a lawsuit for nearly $6 million with Dr. Hatfill for improperly invading his privacy and ultimately ruining his career.

"Hello, Dr. Taubenberger, and I assume congratulations are in order," she said with obvious sarcasm.

"I accept your congratulations on behalf of my entire team, Barbara," he said with sincere pride.

"Well, it appears you all know each other so that saves us the time and trouble of introductions," Secretary Rice said from across the table. "Please sit down. We'll get started very shortly. We're all very busy and we'll try to keep this meeting as short as possible, but we have a lot to cover," she continued when another door that was not visible to the guests in the room opened behind the secretary of state next to the large glass. Unlike the door the scientists entered, this one opened in a typical fashion, appearing to swing open like any ordinary door with one exception: there was no doorknob on the inside facing the conference room. The two men who stepped into the room first made Taubenberger's heart rate rise. Secretary of Health and Human Services Michael Levitt was speaking with Atty. Gen. Alberto Gonzales as they crossed through the doorframe. The four scientists looked at one another, wondering what was going on. Next, Homeland Security Director Michael Chertoff and Surgeon General Richard Carmona entered the conference room, which caused Taubenberger's heart rate to jump further, and when Pres. George W. Bush followed them through the door, his heart nearly stopped completely. The four scientists sprang from their seats in respect.

"Good morning. Please be seated," the president said calmly and in his customary friendly tone, making his way around the table to shake hands and introduce himself to each of his guests, ending with Taubenberger.

"Dr. Taubenberger," he said while extending his hand. "Congratulations on your discovery. It's very exciting stuff. Sorry for the short notice on this meeting, but we felt it important enough to get you all together and over here as quickly as possible," he explained while making his way around the room to his seat in the center on the other side of the large table. His cabinet members sat to either side of the commander in chief who was directly across the table from Taubenberger.

"Let's get right to it, shall we?" the president asked.

"We've been monitoring your impressive progress for years, Dr. Taubenberger," began Richard Carmona who was seated to the president's far right at the table. The surgeon general was complimentary in his tone, but his appearance conveyed an intensity and critical importance to the guests in the room. Carmona was in his early sixties and wearing his military dress uniform, which was adorned with numerous medals on his chest. The balding man with steel-blue eyes and square jaw sat up straight and rigid with his hands clasped across the thick folder he had just opened. His tone was less friendly than the president's and more interrogating.

"You've accomplished a true scientific breakthrough and the accolades are well deserved. What we're interested in discussing with you this morning is when, where, and what can we do about the next bird flu pandemic that you and your fellow scientists feel is a certainty," he explained. "And may I also add that I believe you are correct."

"Well, Mr. Carmona, 'when' is the magic question. The mutation of the virus has apparently been taking place around the world," Taubenberger began when he was interrupted by Alberto Gonzales.

"Before we get ahead of ourselves, there are some of us in the room who are at somewhat of a disadvantage, scientifically or medically speaking," said the country's attorney general, directing the last portion of his statement to the president, who agreed by nodding. "Can we take a step back? I know your research focused on the influenza epidemic at the start of the last century, but I'm confused as to why. What does that event have to do with the H5N1 virus of today?"

"And," began the director of Homeland Security, Michael Chertoff. Seated at the other end of the conference table to the president's far left, he paused, waiting for the entire room to direct their attention at him. "I'd like to know more about the impact the flu had on society, infrastructure, and the government as well as the consequences and lessons learned during the outbreak and recovery."

The purpose of this meeting was now perfectly clear to Taubenberger. He remembered the quote attributed to Japanese Admiral Isoroku Yamamoto after the attack on Pearl Harbor: "I fear all we have done is to awaken a sleeping giant and fill him with a terrible resolve."

Apparently, I've awakened a sleeping giant but filled him with a massive undertaking, the anticipation and possible prevention of the world's next great pandemic, he thought. He looked around the room, then down to his notes in front of him, and then back to the powerful people seated with him at this table. The president of the United States and most of his cabinet sat quietly, waiting for his unprepared, off-the-cuff presentation. He looked to his right at Phillip Campbell, who looked back with an expression that said either "Good luck" or "I'm glad I'm not you right now." He didn't bother looking to his left at Ebright or Rosenberg, who he knew would not offer the same semi-support.

"Is there a problem, Dr. Taubenberger?" asked the president.

"No problem, sir. I'm just a little nervous. I wasn't really prepared to deliver a presentation to this—"

"It's less of a presentation and more of a discussion. We need to understand the severity of this flu, and you all are the world's leading

authorities. There's really no need to be nervous, Dr. Taubenberger,"
explained Rice.

That's easy for you to say, he thought. *You work every day with the
most powerful people in the world.*

"Thank you, Madame Secretary," he said trying to calm himself.
He cleared his throat. "In the spring of 1918, the first outbreak of the
bird flu virus took place. During the months of March, April, May, and
June, large portions of the world's population became sick with flu-like
symptoms. The onset of which were very similar to the common flu,
compared to the latter two waves. It was also not nearly as lethal," he
began.

"The epidemic's first wave hit the armies hard in Europe as
well," contributed the surgeon general. "In fact, German general Von
Ludendorff blamed the failure of a German offensive in July of 1918
on the flu. Thousands of German soldiers were leaving the front lines
because they were too sick to fight. The influenza definitely had an
impact on that offensive and could have helped end the German
campaign entirely."

"Are you saying the flu actually ended World War I?" asked Alberto
Gonzales.

"Not by itself. There were many factors that came into play. Nation
fatigue, costs, and a lack of progress by either side were certainly elements
that lead to the armistice. But the flu just might have been the final
determinant. If you can't field an army, you can't very well fight a war,"
responded Carmona.

A beeping sound from beneath the table interrupted the discussion.
Condoleezza Rice reached down and picked up a phone. She leaned over
and whispered something into the president's ear.

"By all means, let him join," the president responded.

"We have another participant joining our discussion. Dr. Terrence
Tumpey of the Centers for Disease Control could not make it in person,
so he'll be joining us via satellite," said the secretary of state while
motioning to the wall on her left with one hand and hanging up the
phone with the other. The four scientists looked to the same wall on
their right where the large wooden panels dissolved away, revealing the
wall to actually be a large digital monitor. Dr. Tumpey's framed face
appeared, smiling back to the room in the center of the wall with type

beneath him that read, *CDC, Atlanta, GA.* Secretary of State Rice introduced Tumpey to everyone in attendance.

"Good morning. I'm sorry I couldn't make it in person, but I'm honored to be attending. Thank you, Mr. President, for inviting me," Tumpey said from the wall.

"Thank you for taking the time, Dr. Tumpey. Dr. Taubenberger, please continue," the president requested.

"Yes, sir, Mr. President. The second wave began in August 1918 and lasted through December before vanishing again. This time, the onset of symptoms was swift and devastating. A high fever was accompanied by incapacitating aches and pains, severe headaches, sudden collapse, and death within days and sometimes hours. The cause of death was similar to pneumonia and, most times, mistaken for it. The virus would infect and break down the lung's lining, causing them to fill with frothy, bloody mucus, which, in turn, caused the victim to literally drown in his own liquids."

"What made this wave unique and terrifying for the populace was the demographics of those that were succumbing to it," said Dr. Richard Ebright, entering the discussion for the first time. "Influenza usually killed people whose immune system had deteriorated or not yet developed: the very young or the elderly. This flu attacked and killed young healthy adults in the prime of their lives, people whose immune system had typically fought off the flu. It was unprecedented for the medical community in 1918," he continued.

"Correct," Taubenberger agreed. "And to support Dr. Carmona's point about the impact on World War I, of the fifty-seven thousand US troops that died during the war, research shows that forty-three thousand died from complications because of influenza."

"So just fourteen thousand of our boys died on the battlefield," Chertoff stated more than asked.

"That's what the data tells us, yes, Mr. Secretary," confirmed Taubenberger. The president sat back in his chair surprised by the numbers he had just heard. "Without getting bogged down in a World War I history lesson, if we suffered that kind of casualty rate from this virus, it's safe to assume the other countries must have suffered the same. Is this the determining factor you mentioned a moment ago, Rich?" he asked the surgeon general.

"Because of the time and the poor conditions, the numbers can't be confirmed. The records just aren't that accurate. I believe it is safe to assume the countries that had been fighting for years, since the outset of the war, suffered worse. Consider the horrendous conditions in the trenches combined with malnourishment, combat fatigue, and chemical weapons attacks, all this had to severely weaken every soldier's immune system. There are reports of trucks and horse-drawn carts carrying thousands of soldiers on both sides, away from the front lines each day, never to return."

"If I may, Mr. President?" asked Phillip Campbell.

"Please," the president responded, motioning with his hand, palm facing up.

"It wasn't only the soldiers in the trenches who endured the pandemic. In the spring of 1918, President Wilson became bedridden with the flu. There are reports that he was near death," began Campbell. The sixty-five-year-old editor-in-chief of *Nature* magazine addressed his audience like a college professor giving a lecture on a subject in which he was clearly very knowledgeable. His full head of white hair and his tan suit and red bowtie helped that appearance. "Wilson's main advisor and confidant, Colonel Edward House, was sick the entire time they're in Versailles, in the autumn of 1918, during the treaty negotiations. As well, Great Britain's Prime Minister David Lloyd George had a mild bout with the flu that April.

"On the German side, Prince Max von Baden had replaced Von Hindenburg as chancellor and taken over negotiations for Germany, which advance steadily toward peace as Von Baden wanted to end the war as much as anyone. He'd seen enough. They were very close to finalizing the treaty. However, on October 23, Von Baden came down with the flu and was bedridden for two weeks, which pushed the signing of the truce back to November 11.

"In the meantime, soldiers continued dying by the thousands on the battlefields of Europe, and around the world, people were dying by the millions. Almost every individual who was negotiating the armistice had a brush with the flu. They're all stuck in a city inundated with death while being briefed on the growing statistics of their citizens dying back home. There had to be an overwhelming concern for their own health and safety.

"As a result, one of the weakest treaties in human history was quickly signed when Von Baden was healthy enough to return to the negotiating table. The Treaty of Versailles lacked any real military teeth and demanded war reparations from Germany that were basically impossible to repay, which drove Germany and Austria into financial collapse well before the Great Depression. Many scholars believe that all this led directly to Hitler's rise in power and, eventually, World War II," Campbell concluded. He looked around the table as if he were waiting for questions. The director of Homeland Security spoke first.

"You said millions around the world were dying. What kind of numbers are we talking about?" asked Chertoff.

"The numbers vary. One guess is fifty million people worldwide died in that single year. Some believe the number to be closer to two hundred million, especially when one considers that seventeen million people died in India alone," Taubenberger said.

"What can you tell us about right here at home?" asked Health and Human Services Secretary Michael Leavitt. "How did our medical facilities fare during this pandemic?"

"If you don't mind, Doctor?" Carmona, sitting to Leavitt's left, asked Taubenberger while thumbing through his notes.

"Please, sir, go right ahead," Taubenberger offered, feeling relieved that others in the room were taking much of the load off his shoulders.

"The numbers are staggering," he began and motioned to the monitor wall. Dr. Tumpey's image slid to the top right of the wall as statistics began appearing on the left side. "Twenty-eight percent of the US population became ill with flu during the 1918–1919 outbreak. That's over twenty-nine million Americans, of which six hundred thousand died from the virus.

"In New York City alone, twenty thousand people died from the illness during the autumn of 1918," he continued as pictures from the period begin appearing on the wall between the statistics and Dr. Tumpey: civilians wearing protective masks on their mouths and noses walk the streets of New York; fans, players, and umpires at a baseball game wearing the masks; morticians loading lifeless bodies into the back of a horse-drawn hearse while wearing the same masks. The pictures accompanied the surgeon general's stats and descriptions. "Hospitals in Philadelphia, Washington, Boston, and New York were overburdened. Patients were forced to return home because of a lack of space and, in reality, because there was very little that could be done to reverse the course of the virus. Society virtually came to a standstill as schools, movie theaters, churches, anywhere people congregated were closed. The virus was airborne, and they knew that large gatherings helped spread the disease."

"It appeared, each time, almost simultaneously around the world. The Spanish influenza and the Spanish lady were the original names associated with the virus because it was believed it originated in the trenches of World War I," added Taubenberger confidently. His knowledge of the topic and the casual conversation around the table had caused his nerves to subside. "The second theory of origin comes from the first recorded medical history in the United States. On the morning of March 11, 1918, in Camp Funston, Kansas, four soldiers reported to the infirmary with flu-like symptoms. By noon, hundreds at the camp were sick, and within a week, the virus had spread to every corner of the country. This theory suggested that the United States inadvertently sent the virus to Europe on troop transport ships carrying our soldiers who were already sick."

"But you said it broke out around the world almost simultaneously?" Leavitt points out.

"It did," says Taubenberger. "That's why I believe this theory is incorrect. There were reports in Europe, elsewhere around the United States, and indeed from around the world shortly after March 11 that the virus was spreading long before any of our troops could have delivered it.

"Therefore, I believe, that the influenza virus of 1918–1919 was a stain of bird flu that had mutated and jumped directly to humans."

"Explain that. What do you base your conclusion on?" asked the president.

"Without delving into too much science, all viruses are made up of eight genes or genomes. Our research demonstrates that the eight genes that make up the 1918 virus differs from human flu viruses in very important ways, which suggests that none of the genes came from a virus that previously infected people. It is the most birdlike of all mammalian flu viruses and also the most dangerous."

"Which is exactly why the report should not have been made public," interrupted Dr. Barbara Hatch-Rosenberg sitting next to Taubenberger. "You've done remarkable work, Jeffrey, no one denies that. But this information, this formula could be extremely dangerous should it escape, and there is a long history of things like this escaping."

"I agree with Barbara," Ebright jumped back into the conversation. "By publishing the entire sequence, you have supplied the blueprint to anyone who means us harm, how to build perhaps the most effective bioweapon ever known to mankind."

"There is always a risk, Richard," Taubenberger responded but was again interrupted.

"A risk? I'd say it's verging on inevitability, Jeffrey. We must take steps to ensure that this virus is never replicated and produced by people who would use it against humanity!" Ebright said emphatically.

"Well, it's too late for that," said Tumpey from the monitor on the wall.

"What does that mean, Terrence?" asked Hatch-Rosenberg.

"We've already reconstructed the virus here at the CDC," said Tumpey.

"Under whose authority? Jesus Christ!" Ebright mumbled under his breath but loud enough for everyone to hear.

"We consulted with the US National Science Advisory Board for Biosecurity."

"And the NSABB gave you the green light?" asked Hatch-Rosenberg incredulously.

Taubenberger jumped in. "There was an emergency meeting last week to consider the risks. The NSABB agreed that the work is important enough for public health and safety to keep moving forward with our research."

"And now your research includes reconstructing and bringing back to life the most dangerous virus in history," Ebright stated more than asked. "Just out of curiosity, what biosafety lab level did you use while conducting your experiment?"

"Biosafety level 3," Tumpey responded from the wall.

"Just 3, not 4," again Ebright stated rather than asked.

"What's the difference?" asked Rice.

"Biosafety level 4 is the strictest biosafety condition," answered Carmona. "It requires experimenters to wear full bodysuits among other precautions," the surgeon general continued.

"Need I remind you both of the SARS virus escaping from labs in Singapore and Beijing in just the last two years under biosafety level

3 conditions?" asked Ebright, now staring at Tumpey's image on the monitor wall. "Incredible!" he finished his point.

"Richard, I can assure that biosafety level 3 was more than adequate. There was no accidental escape," said Tumpey.

"Well, we don't know that yet, do we? If the NSABB meeting happened last week and we assume you did your experiments following that meeting, you may still be in an incubation period," Ebright pointed out. "What about theft from a disgruntled or disturbed or extremist laboratory employee?" he asked.

Now Tumpey was becoming agitated, "This is the CDC, Richard. It's not some horse-shit, outdated lab in the Ukraine. Sorry for my language, Mr. President."

"That's quite all right. I've heard that word before and actually used it a few times myself. Tell us about your experiments with the virus. I believe you said you were successful in reconstructing it?" the president asked Tumpey.

"Yes, sir. We infected six lab mice with the virus. In four days, their lungs had generated thirty-nine thousand times more virus particles than any modern-day flu strain. A day later, all six mice were dead. Quite frankly, I didn't expect it to be as lethal as it was," Tumpey concluded.

"Nobody ever does, Dr. Tumpey. That's my point," Ebright said.

"All right, its water under the bridge at this point, people," said the president, rising from his chair to stretch his legs. "Stay seated, please," he said to the group around the conference table who began to rise from their chairs. The president walked the length of the room. "So we have this flu virus that's been brought back from the dead. It's the same virus that killed at least fifty million people a century ago, dramatically impacted the world socially, politically, and may have helped lead to the Second World War. Now you believe it may be returning again, Dr. Taubenberger?"

"Excuse me, Mr. President," interrupted Chertoff before an answer could be given. "Can we take a step back? Dr. Taubenberger, you said there were three waves of the virus. When did the third occur?" he asked.

"The third wave had the same virulence as the second and began in February 1919 and lasted until around April that same year," Taubenberger said.

"And what stopped the epidemic each time?" Chertoff followed up.

"That's a good question. It could have been because the virus continued to mutate and was no longer as virulent to humans," said Taubenberger.

"Or it could have burned itself out," added Campbell. "To Jeffrey's point, our immune systems may have finally figured out how to successfully fight the virus off or more likely, a combination of the shutting down of societal gathering places and other precautions limited the number of remaining hosts."

"Explain," instructed Rice.

Taubenberger leaned forward and answered for Campbell. "It may have been too efficient. Death came so quickly that those carrying the illness did not have time to pass it along once they were contagious. The virus burned itself out because of its effectiveness and a lack of opportunity to spread further."

The room remained silent for a moment, absorbing Taubenberger's last statement.

"The doctors and scientists of that era, was there nothing they could do to combat the virus?" asked Leavitt.

"Viruses had not yet been discovered by the scientific community. They were just too small for the microscopes of the day. They didn't know what they were fighting," Taubenberger said softly, almost apologetically.

"Which brings us to today and H5N1," Carmona began. "Explain your findings and how they relate to what is happening today."

Taubenberger adjusted a few papers on the conference table in front of him. "It has taken us ten years to unravel the genetic code of the 1918 virus. While we've been doing this work, we have coordinated with the CDC"—he motioned toward the monitor wall where Tumpey nodded in agreement—"the World Health Organization, and several other international agencies. As you know, the world health community watches, tracks, and studies every kind of viral outbreak anywhere on the planet. While we've been decoding this jigsaw puzzle, we've shared our findings with those agencies who share with us specimens from new outbreaks. We've kept a careful eye on the East and Far East where livestock and poultry mingle with the human populations in thousands of villages in that region. It's called free-range farming. Since 1997, there have been a number of smaller outbreaks here." Taubenberger glanced to the monitor wall and was surprised to see a map of the area with statistics showing the number of sick and those who died in Thailand, Vietnam, China, and elsewhere.

"The full sequence of the 1918 flu virus strongly suggests that it was derived wholly from an ancestor that originally infected birds. When we compare the gene sequence from that strain to the samples from people who became ill in recent years, there are eerie similarities in six of the eight genes. Therefore, our research strongly suggests that the H5N1 virus can trace its ancestral roots to the 1918 virus. Viruses are a living organism, and as such, like us and everything else that lives, they are evolving or, more accurately, mutating. By studying the genetic codes and doing the research experiments that Dr. Tumpey is already performing," Taubenberger turned to his left and stared Dr. Barbara Hatch-Rosenberg in the eye, "I'm hopeful we can stay one step ahead of this potential killer." Rosenberg looked at Taubenberger in disagreement and was about to respond when he turned his attention back across the table to the president. "Mr. President, we are all well aware that technological and medical advances could be misused, but we are trying to understand what happened in nature a century ago, track the current strain that bears a great resemblance to that original strain, and try to figure out how to prevent another pandemic. Simply put, in this case, nature is the bioterrorist we have to fear.

"Mr. President, Dr. Tumpey's work has already shed some light on what can be done," Taubenberger insisted.

"Dr. Tumpey," the president turned to the monitor. "The floor is yours."

"Thank you, Mr. President. First, let me say that after recreating the 1918 virus, we did multiple experiments comparing and contrasting the genes with a number of viruses from today. Our research agrees with Dr. Taubenberger's findings. Both are avian viruses.

"In simplest terms, our experiments included simple gene swapping on the 1918 virus. When we replaced the hemagglutinin gene, which helps the virus enter healthy cells and infect them, the virus was no longer able to kill mice. In fact, the mice fought off the virus quite well. Replacing all three of the polymerase genes, which allows the virus to replicate, significantly reduced its virulence. We found that the hemagglutinin gene may be a key, but there are so many variables and possible combinations, no single change or gene is going to provide the magic answer. We have a lot more work to do," he concluded.

The room sat for a moment again. Taubenberger sensed that Tumpey may have been talking over his audience. "It's a combination effect. Dr. Tumpey has successfully weakened the 1918 virus by exchanging genes or moving sequences around. However, the present-day virus is not the exact same DNA sequence as the one that produced the1918 virus, and finding the combination of genes, nucleic acids, and other variables that may enable H5N1 to start a pandemic will require continued surveillance in the field.

"Up until now, most of the casualties from H5N1 have contracted the virus from birds. With one exception, a mother and daughter in Thailand, the flu has not passed from human to human. And as of yet, we don't know why the Thailand flu didn't spread beyond those two. But the mutation is definitely occurring. Think of it as field testing. The virus is looking for the proper combination to unleash itself on humanity, and when it finds the right combination, it may be deadlier than last time."

Taubenberger's last statement shook the room.

"Why do you think that?" asked Leavitt.

"In 1918, the mortality rate was around 2 percent," Carmona began. He said, reading the stats off a piece of paper on the table in front of him. He slowly looked up and around the room before he continued, "A lot of people got very sick, but only 2 percent of them died. Since 1997, a little over one hundred people have been infected with H5N1, and more than sixty of them have died. Today H5N1 has a mortality rate that's better than 60 percent."

"How do we stop it?" Finally came the question from Secretary of Homeland Security Michael Chertoff. For the first time, none of the scientists in the room supplied an immediate answer. "Can it be stopped?" Chertoff followed, offering a new question.

"That depends," said Taubenberger.

"On what?" asked Chertoff, losing his patience.

Taubenberger took a deep breath. "If our theory is correct, and I believe it is, the flu will originate in the Siberian plains where the largest portion of the world's wild birds nest during their mating season. I've been working with a Russian scientist, Dr. Alexander Shestopalov," Taubenberger paused briefly when a picture of Shestopalov appeared on the monitor wall next to Tumpey. He was shocked and more than just a little taken aback. How did they know he would be talking about a scientist studying bird migration in the middle of Siberia, Russia? Taubenberger looked at the impressive group of politicians sitting across from him, not knowing whether to continue, apologize, or be angry. He felt betrayed and violated. *Were they bugging me?* he wondered. *How dare they? I'm on American citizen doing critically important work for the US government and every citizen in this country. Hell, the entire world population.* His expression change did not conceal the fury welling up inside him.

"Dr. Taubenberger," Chertoff began very casually, trying to defuse the obviously angered doctor. "Do you really think that in the year 2005, after all this country has been through recently, as well as the current threats facing us, that we wouldn't be interested in an American microbiologist performing critically important research on virus mutations contacting a former Soviet bioweapons developer?"

Taubenberger's expression immediately changed. "Excuse me? Alexander Shestopalov is a brilliant and well-respected scientist at the Akademgorodok in Siberia."

"Now he is. But prior to the collapse of the Soviet Union, Dr. Shestopalov spent decades developing bioweapons for the Red Army and the KGB.

"You can relax, Jeffrey. We've been following your discussions and exchanges of information for some time now. We're very confident that there is no reason to suspect anything that could be construed as espionage or treason. Please continue with your explanation," Chertoff instructed.

Treason? Taubenberger was not satisfied. "Doesn't the government have to have probable cause or a warrant or something? You can't just spy on me. I'm an American citizen for Christ's sake."

"The Patriot Act provides us with all the just cause we need, Dr. Taubenberger. You should feel less angry and more secure in the knowledge that your government is watching out for your safety," Chertoff said with a grin.

"Listen, Doctor, you're doing your job and we're doing ours. We have to protect and defend *all* the citizens of this country. Please continue with your explanation. You were explaining bird migrations beginning in Siberia," said Secretary Rice reassuringly.

"Have your lawyer call me. I'm sure I will be able to convince him what we did was proper and legal," offered the president. His smile at Taubenberger conveyed a moment of levity. No lawyer could ever pick up the phone and dial the president of the United States directly. Bush was kidding. Taubenberger smirked in response and finally relented.

"Thank you, but there's no need, Mr. President," Taubenberger said.

"Good. Let's continue," responded the president very seriously.

"The former Soviet bioweapons developer has been tracking wild bird migrations for years. Hundreds of species nest in the open plains of the great Siberian tundra before migrating across the globe. Thanks in part to Shestopalov's research, we've discovered five major flyways the birds travel each year. The East Atlantic Flyway originates in Siberia, then crosses parts of Canada, travels down Western Europe, and ends on the west coast of Africa," he explained. When he was done describing the first route, the monitor wall once again grabbed his attention. Shestopalov's picture was now much smaller compared to the large 3-D map of the world where a red arrow began in Siberia, then traversed the exact course that Taubenberger had just described. The doctor couldn't help but chuckle. *Wow, they not only have been listening, but they've also been paying attention*, he thought.

"The second route is known as the Black Sea/Mediterranean Flyway," he paused to look at the monitor where the original red line faded away and the route he was about to describe began animating across the globe. Taubenberger smiled, shook his head, and continued, "This route, as some of you already know, crosses south over Eastern Europe, then through the Middle East, and ends in Northern Africa.

"Number 3 is referred to as the East Africa / West Asia Flyway. It follows a similar route as the previous one except it concludes in sub-Saharan Africa.

"The Central Asian Flyway travels through central China and into India.

"And finally, the East Asia/Australian Flyway begins in the same location, then cuts across Alaska before heading toward Southeast Asia and ending in Australia. This is the route that poses the most danger for our country. And unless the person running the animation wants to come out and explain why, I guess I'll continue. No? Okay.

"These wild birds have been using these major migratory highways for thousands of years. They vary their courses very little. They also rest in the same areas during their long journeys, usually where there is abundant food and water. These resting areas also attract other migratory birds whose treks are less global and more regional. The birds mingle, and the virus is passed along in these resting locations. It's the perfect bioweapon delivery system: hundreds of species, millions upon millions of birds flying to every corner of the world spreading the virus," Taubenberger leaned back in his chair, signaling he was done.

"Unfortunately for us and the rest of the world, these wild birds do not respect borders. There's just no way of keeping them from reaching their destinations," added Campbell.

"And the clock is ticking. Mr. President, one month ago, Dr. Shestopalov discovered one hundred birds in a relatively small location in Siberia that died from H5N1. It was the largest grouping of birds to die from the virus since we began our research," Taubenberger said, sitting back up.

"Well, apparently, we can't stop the migration of the entire planet's wild bird population. So what *can* we do?" asked the president.

"We can begin stockpiling vaccines for the flu immediately in hopes of inoculating the entire population once an outbreak occurs," suggested Chertoff.

"That won't work, Mr. Chertoff," Tumpey said from the wall. His picture pushed forward from the small corner he had been occupying and was now back to the size it was when he joined the meeting. "You see, as the virus mutates, the vaccines have to change to be effective on the virus's new sequence. We can stockpile hundreds of millions of doses of vaccine, but if it doesn't counter the most current virus, it's useless. The vaccine that works will be specific to the genetic code of the newest and deadliest virus."

"We also don't want to panic the public. Remember the predicted flu epidemic in 1976?" asked Carmona. "Forty-five million Americans were immunized against the swine flu that never materialized. Some of those people became sick with flu symptoms, and a small fraction of them died from adverse reactions to the vaccine. If we start immunizing people with vaccines that don't work, public reaction will first be negative toward the medical community *and* the government, but even more dangerous than that, they will turn into distrust and hopelessness. They won't trust us when the real pandemic hits."

"Suggestions then, people?" asked the president.

"First, I would advise that Dr. Taubenberger and his critical staff join the National Institute of Allergy and Infectious Diseases," Carmona said to the room but was looking at Taubenberger. "We'll get you all the assets you need to continue your current work. You'll have the full power and resources of the US government behind you. Dr. Tumpey, you will continue to coordinate from the CDC in Atlanta. You will work with and report to Taubenberger. Dr. Ebright and Dr. Rosenberg will return to their civilian work but will make themselves available for consult concerning the development of our nationally coordinated response if and when you are needed. Your participation is contingent on your public silence."

The two doctors nodded in agreement.

"Dr. Shestopalov will be contacted about Dr. Taubenberger moving to the NIAID. We have already had discussions with the Vector Research Institute and the Russian government who has agreed to provide any and all support in our efforts. Shestopalov will receive additional research funds from both governments. He'll also get the support of the Russian military for additional manpower and will continue tracking the flu from its ground zero, Siberia.

"There will be further instructions shortly, but you people are the point of the pyramid. I expect everyone to use good judgment and not speak publicly about any of this. The last thing this country needs is to be traumatized again with panic and fear. I'm asking you to keep this as quiet as possible. Understood?" Carmona's question was more of an order that would be enforced, and the four scientists in the room knew that.

They agreed.

"Good. Thank you, everybody. You will be hearing from us very shortly," concluded Carmona. The four scientists placed their notes and other documents back into their bags and stood to leave the conference room, thanking their impressive hosts for inviting them to the meeting. Dr. Tumpey said his goodbye and then disappeared from the monitor wall. The wall returned to the image of the wood panels that were there at the start of the meeting.

"Oh, Dr. Taubenberger, would you mind staying for a few minutes longer?" asked the surgeon general. Taubenberger noticed that no one from the other side of the table had budged from their seats. He returned to his. The door closed behind Ebright, Rosenberg, and Campbell.

"Dr. Taubenberger," began Secretary Rice, "you will have unfettered access to the White House and, in particular, everyone in this room. Your day-to-day science contact will be Dr. Carmona. We would like you to report as often as necessary."

"Understood. That won't be a problem," responded Taubenberger to the group.

"We've also begun the process of moving you and your staff to the NIAID," Carmona said. "There won't be any kind of announcement or press material sent out. We'd like to keep this quiet because we don't want any questions coming back as to why we're making these changes."

"Understood," Taubenberger said, becoming slightly overwhelmed from the speed in which everything was moving. His concern was obvious to everyone sitting across the table.

"Dr. Taubenberger," began the president in his most soothing and reassuring tone. "You know now that we've been following your progress. You've been on our radar for some time. What you've been able to accomplish with limited resources has been impressive. Your country and perhaps the entire world already owe you a debt of gratitude. However, if what you're telling us becomes a reality, well, I don't think any of us wants that to happen now, do we?

"In my speech next week to the UN, this pandemic threat will be brought to the world body. I'm going to warn the leaders of every country that they need to get on board now.

"We'll start prepping our major pharmaceutical companies. They will know that they need to have action plans ready at a moment's notice to start manufacturing whatever vaccines are needed. We're not going to let this virus surprise us. And if at the end of the day, there's nothing that can be done, well, history won't judge us on our inaction. Everything that can be done will be done in preparation, that, I promise you, Doctor."

"Thank you, Mr. President. I appreciate your kind words to me, and I want you to know that I'm ready and up to this challenge. So is every person that works with me."

"We will provide you with two telephones," added Chertoff. "They're secure landlines, one for your office at the NIAID and one for your home. The phones are preprogrammed with the direct contact information of everyone in this room."

"Wouldn't a cell be more efficient?" asked Taubenberger.

"Probably, but we can't have you losing a cell phone with speed dials to the president of the United States and his senior staff."

Good point, Taubenberger thought.

"This disc contains secure e-mail addresses for Dr. Carmona, Secretary Rice, and myself." Chertoff slid what appeared to be a mini DVD in a plastic case across the table to Taubenberger. "Download it to your computer and then destroy it. To e-mail us, all you have to do is type our first names and the program will finish the address."

First-name basis with the White House staff, he thought. *Even I'm impressed with that.*

"Do you have any questions, Dr. Taubenberger?" asked Rice.

"Is there any reason for concern for my safety?" he asked.

Chertoff smiled. "The Secret Service has added you to their list of priorities," he told Taubenberger and saw a slight exhale of relief. "Do you want to know your Secret Service code name?"

Taubenberger nodded yes.

"Scarecrow."

15

Nobody Wins

Seattle

April 2, 1919

The shot glanced off the goalie's left skate and slid wide of the goalpost and then to the backboards behind the net. Newsy couldn't believe he missed from such a close range. He was less than ten feet away from the front of the net and perfectly positioned to score the go-ahead goal. His frustration was mounting because neither team had scored and the third period was winding down. He knew that overtime would not favor his Canadien teammates who were all still battling flu symptoms. If they couldn't score in regulation, their chances of winning the Stanley Cup may be slipping away.

Cleghorn retrieved the puck and quickly snapped a pass to Newsy, who had moved slightly to his left, opening up a passing lane for his teammate. The puck slid purposely and forcefully to Newsy's stick. He stopped its momentum by sliding his stick back a few inches, softly cradling the puck against his lumber, and then unleashed his deadly wrist shot toward the net. It seemed to move in slow motion toward a wide-open portion of the goal. This was it—Newsy was about to score the go-ahead goal and win Lord Stanley's Cup for the second consecutive year. The flight of the rubber wasn't smooth as it approached its target. It wobbled slightly, something Newsy was unaccustomed to seeing with his shot. Even with the imperfect flight, he felt the excruciating weight of frustration start to lift off his shoulders. He raised his hands in early celebration. The Seattle goaltender was beat. He couldn't make up all that ground in time. This was it!

He was right; the goaltender couldn't get back to the point that Newsy had picked to place the puck, but his stick might. Seattle's goalie lunged as far as he could, fighting fatigue and fear, thrusting his stick toward the path of the flying rubber. Newsy calculated the rate of the puck approaching the open area and the goalie's stick returning to ruin his glory. It was going to be close.

Newsy could have sworn that the stick missed, but the puck changed direction anyway and skipped off the goalpost with a loud *ping*. The crowed oohed and then cheered. His momentary euphoria quickly vanished, and Newsy felt the weight of the world on his shoulders again. He had never experienced this type of failure on the ice before, and he couldn't understand how he had missed such easy but critical shots. The game continued as the puck ricocheted and rolled around the corner boards back out toward the blue line. Newsy played on, following the puck's journey until it was stopped by Joe Hall just inside the zone.

That's weird. I thought Joe was still in the hospital recovering from his bout with the flu, Newsy thought. The surprise was quickly replaced by anticipation. Joe was gifted with an expert touch of flipping the puck at the net at the perfect speed and location so that Newsy could tip it at the last second, deflecting its angle and beating the best goaltenders on the planet. He looked up in Newsy's direction, and just before wristing the puck toward the net, Newsy thought he saw Joe wink at him.

It came in low and hard, the perfect shot/pass from the point. Newsy knew the goaltender behind him was in the process of dropping to the ice to stop the shot. All he had to do was tilt his stick slightly and lift the puck over the helpless defender. Joe knew he'd be able to provide Newsy with the perfect setup. *He did wink*, he thought.

The puck smacked against Newsy's stick and redirected toward the top of the goal. It all happened so quickly this time, Newsy didn't have time to turn around and follow the puck to the net. He didn't have to because he heard the *ping* of the puck bouncing off the crossbar again before sailing into the crowd.

"Damn it!" he yelled, lifting his stick high over his head. He brought the stick down toward the ice with both hands, providing enough force to shatter an oak tree, and just before slamming it to the frozen surface, Newsy sat up in bed. His cough burned deep in his chest, helping his return to reality. The pain of frustration was now replaced by the aches of fever and fear of the unknown. Slowly lying back in his bed, he glanced around the hospital room. Odie Cleghorn was in the bed next to him, lying on his side, facing Newsy.

"Bad dream?" he asked.

"Not as bad as what I've awaken to. How long have I been out?" Newsy asked.

"A while. You just missed Kennedy. Lots of talks going on with Seattle," Cleghorn informed his teammate.

"About?"

"About tonight's game. Looks like we're going to have to forfeit the cup. There's not enough of us healthy to put a team on the ice. How you feeling?"

"Like crap. You?"

"Not as bad as most of you guys," Cleghorn said, muffling a slight cough. "Doesn't matter though. I can't play the game by myself."

"The entire team is sick?" Newsy asked.

"Vezina and Corbeau are okay. Everyone else has been admitted to the hospital. Hall, Pitre, Couture, McDonald, Berlinquette, you, me . . . Am I missing anybody?" Cleghorn asked.

"I don't think so," Newsy said with a large exhale followed by several violent coughs.

"You don't sound too good."

George Kennedy knocked at the door and poked his head into the room. He surveyed the two patients. Newsy on his back with his eyes closed and Cleghorn on his side, looking in Newsy's direction before George got his attention.

"Is he still asleep?" Kennedy asked softly, coughing.

"No, he's not, George. Come in. What's going on?" Newsy responded with impatience.

"How you feeling, Newsy?" Kennedy's tone was sincere and worried.

"Sick. What's going on?"

"We just concluded a meeting." Kennedy began closing the door behind him and walking over to a chair next to Newsy's bed. On the way, he coughed into a handkerchief several times, checked the spew, and folded it before placing it back in his pocket.

"It's obvious we're not going to be able to play tonight, and with this influenza, there's no telling when we'll be healthy enough to play again," Kennedy began. "Therefore, it's been decided to cancel the series."

"And Seattle wins the Stanley Cup because of our forfeit," continued Newsy, finishing what he thought was the rest of Kennedy's update.

"They did offer Seattle the cup, yes. But they respectfully declined," Kennedy said.

"Declined?" Newsy and Cleghorn asked in unison.

"Why?" Newsy added.

"They said they didn't win the cup on the ice, and they don't want to have it handed to them like this. I have to admit, it's the most sporting and gentlemanly act I've ever seen in hockey. Rules say that because the series is cancelled and Seattle declined the cup, the Montreal Canadiens are champions again. And so they offered to present the cup to us again."

"What did you say?" Cleghorn asked.

"Just didn't feel right, Odie. After what you boys have been through to this point of the season and then Seattle's incredible act of sportsmanship, I didn't feel it was appropriate for us to accept it either," Kennedy apologetically explained.

"You did the right thing," Newsy said. "No doubt about it."

"Agreed," said Cleghorn.

The three men sat silently for a long moment, staring at nothing in particular.

"Thanks, boys," Kennedy finally said.

Seattle

April 5, 1919

Lord Stanley's Cup had been packed up two days earlier and began its long trip home to Montreal. An asterisk would be placed in the record books for the 1919 Stanley Cup Championship with a simple factual notation that failed to tell the story of the Canadiens' emotionally exhausting season or the dramatic disappointment at its conclusion: "No decision. Championship cancelled because of influenza."

Odie Cleghorn had been released from the hospital the previous day, as were most of his teammates, and Newsy was alone with his thoughts now. Lying in his hospital bed with his hands clasped behind his head, staring at the white ceiling, he couldn't help but wonder what would be engraved on the cup under the year of 1919. An entire season of bruises, broken bones, stitches, and now heartache. The Stanley Cup was the record keeper, showcasing the names of champions from each season dating back to 1893. He wondered how long that tradition might continue and if anyone would remember those who battled so long and so hard for the right to have their names engraved on the cup in 1919. Two words continued to pop into his mind: "in vain." Perhaps that should be the engraving. "They battled in vain because another opponent was unbeatable." He shook his head and rolled over on to his side.

It took all his strength and concentration to swing his legs off the side of the bed and sit up. It had only been a few days, but he felt as if someone had used a two-by-four and beat every muscle in his aching body. His cough had finally cleared up, but the aches persisted. He rose to his feet, clutching the bedpost to steady himself. After a moment, he felt as if he could take a step and was surprised when his body reacted to his command. He walked around his bed several times in case he needed to fall down, hoping he would hit the soft mattress. But his strength slowly returned as did his confidence. Newsy took a deep breath and headed for the door to his room.

It was quiet in the hospital's hallway. Newsy looked to his right where a window about ten feet away at the end of the hall revealed the sun's rays shining brightly. He couldn't remember the last time he saw the sun, and it hurt his unaccustomed eyes. He winced in pain and turned away from the bright light. To his left, the hallway seemed to stretch for a mile. He slowly walked in that direction, sliding his left hand on the wall for security. His eyes struggled to focus but slowly returned to normal function as he made his way down the hallway. As he approached a nurse's station, a sound unfamiliar to this place became louder. It was music, he realized. He crossed the hall to the opposite side where the nurse's station was located and leaned on the counter. Behind the desk, two young nurses were busy with their work and had not yet noticed Newsy. The music came from a wooden box next to one of the nurses.

"He's not worth what I have to pay him,
But I'll never complain;
I've agreed to give him $50 per

It's worth twice as much to hear him call me Sir."

A sudden tug at his elbow shook him from his momentary musical enjoyment.

"Mr. Lalonde, are you sure you should be out of bed?" asked another nurse who had approached him from behind.

"I'm feeling better, yes, ma'am. Thank you. What is that?" he asked, pointing to the origin of the music. "Why, that's Al Jolson singing his latest hit. Do you like it? It's called 'I've Got My Captain Working for Me Now.'"

"Yes, it's delightful. But that piece of furniture where it's coming from, is that a radio?" he asked, becoming more than a just a little annoyed.

"Yes, Mr. Lalonde, an RCA radio. It just arrived last week. We thought it would help cheer our patients. Is it working?" she asked in an overly cheery and optimistic tone.

"Not one damn bit," answered Newsy. *Fucking Gladstone*, he didn't say out loud. He turned away from the popular technology and looked down the hallway. Not able to find his bearings, he turned back to Nurse Happy. "Could you tell me where Joe Hall's room is, please?" he asked, trying his best to hide his anger.

"Certainly," said the confused nurse. "Straight down that way, about halfway down the hallway, on your right," she pointed out.

"Thank you," he managed. He headed slowly toward Joe's room, now in a completely foul and ornery mood, even for Newsy. He thought about breaking his hockey stick over his brother-in-law's head the next time he saw him. Thanks to Gladstone, Newsy had probably missed the opportunity of a lifetime, he thought. What he needed was a good dose of Joe Hall to snap him out of his mood and cheer him up.

When he was ten feet away from Joe's room, the door opened slowly, and a nurse stepped out and then slowly closed the door behind her. She held her head down, staring at her shoes before finally releasing the doorknob and turning toward Newsy. He had stopped just a few feet away. When she picked her head up, Newsy knew something was wrong.

"Mr. Lalonde! You startled me. You seem to be feeling better, but are you sure you should be up and around?"

"Yes, I'm fine, nurse. How is Mr. Hall?" he asked, and for the first time, fear gripped his chest and tugged the breath from his lungs. He already knew the answer from witnessing her exit Joe's room, but he asked anyway. She looked at Newsy for a moment, trying to find the right words. She could already see the pain growing in his eyes. There was no easy way to say it.

"Mr. Hall just passed. I'm sorry. I know he was your friend."

"He is my friend," Newsy corrected her. Even though he knew he was wrong, he couldn't let this stranger be the one to talk that way about Joe Hall. He pushed by the nurse, who stepped out of the way, knowing there was nothing she could do to stop him. He grabbed the doorknob and hesitated, trying to emotionally steady himself for what he was about to walk into. Turning the doorknob seemed difficult. It required what little energy he had. He pushed the door open, revealing the room's shocking contents. It seemed larger and colder than it was just a few days earlier when Newsy and his teammates paid the Bad Man a visit. Everything had changed since then. Things would never be the same.

It all seemed impossible. Just days earlier, Hall was the most feared player in all of hockey. Nasty and relentless on the ice, his reputation proven to be warranted each time an opponent dared to challenge this living legend. Newsy entered the room and walked around to the far side of the bed where Joe was curled up on his side, facing the stark, bare hospital wall. Joe's hands were curled up by his neck, a few of his fingers inside the collar of his hospital gown. His mouth was open as if he was still desperately gasping for breath that his lungs could not accept. His eyes were closed and clenched as well. Joe Hall died a painful, agonizing death, and he was alone.

Suddenly, Newsy feared for his own life. He was finally feeling better, just as Joe appeared to be getting better a few days ago. Before most of the Montreal Canadien hockey club became ill with the flu, before the Stanley Cup Challenge was cancelled. Before life, as Newsy Lalonde knew it, had permanently changed.

Newsy reached under the hospital bed, his hand searching along the inside of the bed frame. He felt the bottle and pulled it from its hiding place. Yanking the cork out of the neck, he raised the bottle to his friend and then took a long drink, draining the bottle of what had remained.

"That's a first," Newsy said, looking at the bottle. "Don't tell anyone about this, Joe. It's just between you and me," Newsy said to his friend, placing his free hand on his friend's cold skull.

He took another long drink. He wiped his lips, placed the cork back into the bottle, and put the bottle back into its hiding place beneath the bed. Joe's wilted and punished body barely resembled the man he knew. This man that Newsy battled against and alongside was the most feared man in the sport. And now he was gone. Newsy felt the guilt of not being there at the end, wondering if Joe was awake or just passed away while he was unconscious. He wondered if he'd be haunted by this thought for the rest of his own life, as he was now.

"See ya around, Joe," he said and turned away.

He walked slowly for the door before turning around for one last look. This wasn't the way he wanted to remember his friend. He turned away in disgust and grabbed the doorknob, pausing again. His head hung from the weight of his own recent illness and from the weight of the moment he was leaving. He'd never see Hall again. It hurt him to his bones. He'd never see Joe Hall again. He turned the doorknob and left the room.

Newsy Lalonde recovered and returned to hockey the following season. Before he retired, he set the NHL scoring record, which stood until another Canadien great, Henri "Rocket" Richard, broke it a few decades later. In 1960, Lalonde was elected to the Hockey Hall of Fame and the Lacrosse Hall of Fame. After the 1919 final, he would never play for Lord Stanley's Cup again.

Following the 1919 Stanley Cup, George Kennedy's health stabilized, but he never fully recovered. Kennedy died a year later.

George Vezina had evaded the flu and helped the Canadiens win the Stanley Cup in 1924. He died of tuberculosis on March 27, 1926. When the Hockey Hall of Fame opened in 1945, Vezina was one the original nine inductees. Today the Vezina Trophy is awarded each season to the NHL's top goaltender.

16

Condemned to Repeat

Secaucus, New Jersey

September 11, 2012

Jim Wright waited patiently for the traffic light to change. The sun had been up for less than half an hour, and the only other vehicle on the road was a street cleaner. Why towns in this part of New Jersey still spent taxpayer's dollars sweeping their streets was a mystery to Jim. He rubbed the sleep from his eye and checked his rearview mirror, and even though nobody was around, he decided against running the red light. Peter Frampton's "Do You Feel Like I Do?" blared from Q-104.3 on his radio, and with his car windows down, he shouted the lyrics over the noise of the street sweeper. To his left were two brown nondescript brick buildings marking the end of the office park on Harmon Meadow Boulevard. The taller building was a typical four-story office building connected by a short glass walkway to a two-story windowless structure. The NBA had built the television studio next to their satellite office over a decade before using the same construction process as every other structure erected in the Mill Creek Marsh. The technique had been developed and mastered by the Romans two millenniums earlier. Massive timbers were driven through the soggy meadowlands and into the bedrock below, supporting the foundation and keeping it from sinking into the marsh.

The light turned green, and Wright shifted his 1992 Toyota Celica into first gear, turning left onto the overpass that brought him over New

Jersey Turnpike and into another sprawling complex of retail stores, office buildings, restaurants, and acres of parking spaces called the Mill Creek Mall. Turning right at the next light, he entered the parking lot for a row of retailers. Toys-R-Us, TJ Max, the Sports Authority, and Bob's Furniture stores sat empty for the moment, but in a couple of hours, this scene would be completely different, and parking would not be quite so easy. He pulled into a space next to Bob's Furniture, the northernmost store in the mall and waited for Frampton to finish his 1976 classic.

A four-foot-tall chain-link fence was all that separated the sprawling suburban madness from the tranquil scene spreading out in front of Wright. Mill Creek Marsh was a ninety-acre ecological oasis in the middle of twenty-first-century man-made madness. Two decades earlier, federal and state governments joined with private business, spending over $10 million reclaiming the marsh. For five years, heavy equipment and dozens of workers removed the garbage, hazardous materials, human remains, and invasive plant life called phragmites and a rebirth occurred.

Wright grabbed his binoculars and high-powered Nikon digital camera from the back seat of the car and opened the door. His forty-nine-year-old bones creaked as he stood and stretched in the early morning light. At six feet two inches tall with a square jaw, rugged features, and a slender, athletic physique, Wright was not the typical bird-watching enthusiast.

The fog was lifting off the marsh, and the darkness was replaced by a surreal orange glow across the tiny valley. The Jersey summer was over but offering one last stretch of warm sunny weather before succumbing to autumn. Wright loved it here at this time of day. As communications officer for the New Jersey Meadowlands Commission, part of his job was to update the Mill Creek Blog with daily postings from the site. A woman in jogging gear ran past him and through the gate after saying good morning. Running along the raised red gravel paths snaking through the marsh for miles, she was soon out of sight. Wright followed her into the marsh and noticed that the phragmites growing just inside the entrance were in need of removal.

This stubborn, invasive species of weed grew to nearly eleven feet tall and resembled a giant mascara brush. At least, that was how a female reporter from a local newspaper described them earlier in the summer.

Similar to the tall sea grass commonly found along the eastern coast line, the weeds were much more rigid, and they spread at an alarming rate, causing the ongoing battle to keep them from reclaiming the marsh. Wright made a mental note to have a large patch of phragmites removed from the southern end of the marsh along the fence line.

As he walked along the jogging path, a slight breeze blew the seedlings off the groundsels. The bushes lining the man-made path grew to about four feet and were now covered with the white seeds that became airborne with the slightest wind, causing a snow flurry effect in the unusually warm 85-degree air. It was low tide, and the remnants of the great cedar forest that stood here for a thousand years were visible above the water line. Spaced about ten feet apart in the brackish water, the stumps appeared prehistoric and were testament to how this thick forest with trees eighty feet tall once flourished here.

Stories and theories about the demise of the great cedar forest were very familiar to Wright. The stumps, which are remarkably resilient and resistant to decay, were discovered by workers during the reclamation project. It was these properties along with an appealing fragrance that probably helped cause the forest's decline. As early as the 1700s, the wood was harvested for the production of boats, housing materials, buckets, channel-marking posts, and one of the original roads in the area built entirely out of cedar plank called Paterson Plank Road. In 1985, the roof of an old Quaker meetinghouse in Crosswicks, New Jersey, was removed after nearly two hundred years of exceptional service. The cedar shingles were still in excellent shape, but a new roof was ordered and the shingles became kindling for neighbors' fireplaces.

By the 1920s, North Jersey's population was exploding with suburban sprawl. New neighborhoods practically sprang up overnight, and these towns needed a water supply. To accommodate the massive new need, the state dammed the Hackensack River ten miles north in Oradell, cutting off the fresh water supply to what remained of the forest. The water turned brackish, and the great Cedar Forest literally became a buried memory.

Wright, however, never failed to recount the forest's more romantic and earlier stories to the tours of bird-watchers he escorted around the marsh. Centuries earlier, pirates were enjoying their heyday all along the eastern seaboard. By the 1600s, they had ventured north to New York, ransacking ships moored on the Hudson River and in Newark

Bay, playing havoc with the economic fortune of England. By the end of
the century, London had had enough and ordered the governor of New
York to rid the city of the thieves, so in 1690, the pirates sailed across the
Hudson River and found the perfect refuge in the 5,500 acres of thick
cedar forests and murky swamps of the Hackensack Meadowlands.

At first, the locals took a liking to their free-spirited, hard-partying
neighbors who lived peacefully among them as folk heroes. Wright
would quote Philip Longman, a writer for a local newspaper during
the period, who warned, "The law dared not enter into this quagmire
of thieves and so travelers did well to go armed, if at all." Commuting
to New York was difficult and dangerous even back then. The pirates
continued to loot and plunder ships, and their success helped power a
prosperous, albeit somewhat seedy, local economy. By the late 1700s,
the pirate problem was so rampant that even the locals were not safe,
and state officials decided it was time to clean out the forest.

In 1791, a massive force comprised of hundreds of law enforcement
officers from all over New Jersey, cooperating with local militia, laid
siege to the meadowlands. Fires were strategically set around the forest
to smoke out the pirates, who were either captured or killed as they
escaped the burning timbers, and their free reign came to an abrupt and
violent end. The fires had worked well, but they quickly burned out of
control, and more than half of the forest was destroyed.

Wright viewed the stumps from a wooden bridge that carried bird-
watchers, joggers, and local nature lovers over one of the many ponds.
To his right, modern-day travelers on the New Jersey Turnpike sped by
at blinding speeds, totally unaware of the history and natural beauty
that once was this place and now is again. Behind him and to the south
just beyond the shopping complex, traffic was already building on Route
3, the main thoroughfare bringing tens of thousands of commuters
through the Lincoln Tunnel and into Manhattan. Today's commute
was much less dangerous than during the days of the Meadowlands
pirates but just as time-consuming and much more frustrating. To
his left, a housing complex filled the view that was the western ridge
of this valley and to the north, the western leg of the turnpike joined
with the eastern, creating a man-made barrier for the ninety pristine
acres. He turned to the southeast where the Twin Towers had burned
and crumbled eleven years earlier to the day. He remembered being in
this exact spot at that moment, watching the smoke billow from the

towers. He lowered his head and said a brief prayer for all those who lost so much on that tragic day and wondered how in the midst of this modern insanity, Mother Nature continues to lead her migrating masses to this tiny speck of land carved out and preserved by so few. It was a miracle the birds were even able to find Mill Creek Marsh. From above, it must look like a tiny speck, surrounded by ten thousand acres of homes, industrial parks, highways, office buildings, and a sewage treatment plant.

There were now 280 species of birds visiting the marsh, and that number continued to grow every year. First, the various species of migrating ducks returned, followed by the inevitable raptors. The ducks find refuge, rest, and most importantly, food in the muddy swamp during low tide. Benthic organisms began their comeback a few decades earlier when then governor Christine Todd Whitman ordered new EPA regulations forbidding the toxic dumping that had gone on, unimpeded, for decades. The bottom of this diverse and fragile food chain, the benthic began to flourish, and where there is food, there is sure to be other wildlife. Wright marveled at what he helped create and now was confident he could preserve. A snowy egret stood tall and proud to his right just beyond the cedar stumps. With summer coming to an end, the egret would be leaving Mill Creek very shortly. The endangered red knots were just taking flight, continuing the longest migration on the planet from the Arctic Circle to Chile. Red-winged gulls, raider yellowlegs, greater yellowlegs, green-winged teals, and northern shovelers either swam or walked the shallow ponds, feeding and socializing.

A billow of smoke rising to the east on the far side of Route 95 caught Wright's attention. It was coming from the back of the enormous Walmart. Probably burning the extra shipping crates, illegally, Wright assumed. He followed the trail of the smoke as it rose in the cloudless sky when something else caught his attention. He raised his binoculars and viewed a young bald eagle soaring five hundred feet in the air above the Walmart. In one smooth motion, he dropped the binoculars, which caught by their strap around his neck, and swung up the Nikon, snapping off several shots of the majestic bird.

He checked the digital pictures in the viewfinder on the back of his camera, pleased with his work.

He looked up again to see the eagle moving off toward the city. In the distance, several helicopters raced over the New York skyline, appearing to be the same size as the much closer eagle. He shook his head, marveling at the ability of nature to live in such close proximity with man.

"A great morning on the marsh," Wright said to himself as he turned to head back to his car. He wanted to blog about the sighting of the bald eagle as quickly as possible, but something stopped him after just a few steps. It was nothing more than a blur, but Wright knew immediately what he was witnessing. A peregrine falcon was making a feeding dive toward something it had chosen in the marsh. Wright knew there was a pair nesting under an overpass nearby on Route 3 but had yet to see one in his marsh. About the size of a rabbit and reaching speeds up to two hundred miles per hour in its dive, the peregrine was the fastest animal on earth and capable of carrying a duck equal to its own weight. Wright swung the Nikon up again, but this time, it was too late. The falcon swooped down, disappearing behind the groundsels in front of the pond to the north, and then reemerged about twenty feet to the left from where he vanished. In his talons, Wright identified the green-winged teal and snapped off five quick pictures. The falcon arched to its left above a small tree line and was now heading straight at Wright, shaking the duck violently. The green-winged teal did not struggle against the raptor, its head hanging oddly down and limp. The peregrine shook its morning meal again, and again, there was no response. Now, about a hundred feet above the marsh, the falcon's head turned to the side and dipped to take a peek at his breakfast. After a few more seconds, it released the duck, which tumbled back to earth, lifeless. The duck splashed into the mud in front of Wright, spraying him with the wet swamp. He looked up and over his shoulder.

"Thanks a lot," he said to the falcon flying south, who seemed to be returning to his nest, empty-handed.

Wright returned his focus to the duck, now a feathery mess in front of him. He walked down the embankment and into the pond, his feet sinking six inches into the slop with each step. As he approached, he noticed the green-winged teal's eyes were still clear, an indication that the duck was alive until this morning. He grabbed the duck by the legs and lifted it out of the mud, holding it for a second in front of his face in order to inspect it a little closer. The duck seemed healthy, which made the events he just witnessed very curious. *Why would the peregrine drop such an easy kill and what, in fact, killed this bird?* he wondered.

Wright made his way back to his car and popped the trunk. He placed the green-winged teal on the pavement and removed the information fliers he passed out to his tours from a cardboard box. Next, he gently picked up the duck and inspected it again. He held the bird up in his right hand and rotated it with his left. *Curious, it looks healthy enough,* he thought and placed the carcass into the box. He slammed the trunk, climbed into the driver's seat, and started the engine. It was nearly 8:00 a.m., and Wright knew he now had much more to blog about than the bald eagle. He drove out of the parking lot and on to Harmon Meadow Boulevard. It was a short fifteen-minute drive to the office where the coffee was horrendous, so Wright pulled into the Starbucks parking lot before getting on the highway.

It was a sensory bombardment. Josh Groban played on the house audio system inside the Starbucks while sweet-smelling baked goods mingled with the aroma of the planet's strongest coffee.

"Can I help you, sir?" the barista asked from behind the counter.

"Yes, I'll have a grande skim latte, extra shot, extra hot, please," Wright ordered.

"That will be $4.59," the teenager answered and repeated the order to the person making the hot beverage to his left.

Wright pulled his wallet out of his back pocket and a pen dropped to the floor unnoticed by him. The tall African-American behind him tapped Wright's shoulder, bent down, and picked up the pen.

"Yo, buddy. You dropped this."

Wright turned around, smiled and took his pen back. "Thanks a lot," Wright said.

"No worries," replied Andy Thompson, a twenty-year veteran television producer for the NBA, who was getting his morning fix as well. Thompson was in a rush to get to the office because he had an early afternoon flight to Miami for tonight's game against the Knicks. Located just across the street from Starbucks, the NBA's Secaucus office housed nearly five hundred production, marketing, and licensing employees in a modern environmentally controlled building. If this line moved quickly, Andy might just make his production meeting about the documentary he was producing, featuring LeBron James and the Heat. His plan was to leave the office by 11:00 a.m., drive fifteen minutes down the turnpike to Newark International Airport where he and 178 other passengers and flight crew would spend two-plus-hours on a Boeing 757 aircraft. Once arriving in Miami, he'd have just enough time to check into his hotel, shower, and change into his suit before rushing off to the arena with eighteen thousand hoop fans.

The guy in front of him finally paid, and Andy stepped up to order his coffee and egg sandwich.

Wright walked down to the end of the counter to wait for his latte, where two overweight businessmen were discussing the upcoming Giants game against archrival Dallas. Wright was thinking about the scene he had just witnessed and thought about having the duck autopsied. The lattes were just not flowing out quickly, and Wright couldn't help but listen to the two businessmen. One was in town for a Morgan Stanley/Dean Witter conference in North Jersey. Over one thousand brokers and money managers would be in attendance, the furthest businessman from Wright commented. He had checked out of his Secaucus hotel and was staying in New York tonight after the conference. He mentioned that he was trying to get tickets to the theater before he had to fly back to Nashville tomorrow. The nearer fellow offered to help out with the theater tickets because his sister worked at Radio City and knew several people on Broadway. Wright realized he was looking at the two men who suddenly stopped talking and glared at him. Wright politely and apologetically smiled and looked the other way where Thompson impatiently checked his watch and glared at the young man behind the coffee counter as if that would help deliver their orders quicker. Another ten minutes later, all four finally left Starbucks and went their separate ways.

However, their fates were one and the same.

One green-winged teal would cause tens of thousands of people to become infected in the next twenty-four hours with nearly half of them dying in the coming days. Around the globe, millions of birds were infecting tens of millions of people with H5N1.

17

Those Who Fail to Learn from History

Montreal, Quebec

September 13, 1969

Newsy felt better this morning than he had in a long time, as long as he could remember. At eighty-two, he had accepted that his time on this earth was growing short. Perhaps it was seeing his granddaughter or taking his great grandson to hockey practice. Whatever the reason, Newsy welcomed this good day.

Eight-year-old Brett sat in the back, buckled into his seat, wearing all his hockey gear, ready for his early morning practice. Newsy was thankful that his mom had gotten him dressed. What an ordeal that is!

It was barely 7:00 a.m., and the sun had just peeked over the horizon.

Newsy thought about Brett's dedication to the sport he once dominated. The Canadiens never had to practice this early in the morning. *The boys would have revolted if Georgie asked us to just wake up this early, let alone practice.* Newsy smiled at the thought.

The ride to the practice rink was quiet as both driver and passenger tried to shake the cobwebs. Newsy pulled up to a stop sign, looked to his left at a densely wooded area, and made the sign of the cross as he did every time he stopped here.

Brett noticed his great-grandpa's gesture and perked up.

"Papa?"

"Yes, Brett? I thought you were sleeping back there," Newsy replied, finding the boy in his rearview mirror.

"Why do you cross yourself at stop signs?" Brett asked.

"I don't do it all stop signs. Just that one, Bretzky."

"Then why do you do it at *that* stop sign?"

Newsy smiled at the innocence of youth. *If you only knew*, he thought.

"I'll tell ya what, why don't you concentrate on your hockey practice, and afterward, I'll tell ya why I cross myself at that stop sign. Deal?" Newsy asked, believing an hour on the ice with his buddies would help Brett forget about the stop sign.

"Deal, Papa."

Brett and Newsy arrived early as usual. *Old habits die hard*, Newsy thought. He snapped Brett's chinstrap into place and lightly patted his helmeted head. "Ready?" he asked the now fully awake and excited boy.

"Ready, Papa!" Brett said, turning away and half jogged, half waddled in all his gear down the padded walkway, jumped through the doorway to the rink, and darted out onto the resurfaced ice. Newsy smiled with pride.

He went to the far end of the ice and took his customary position at the bend in the glass. *This is the best place to see the entire ice, and being at the farthest end of the rink from the entrance, other parents will leave me alone,* he reasoned. The boys practiced for an hour, and for a man who had forgotten more about hockey than all the coaches on the ice knew about the sport, the only advice Newsy yelled was, "Brett, head up. Keep your head up!" but to no avail. The invisible hip checks were rampant, and every time Brett or a teammate hit the ice, a big smile formed on their face. The game was still fun at this age.

The practice ended just as the next team was gathering for their turn on the ice. Brett exited the ice at the Zamboni entrance while peeling off his gloves and helmet. He hopped onto the rubber mat, looked up at Newsy, and said, "Let's go to the stop sign, Papa," never breaking stride or looking back. Newsy just shook his head.

Lalonde pulled the car over about twenty feet short of the stop sign and sighed heavily, wondering if he should distract Brett with the promise of ice cream before breakfast and face the wrath of his mother. He quickly decided against that.

"All right, here we are," Newsy announced, opening the car door before walking around to the passenger side rear door and freeing Brett to explore the area around the stop sign. Newsy called him over to the rock wall where he was now sitting. Behind him appeared to be a thick forest, but Newsy knew better.

Brett did his best to hop up on the wall next to his papa, but his hockey pants wouldn't allow it, so Newsy grabbed him under his arms and swung him up.

"What do you see behind us?" Newsy asked.

"Trees and bushes," Brett responded.

"Look closer."

Brett stood up on the two-foot-thick crumbling wall and turned to face the forest. For the first time, he was able to see what his papa clearly knew was there. Old headstones. Most of them weathered and crooked; some had trees, bushes, and other plant life overgrowing them.

"It's a cemetery, Papa?" he asked.

"Yes, a very old one."

"Why does it look so bad? It doesn't look like any other cemetery I've ever seen. Pretty spooky."

"That's because the people who are buried here died a long time ago from a very bad disease. And after they were buried, people were afraid that they'd catch the disease if they went back in there to take care of the cemetery. So nobody took care of it. I've never spoken about this with anyone else. So this will be our secret, okay?"

Brett looked back at his papa and could see how serious he was. "Okay, Papa. But why haven't you ever told anyone else?"

Newsy thought hard about that question. *Why didn't anyone speak about it? It was just too painful. We all did our best to forget and move on. How do I describe the fear, the desperation, the helplessness, and the incredible amount of death to an eight-year-old?* The emotions came flooding back to Newsy who felt a tear form in his eye. He quickly wiped it away, stood up, and grabbed Brett off the wall.

"Well, Bretzky, that's a story for another time. When you're a little older. Right now, you have to remember to keep your head up at all times on the ice. You drop your head, and that's when you get blindsided by some *big ugly goon*!"

Brett giggled at Newsy's description and the tickle under his arms. "Hey, Papa, could the disease ever come back?"

THE END

Sources

Books

Kary Mullis "Dancing Naked in the Mind Field", 1998
Published by Pantheon Books, a division of Random House, Inc., New York.

Gina Kolata "FLU; The Story of the Great Influenza Pandemic of 1918 and the Search for the Virus that Caused It", 1999 Farrar, Straus and Giroux, New York.

Charles L. Coleman "The Trail of the Stanley Cup" Vol. 1, 1966 National Hockey League

Periodicals and Online Articles

"The Habs and Their History", Part two, by Vince Lunny, A Sports Magazine Featurette

Lalonde Shaken by the Attack; The Star, Vancouver, B.C., 1919

Lalonde is Noted Financial Star, Says Kennedy; Victoria Times, c1919

Lalonde Says We'll be Champs; The Star, Vancouver B.C. 1918

Proceedings on Discharge; Harry Lawton Broadbent, National Archives of Canada

Frank Nighbor Wikipedia Page

Frank Nighbor Biography, *www.legendsofhockey.net*,

Lalonde Family History: Hockey Superstar; by Eric Lalonde, *elalonde@odyssee.net*,

Odie Cleghorn page, Yahoo GeoCities, The NHL History Book

Georges Vezina page, Montreal Canadiens Hall of Fame

Didier Pitre page, Hockey Hall of Fame

The Montreal Canadiens 1918-1919 Season, By Eric Lalonde, November 16, 1999

Hall of Famer 'Newsy' Lalonde Dies; newspaper article

1919 in Review- Club History Ottawa Senators; *www.ottawasenators.com/1919*
"On the Threshold of a Dream", The Bergen Record- Section L, 5.25.10

"The Postal Service Begins", USPS.com

Seward Peninsula Wikipedia page

The History of Brevig Mission, *www.explorenorth.com/library/communities/alaska/bl-Brevig.html*

The History of Nome,
www.explorenorth.com/library/communities/alaska/bl-Nome.html

Marshall, Fortuna Ledge and the Mining of Willow Creek, by Jeanne Ostnes Rinear and Elanor Ostnes Vistaunet,
www.explorenorth.com/alaska/history/marshall-history.html

Permafrost Preserves Clues to Deadly 1918 Flu Article #1386, *www.gi.alaska.edu/scienceforum/ASF13/1386.html*

Polymerase Chain Reaction- Xeroxing DNA, National Center for Human Genome Research, National Institutes of Health. *www.accessexcelllenc.org/RC/AB/IE/PCR_Xeroxing_DNA.php*

Fort Jackson(SC) United States Army Training Center, *www.columbiasouthcarolina.com/fortjackson.html*

The Beginning- 1917, *www.jackson.army.mil/Museum/History/CHAPTER%201.html*

Nome, Alaska- *http://explorenorth.com/library/communities/images/n-nome4.html*

Piper J-3 Wikipedia page, *http://wikipedia.org/wiki/Piper_j-3*

The History Of Wales, *www.explorenorth.com/library/communities/alaska/bl-Wales.htmo*

The Virus Detective: Dr. John Hultin had found evidence of the 1918 flu epidemic that had eluded experts for decades, By Elizabeth Fernandez, 2.17.2002
www.SFGate.com

Thailand on the alert for bird flu cases, USA Today page 10A, 9.29.04

Army of a million volunteers pitches in to tackle bird-flu, The Independedent, by Jan McGirk, 10.1.04

'Bird flu' deaths in Hong Kong spark fears of global epidemic, The Independent, By Jeremy Laurance, Health Editor, 2.20.03

Tracking the Next Killer Flu, By Tim Appenzeller, National Geographic.com, October, 2005

Barbara Hatch Rosenberg's "Political Campaign" or Rumor Mongering for a cause, by Ed Lake, 7.30.03

Flu, by Any Name, Is Serious Business, by M.L. Faunce, *www.bayweekly. com/reflect6_3.html*

Is Another Influenza Pandemic Coming Soon?, May 1997, *www. slackinc.com/general/idn/199705/pandemic.html*

Nature Magazine article, October 6, 2006

Experts Unlock Clues to Spread of 1918 Flu Virus, The New York Times, 10.06.05

Laboratory of Infectious Diseases, Jeffery K. Taubenberger, MD, PhD, National Institute of Allergy and Infectious Diseases

The Spanish Lady and the Newfoundland Regiment, by W. David Parsons, MD, CM, FRCP(C), 7.27.99, file:C:\WINDOWS\TEMP\-0064853.htm

U.S. flu strain resistant to popular drug, The Bergen Record, 3.3.09

An early look at migratory birds in area, The Bergen Record, 3.13.10

Migratory Birds and Flyways, Birdlife International, *www.birdlife.org*

Migratory flyways in Europe, Africa and Asia and the spread of HPAI H5N1, by Ward Hagemeijer & Taej Mundkur for Wetlands International, *www.fao.org*

Virological Evaluation of Avian Influenza Virus Persistence in Natural and Anthropic Ecosystems of Western Siberia (Novosibirsk Region, Summer 2012) by Maria A. Demarco, Mauro Delogu, Mariya Sivay, Kirill Sharshov, Alexander Yurlov, Claudia Cotti, Alexander Shestopalov *www.journals.plos.org*

H5N1 Influenza Virus, Domestic Birds, Western Siberia, Russia, by Alexander Shestopalov, Centers for Disease Control and Prevention, wwwnc.cdc.gov, Volume 12, Number 7- July, 2006

Interviews and Personal Communications

Eric Lalonde
Richard Quintal
Bob Quintal
Jane Rodney- Hockey Hall of Fame
Jim Wright- New Jersey Meadowlands Commission, Communications

CPSIA information can be obtained
at www.ICGtesting.com
Printed in the USA
LVHW091110120420
653141LV00007B/701/J